In loving memory of my Uncle Murray and Uncle Bruce.

I think this story would've made them smile.

the

kindness
of it all

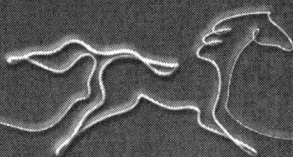

gina flewelling

Gina Flewelling Publishing

Gem, Alberta

https://ginaflewelling.com

ISBN: 9798838415967

Imprint: Independently published

Design: by Jess Creative [https://jesscreative.ca]

ACKNOWLEDGMENTS

Braden

Your calming, reassuring presence in my life helped me find the courage to publish this story. Thank you for believing in me and pushing me to follow my dreams.

Mom

When you wrote and published your own book, it inspired me to do the same. We come from generations of gritty, hard-working women. I can't imagine a greater honor than to carry on that family tradition with you.

Tel and Tyrel

My two big brothers who are also my two best friends. Thanks for listening to me talk about this book for years. It meant more than you guys know.

Dad

Thanks for letting me use some of your best lines in this book. And thanks for being the first person to teach me how to tell a great story. Your daughter loves you.

JJ

I've always looked up to my big cousin. I thought you were the coolest person ever. Now you are the sole reason this book is in someone's hands in this beautiful, physical copy. I guess I was always right about you.

Dana and Taylor

The only two people I would trust with a first reading of this book. I love you both and I am so lucky to have friends like you.

Carla, Gus, and Collins

My heart. You guys are an example of all the joy and love encompassed in a rural family. I hope I captured some of that in this book but I know I never properly could. Thanks for being an inspiration.

CONTENTS

A NOTE FROM THE AUTHOR   1

PART ONE: 1959

1. EUPHORIA   5
2. MAGIC   13
3. HOLLERING   21
4. TICKLISH   27
5. INDULGENT   37
6. PRAISE   47
7. SWIRLS   53
8. NERVE   61
9. BLURRY   67
10. MEMORABLE   73
11. FORGIVING   85
12. EASY   89
13. TOUGH   95

PART TWO: 1981

14. UNCOMPLICATED   103
15. PASSIONS   109
16. CELEBRATING   115
17. FROZE   119
18. SALUTE   121

19. COINCIDENTAL   127
20. MEMORY   131
21. BRUTAL   137
22. DESPERATE   143
23. DISAPPROVAL   151
24. JUDGEMENTS   163
25. LOYAL   179
26. DISCONNECTED   185
27. INDISCRETIONS   191

PART THREE: 2019

28. LOVING   199
29. EXHAUSTED   207
30. EXCITEMENT   219
31. COMPOSURE   225
32. BETTER   233
33. RESPECT   243
34. REASSURANCE   251
35. SLOWLY   259
36. LIGHT   265
37. GOODBYE   271

A NOTE FROM
THE AUTHOR

When my Uncle Bruce was 17 years old, he left the family farm in Lacombe to go work at the Calgary Stockyards. That family anecdote has always captured my heart. So that is where this story begins and it is based upon a real event. However, everything after that and all of the characters are simply figments of my imagination.

Some references in this novel are historically accurate. Some are made up for the convenience and magic of story telling.

To professional chuckwagon drivers and all those involved in the industry – I hope you don't mind that I wrote about your sport. I took a few liberties with the rules and the history of chuckwagon racing in hopes that this novel can be understood and enjoyed by a reader who has never been around the event. It is to note that chuckwagon racing had 4 outriders up until 2011.

Lastly...

After I trained and sold my first horse, my dad told me that I did a good job and all I could do now is try to make the next horse a little bit better.

I think the same concept can be applied to novels.

Happy reading,

Gina xx

1

1959

"Live life as though it is rigged in your favor."

~ Rumi

euphoria

The best place for any story to begin is with a goodbye. I suppose that's why they put "good" right in the word. More often than not, some good comes out of leaving. Of course, it isn't always easy at the time. But this isn't a story about life being easy.

I said my first real goodbye when I was 17 years old. It was the early spring of 1959 and an uncharacteristically warm day for central Alberta. You could hear melting snow splash on the ground as it slid off tree branches. I paused and felt the sun beat down on my face; always a welcome sensation after a long Canadian winter. I'd like to say there were robins chirping but that might be a figment of my imagination. My point is that it was a real pretty day.

I carried two bags out to my truck. One bag held my blue jeans, button down work shirts, socks, underwear, and some wool sweaters. The other bag had my comb, toothbrush, razor (which was barely used), some pen and paper, and my bible (also barely used). In my wallet, I had $173 and a torn newspaper ad for hired help. In those days, that was everything you needed to start a life.

I threw the two bags into the passenger side of my pickup and glanced back at the house I'd grown up in. It was a two-story farmhouse with a wrap-around porch. That might sound fancy but I promise you, it was fairly plain. Everything was tidy and respectable but the financial status of my family managed to seep through in hints like the disintegrating wooden porch and the dated yellow paint on the house. None of that ever bothered me. Your first home is a lot like your first crush on a girl - you're going to be blind to any flaws until you're exposed to something better.

I could see my mom looking at me through the window as I walked up to the front door. She wiped a tear away with the tea towel she was holding and kept watching me as I approached. I swallowed a lump down that had been building up in my throat. I was ready as ever to leave but there's just something about watching your mother cry that makes it about impossible to keep yourself composed.

I paused and took a deep breath, my chest shakily rising, before I turned the door handle and walked in.

"Where's Dad?" was all I managed to say.

She looked me in the eye and said, "Out in the field. He wanted to check the mares. It would be a good day for Young Mare to have her foal. This warm weather won't last too long."

I nodded my head. Young Mare wasn't all that young anymore. She'd adopted the name as soon as we bought her and it seemed to stick. In the 8 years that we'd owned her, she'd had trouble foaling three different times. But every time, my dad managed to keep her alive. He only lost one foal.

Even so, Mom and I both knew that Dad could've seen me off if he had wanted to. The man wasn't big on emotional moments. He would stay out in the field until he knew Mom was finished crying and had his lunch ready. Just the way he was.

"I wish you'd stay one more day so you could join us for church tomorrow," Mom said. She had the tea towel held tightly in both hands as she looked at me.

"Sorry, Mom. I need to get down there before the spot is filled. I'm sure they got a church in Calgary."

"Charlie, I'm sure they *have* a church in Calgary. They don't *got* a church in Calgary. I do wish you would remember your schooling; I

6

know you're capable of it. And, dear, remember your grammar while you inquire about the job. I'm sure that even a stockyard isn't interested in hiring a young man who doesn't take care to think before he speaks."

I just nodded again and smiled. Even when Mom was reprimanding me, she spoke in such a gentle manner that you couldn't take much offense. She'd always been that way. Real easy going and full of love at the same time. The more women I met throughout my life, the more I realized that my mom was something special. I think you would call it grace. She always spoke with grace.

"Your brothers are in the barn," she said. "They'll be expecting you to say goodbye before you leave."

"Yes, Mom. I'll stop in there."

At that point, I couldn't take it much longer. I stepped over to her and bent down to give her a hug. She was short and slender but she latched on to me and squeezed harder than I was expecting. She stroked the back of my head a few times and I felt a little foolish just standing in the kitchen hugging my mother but I sure didn't want to let go. Finally, she pushed me back and held my shoulders.

"No one prepares you for how hard it is to say goodbye to your first born. Charlie, you've been one of the greatest joys in my days throughout the last seventeen years but I know it's time for you to make something of yourself. You can't stay here but I do wish you could. Now go ahead, go on. You better get on the road. I love you as much today as I ever have."

I didn't trust myself to say a word so I just stepped out of the kitchen silently. I pulled my boots on and roughly placed my work cap back on my head, covering up my sandy blonde hair as I cleared my throat. I tried to shove down the feelings of regret and sadness that were bubbling up. I didn't dare look back as I strode over to the barn. I knew Mom would still be standing there and watching me through the kitchen window.

I rolled open the big side door of the barn and stepped into the cool air that had yet to be warmed by the spring sun. There were three box stalls in the barn and each of my brothers was cleaning one out. It was the first day it was warm enough to shovel everything out that had been piling up over the winter.

"Well, it's a good thing I'm leaving," I said loudly. "There isn't enough work in this barn for the four of us. Hell, maybe Philip will finally start pulling his weight around here."

I ducked as Philip lunged out of the boxstall and swung his fist over my head. Then he immediately followed up with his left fist and cuffed me in the shoulder. We both grinned at each other. The real joke was that Philip, the youngest of the four of us, had more grit and work ethic than all of us combined. He would probably be the first one done cleaning out his stall and then on to the next job by himself. Philip always seemed to have endless amounts of energy. He loved working with his hands and could stay outside all day. I remember Mom teaching Philip how to walk when he was a baby. She coaxed him into taking his first steps the day he turned 8 months old. After that, he never seemed to stop. Philip just had a limitless enthusiasm for life. That's probably why he'd always been my favorite brother.

Walter and Grant came out of the boxstalls they were working on to join us in the barn alley. We all stood in silence for a short moment before Grant piped up.

"Shit Charlie, don't tell me you're gonna shed a tear saying goodbye to us. My guess is that you already cried with Mom. But we won't even hardly notice that you're gone."

"I'll just be happy to eat your portion at supper tonight," said Walter.

Grant eyed him up and down and said, "Walter, you know if you eat any more, Mom is gonna have to let your pants out."

"Again!" Phillip laughed, with his bright eyes clearly amused.

I laughed along with them and said, "I'm glad I won't have to listen to you jackasses bicker at each other until Christmas."

They all looked at me then and Grant said, "What if you don't get the job?"

"I don't see why I wouldn't. Seems like I could do just as good of a job as anyone else. Once you've worked for a hardass like Dad, you probably can make a go of it at any job," I smirked. "And besides, Uncle Bob already put in a good word for me. He made it sound like the job is as good as mine."

We all just stood there for another moment. I watched my three younger brothers as they aimlessly toyed with the shovels in their hands. Truth be told, I already had plenty of job experience. I'd been in charge of organizing Walter, Grant, and Philip for as long as I could remember. Dad would give us our list of jobs that needed to be done for the day and it was my responsibility to make sure it all happened. I wondered who would take over my role when I left.

As we stood there, I knew it was going to be up to me to speak first. They all waited silently; knowing I would take control. "Well, boys," I finally managed, "This barn won't clean itself and I'd better hit the road."

This time Philip was the first one to act. He reached out to shake my hand. "Mind if I come visit sometime?" he asked. "I think those Calgary girls might really love me if I give 'em a chance."

We all burst out laughing as Walter and Grant followed suit by shaking my hand.

There was a chorus of "good luck" and "see ya" and "work hard" as I headed back out the barn door I'd entered through. As I left the big, red barn and the boys standing inside of it, I felt one thing that has remained with me throughout my entire life: I am pretty god damn proud of my brothers.

I strolled over to my pickup and fired her up, letting the engine idle. I almost reached for a pack of smokes before noticing that Mom was still watching through the window. I didn't want her last image of me to be lighting one up. I gave her a wave as I eased out of the yard. She smiled and waved back with that same tea towel still in one hand. No more tears. It was the purest send-off I could've ever asked for.

I coasted along the dirt roads, enjoying the scenery. Most of the neighbors were outside working, taking advantage of the nice weather. They all waved as I drove by. I rolled down the window and smoked. It was hand rolled tobacco that my old man had silently handed over to me the night before. I figured his way of saying goodbye was just as meaningful. Sometimes a small action speaks louder than any words ever could. My dad taught me that.

Eventually, I passed the big sign that said "Welcome to Lacombe." The wooden blue sign had never stood out to me before but now I looked at it and said a silent goodbye to my hometown. I was heading about 100 miles south to the Calgary Stockyards. At that naïve time in my life, I was just happy to be on the open road. I didn't know that I was going to one of the most special and historic work places in Alberta. I didn't know that after the construction of the railroads, major stockyards were built at railroad terminals. You see, the railroad arrived in the city of Calgary in 1883 and in 1890, the many growing ranches in southern Alberta had established a meat trade where cattle were shipped from Calgary to all over Alberta, Eastern Canada, and some US destinations. It didn't take long for a few businessmen to realize that with all of this cattle activity, Calgary should have a major stockyards operation. I didn't realize that the Stockyards was an integral part of Alberta and Canadian history. I just knew it was a place where I could go to make some money.

When I pulled on to the highway, I started to fiddle with the radio knob. It didn't take long for Johnny Horton's rhythmic voice to take over the whole truck. I turned it up and started singing along with Johnny.

In 1814, we took a little trip

Along with Colonel Jackson down the mighty Mississip

By the time Johnny was half-way through the song, I was belting out every word. I was hitting my hand on the steering wheel and keeping time with Johnny's drummer as if I had been right there with those boys in The Battle of New Orleans. I practically shouted the lyrics.

Yeah, they ran through the briars

And they ran through the brambles

And they ran through the bushes

Where the rabbits couldn't go

They ran so fast

That the hounds couldn't catch 'em

Down the Mississippi to the Gulf of Mexico

To this day, that song takes me back to that moment. I can't hear ol' Johnny sing about the *Bloody British* without a sense of freedom and euphoria washing over me. Looking back at that moment, I wouldn't change a thing. I barely had enough money to get by and I didn't have much of a plan. But none of that mattered in the end. From that moment on, my life truly began. I'd been doing my part at home and raising a few cows to make a little money. But I was mainly just biding my time. I knew that I was never meant to stay there. I was meant to go out in the world. Grant or Walter might take things over on the farm someday. I'm sure they'd do a fine job of it, too.

At that time, I never could've guessed what my life would go on to entail. If the course of your life doesn't surprise you, I don't think you really did enough livin'. I would live as a poor man and as a rich man. I would work with great men and imperfect men and I would come to learn that it's a fine line between the two. I would see the way of the world change drastically throughout my generation. I would experience absolute devastation in the span of a few moments and I would carry that feeling with me until the end of time. And I would kiss the most beautiful woman I ever laid eyes on.

But, hell, I'll get to all that soon enough.

magic

"Good afternoon, ladies. My name is Charlie. Charlie Hyde."

Three women looked politely back at me. They were the head office ladies at The Stockyards. Just a few seconds ago, they all had their heads down at calculators or calendars or notepads. Now I had the attention of all three as they eyed me up with a slight smile on their faces. There's something special about a person who can manage to give you their full attention when they're visibly busy. I think every secretary I've ever known embodies that quality.

"Well, good morning Charlie," said the first one.

"Aren't you just the picture of handsome," teased the second one.

"Any relation to Robert Hyde?" asked the third one.

I avoided the handsome comment altogether. But I liked those three women immediately.

I looked at the third one as I said, "Yes, that's my Uncle Bob. He's actually part of the reason why I'm here. I found the ad in The Calgary

Herald that the Stockyards was hiring. *Uncle Bob made a few phone calls on my behalf to inquire about the position.* And I believe that someone here was expecting to hear from me."

I remember noticing the way the women warmed up to me as I spoke. I'd been rehearsing that line for the last half hour of the drive: Uncle Bob made a few phone calls on my behalf to inquire about the position. That was a line that would've made my mom proud.

"Pat is in charge of hiring new workers for the back. I believe he's up in his office right now," said one of the secretaries as she dialed numbers on the phone. She held the bulky, black receiver up to one ear and paused.

"Pat," she said. "I'm sending a young fellow to your office about working in the back." Another pause. "Very good," she finished and hung up, turning her attention back to me. "You head straight down this hall toward the sale ring and take your second left. You'll find his office if you go up that flight of stairs. Good luck!"

I thanked them and carried on. As I walked away, I heard the sounds of the office resume behind me. The clicking and clacking of calculator buttons, pages flipping, and phones ringing. Things were moving fast. Climbing up the wooden stairs, I wondered about the man I was going to meet. I didn't know how high up the chain of command he was, but he must be some sort of a big deal if he was in charge of hiring. I realized that I had never actually spoken to a rich man in my life. I had worked at the gas station off the highway for a short while and every now and then, a fancy car would roll up. I was never too interested in cars but I was always intrigued by the men driving them. What did they do for a living? Where were they from? How did they carry themselves? Of course, my questions were never answered and there would only be a few words exchanged between us. *Fill 'er up, kid,* they usually said without ever really looking at me. I didn't last long working at the gas station because Dad needed help one weekend fixing fence after his cows had got out into the neighbor's crop. They fired me when I missed my shift.

Before I reached up to knock on Pat's office door, I took a deep breath and steadied myself just as I had before I entered my mom's kitchen earlier that day.

"Come on in," a voice said behind the door.

I opened the door and saw a short, stocky man behind a desk. He slid a few papers to one side as he stood up to shake my hand.

"Very pleased to meet you. I'm Charlie Hyde," I said as I grabbed his hand. I was surprised to notice I was taller than him.

"Yes, you as well," he said and motioned for me to sit in the chair opposite his desk. "You smoke?" he asked.

"Well, yes, whenever I'm not around my mother." I silently cursed myself. *Get it together*, I thought, *that is not the reply a grown man would give in a job interview.*

To my relief, the man threw his head back and gave a short laugh.

"Smart thinking. There's still quite a few things I wouldn't do in front of my mother, either," he said with a sly wink.

As he took out a pack of smokes and silently handed me one, I exhaled a little; feeling more relaxed. It's funny how some people have the ability to put us at ease with a just a few words. I'm not sure if that talent means they are a good person or a good conversationalist. And to be completely truthful, to this day, I'm not sure if you can ever really tell the difference between those two things.

We sat in silence for a moment as he lit his cigarette and then passed the lighter over to me.

"How old are you, son?" he asked after we were both puffing contently.

"Seventeen," I responded.

"Did you finish high school?"

"No… I didn't." Although he didn't say anything, I could sense his disappointment which surprised me. I didn't think the back worker at a stockyards would be questioned about his high school education. Besides, I hardly knew any boys my age that completed their schooling. In a rural area, most boys either bored of school or were expected to start working. I was a little bit of both.

"Robert Hyde is your uncle? Your Dad's brother I presume?"

"Yes, that's right," I said, glad for the subject change.

"Yah, I know Robert. Good guy. He sells his calves here. Runs a good operation. He called me about a week ago and said you're a heck of a young stockman."

I thought he might say something else but he just took another puff of his smoke.

"Uncle Bob takes a lot of pride in his herd," I replied, without acknowledging the compliment he'd given me.

He seemed to take notice because he gave a small smile. Then he said, "Son, thanks for having a smoke with me. The job was yours before you stepped foot in my office. I've got a few more things to tend to in here but why don't you go out back and introduce yourself to some of the boys. Things should be slower today. That will give you time to see how things work. You will be on the payroll beginning Monday morning. Be sure to give all your information to the ladies in the office."

A big smile spread across my face but before I could speak, the telephone interrupted with a loud ring. He was reaching for it as we gave a quick hand shake and I professed a hurried, "Thank you, thank you very much," before heading out the door.

As I walked back down the stairs, I recalled the final comment. *Son, thanks for having a smoke with me.* The man had just given me a job. And then he thanked me for it. I knew I was the one that was supposed to be grateful. I figured I'd show my gratitude simply by proving that he'd made the right decision in hiring me.

I got lost a few times on my way to the back pens. The stockyards were more expansive than I had imagined. There were two sale rings and it seemed like miles of wooden pens for the cattle. But this place wasn't just an auction mart. There was a packing plant, too. The Stockyards and Burns Foods were interlinked. They joined each from the railroad tracks on the east side to Portland Street on the west side. There were several buildings, most of which I had no idea what their purpose might be. There were tall hay sheds filled with hay and straw for the livestock. There were load out facilities and, for the first time in my life, I saw a truck and cattle liner. I'd never seen anything so big. It must've been about 26 feet long. These days, that's pretty dang small. But before then, I'd only seen cattle hauled in the truck box with racks.

When I made my way through the wooden pens, I passed a few men who simply gave me curt nods and kept walking. Everyone seemed busy and I was still working up the courage to stop someone and ask them for help. I stared at the wooden pens as I walked along. There were holding pens, sorting pens, and overnight pens. The long alley that led up to the sale ring was easily accessed from all different areas. Finally, walking down one of those alleys towards the weigh scale, I saw two guys leaned up against the fence beside the scale house. One looked to be about my age. He had a carefree laugh as he chuckled about something he had just said. The other man was older - maybe 50 - and he barely smiled at whatever had just been said. To his left, lay a blue heeler dog. I knew I'd found the people I could introduce myself to.

I approached the younger one first and stuck out my hand. "Morning. I'm Charlie Hyde. I've just been hired on. I was told to find someone out back who could show me around."

"Heya, Charlie, good to meet ya. I'm Rich Malaney," said the younger one as we shook hands. "This is Gene Weisgerber," he said gesturing to the older man. "And this good ol' boy is Blue," he finished by bending down and affectionately patting the dog's head.

Rich seemed my age and about the same height as me but his body was slim compared to my own. He didn't have the broad shoulders that I had earned from working on the farm every day.

Gene squeezed the hell out of my hand as we gave a quick shake. He only briefly looked me in the eye as he said, "Mornin'." His face was weathered and wrinkled, making it hard to guess his age. He looked like he'd been working out in the elements his entire life. Canadian weather was hard on skin that was constantly exposed. In the winter, you dealt with freezing temperatures and winds. In the summer, you had relentless sun and heat. Both would leave your skin dry and cracked; the trademark of a hard-working man in Alberta.

Rich carried on the conversation easily. "Gene is a brand inspector. Try not to judge him by that. I promise he ain't as much of a nuisance as most of them are," Rich said as he chuckled at his own joke again. He either didn't notice or didn't care that Gene wasn't laughing. "I can show you around since you'll be working with me. A fellow alley rat!" he smiled as he slapped me on the back. I frowned, just a little. I knew that working in the back pens would mean I was low man on the totem pole at the stockyards. But I didn't realize it would mean that we were referred to as alley rats.

Rich started walking so I followed in step with him. Then he turned back towards where we'd come from and called out, "Thanks for all the laughs, Gene. Let's do it again Monday." Gene gave a brief wave and shook his head without looking at us. Blue was still laying by his side.

"Good guy, that Gene," Rich said to me as we walked. "The best there is at his job, too. He barely ever has to clip cattle to see the brands. He must have some sort of vision superpower when it comes to spotting brands on cattle. Not like some of those brand inspectors who make you run a cow through the chute and clip their hair in three different spots just to find the ownership brand. And he's a man of few words, Gene is. If you've got a secret just burning you up, I'd recommend telling it to him. It would be as safe as if you confessed to the priest." Rich poured all of these words smoothly out of his mouth without seemingly taking a breath. He had a natural knack for saying a lot of words without ever seeming like he was talking too much. If Rich took ten minutes to tell a story, you would sit there completely consumed by it without ever realizing how much time had passed.

Rich continued the tour, walking me up and down the alleys, pointing out buildings, and explaining how everything works. He added his own commentary and witty remarks as he went. He also asked me plenty of questions about how old I was and where I was from. I asked him similar questions in return. Rich seemed to smoothly avoid questions about his family but he did it in such a manner that I wasn't sure if I was imagining it or not. I thought about his earlier comment regarding secrets burning you up inside and wondered how many secrets Rich had ever confessed. My guess was not very many. Sometimes the people that talk the most are the ones avoiding what they truly want to say.

Eventually Rich asked, "Where you planning on living?"

"Not exactly sure," I said. "I never really made a plan other than to get hired on. I suppose I'll start looking for places to rent in the paper and sleep in my truck a few nights."

"Well, sumbitch," Rich smiled. "Say hello to your new landlord. I got a couch with your name all over it."

Once the tour finally ended, we started in on the work. Fridays were sale days and Saturdays were for taking care of everything that had happened yesterday. Cattle were being shipped out and moved and the pens were being emptied and cleaned. Rich and I wouldn't have to work on Sundays and I was beginning to get a better grasp on what would be expected of me Monday morning. Eventually, Rich said we could head out and I could follow him back to his house in my truck.

"My truck's parked in the front. Why don't I meet you up there? I gotta run back inside and talk to the secretaries about getting on the payroll," I said.

As I walked inside and up towards the front office, I made a mental note of each doorway and each sign. The vastness of the stockyards was starting to sink in. The biggest auction mart in all of Canada. Not to mention the best. There was a reason that Uncle Bob sold his cattle at this place instead of the number of smaller county auction marts that were continuing to pop up. There was something downright magical about it. The history ran so deep that you could feel it pulsing through the walls. Even on a quiet day with no sale, you still felt like you could hear the echo of an auctioneer's ramble. Or the happy clap of a rancher who just got top dollar for his bred heifers. Or the laugh between two old friends who happened upon each other in the seats surrounding the sale ring.

Of course, an auction mart isn't always surrounded with good intentions and happy feelings. During a low time in the agricultural market, an auction mart becomes the living representation of hard times. But that only contributes to the magic of the place. During The Great Depression, the stockyards survived. They carried on. There's an odd sense of comfort in the fact that no matter how bad a sale goes or how low the prices get, the next week there will be another sale. Same time and same place. Life continues and cattle sell. Folks still need to eat, no matter what the economic climate is.

I may have been young and foolish. But I knew magic when I felt it. And walking down that hall, I felt like I was exactly where I belonged.

hollering

Rich's couch was as uncomfortable as all hell. I rolled over onto my side and felt a lump pushing into my ribs. Eventually, I gave up any hope of sleep. Slowly standing, I yawned and stretched and rubbed my eyes. It was Sunday morning and I didn't have to do a damn thing all day. No horses or cows to look after. No jobs listed out from Dad. Not three brothers to organize and set to work. I came fully awake when I realized I didn't even have to go to church.

I ambled over to the kitchen table and found a pack of smokes from the night before. I lit a cigarette and savored the thought of doing nothing. The euphoric sense of freedom had returned. Rich's house was only a 20-minute drive from the stockyards. It was a small, white, one level house in a nice neighborhood. Calgary's population was over 200,000 people but this neighborhood felt as small and friendly as my hometown. Rich's house was smaller than the others on the block but it was on two lots. The house took up a small space but the backyard was huge. It was fenced in with a white wooden fence that matched the house. The outside was neat and tidy but the inside of the house looked as you would imagine. There were remnants scattered about that revealed someone had once tried to decorate the place – a painting hanging or a doily sitting on a coffee table. But for the most part, the house was neglected and bare and fairly messy. I didn't know who owned the house but Rich had mentioned that I could make the rent cheque out to him without sparing any further details.

Rich woke up a few hours after me and we laid about in sloth, doing nothing except enjoying each other's company. We swapped stories about girls knowing full well that both of us were embellishing the truth a little. It was the first day of my life that I was in good health and didn't do a moment of work. We barely even left the house other than to grab a milkshake in the late afternoon.

The next day, we took my truck to the stockyards. We wanted to be there in time to have breakfast before work started. Rich had advised me that it was best to fill up with food on work days because your meals were paid for. "Eat on their dime so you can spend your money on important things. Like booze and women," was how he said it.

As I drove us, Rich ventured, "I've been meaning to ask you something. How does a seventeen-year-old, small-town farm kid afford a truck like this?" He tapped the dash and whistled briefly in appreciation.

I knew this question had been coming. Rich had been eyeing my truck up since the moment he saw it. I was surprised that it had taken him this long to ask me about it. I couldn't contain my pride and my chest puffed up a little before I even started to tell the story.

"Well… About two months ago, my Grandma took me and my brothers over to the local horse racing track. My grandma loves watching the races. She's a real horsewoman, to tell you the truth. When my Grandpa died and she was left a widow with a bunch of mouths to feed, she trained and sold horses for extra money. She did fairly good at it. She pretty well taught me and my brothers everything she knows about a horse and made sure we rode some nice ones," I paused, knowing that I had captured Rich's full attention. It felt good to be the one doing the talking.

"Anyways," I continued, "We were at the track, minding our own business. After the races were over, all the jockeys and owners head out to the parking lot and pass bottles around. One of the owners must've known Grandma because he waved at her and called her over. She told us to wait where we were and she headed over to him. They hardly chatted a minute before she called me over to join them. I remember Grandma saying "Charlie, what do you say we take advantage of an old fool today?" and I couldn't figure out what she was talking about. But it turned out Grandma and this owner had struck a deal. I would race against this guy's top jockey. Grandma got first pick of which horse I ran. And if I won, we would get the owner's brand-new pickup. If the jockey won, the owner would get three of Grandma's thoroughbred brood mares that local men had been trying to buy for years."

I let the story taper off at that point. I figured the fact that I was driving this truck right now pretty well told the rest of the story on its own.

"No shit!" Rich said loudly in disbelief. Then followed it up, more quietly, almost to himself, "Ain't that some shit."

It was the first time I'd seen Rich at a loss for words. My mind wandered to my grandma and the parts of the story that I'd left untold. The horse she picked for me to run didn't win its heat earlier that day. It lost by a nose. The owner picked the horse that had won earlier. Grandma had a sixth sense when it came to reading a horse. She said that the mare I was running was a fighter. I remember after the race the owner was still in disbelief as he handed his truck keys over to me. Grandma had a smile on her face as she said to him, *"Ability wins the first race. Heart wins the second race."*

Later that day after I had drove the truck home and Grandma and I were alone, she asked me if I knew why she picked me to run the race. I shook my head no. She said it wasn't for the way that I ride. *"You and all your brothers ride like a wild bunch of banshee's,"* she said. *"All four of you could have easily won that race. I didn't pick you to win. I picked you in case we lost. You're the only one that would be able to carry his head high and continue on if I had to give my mares away. Charlie, knowing how to lose will get you a lot further than knowing how to win. 'Cause life sure can be cruel."* Coming from a woman who had married young and then lost her husband in a freak accident after having five little kids, I figured that wisdom really meant something.

I also remembered my dad's reaction when we told him what happened. Phillip was talking a mile a minute and explaining the whole story. As soon as Dad got the gist of things, he said, *"You're returning that truck,"* to which Grandma quickly fired back, *"To hell he is."*

I kept the truck but it never quite sat right with Dad. He didn't think bets should be placed with men who were drinking. If you put my dad in that situation a million times over, he still wouldn't have taken the owner up on his bet. I don't know what it is about Grandma that makes her love a challenge. Maybe it's courage or recklessness or her fiery spirit. But whatever that quality is, I think it might skip a generation sometimes.

I was lost deeply in my thoughts as we pulled up to the stockyards. Rich must have noticed because he had been quiet for the rest of the drive which was pretty uncharacteristic. But when I glanced over at him, I caught a glimpse of something else on his face. It looked like sadness or maybe remorse. I was reminded that Rich and I had only met each other two days ago. As much as we hit it off, there was a lot that we still didn't know about one another. I figured someday I'd ask him about it.

All was back to normal as we headed in to get some breakfast. Rich had his strut back. We ordered some bacon and eggs and I looked around at all the men gathered there to eat breakfast. It was a bit of an offbeat crew. You could pick out the ranchers and cattleman who came to sell or buy cattle. They were dressed just a touch nicer than the rest of us. The order buyers were surrounding the ranchers. Those guys all had an easy disposition and they seemed to be controlling the conversation. The cowboys were sticking to themselves at another table. Rich had told me that the local cowboys were mostly day workers. You weren't ever sure if they would show up but if they did, you could almost bet that they hadn't won much at the rodeo on the weekend. The cowboys wore their hats and boots and spurs even though they would mostly be working on the ground today.

When the cook called out that my order was ready, I grabbed my plate and chose to go sit beside Gene because he was the only person I'd already been introduced to. Gene's dog Blue wasn't more than a couple inches away from his feet. He was laying quietly with his head on the ground. As I sat down, Gene tore off a half of piece of bacon from his plate and held it by his knee.

"Blue," he said quietly and his dog quickly stood up, snapped the bacon into his mouth, and was happily munching as he laid back down by Gene's feet again, all in a matter of moments.

I smiled and said, "I'm glad Blue gets to eat on the company dime, too."

To my surprise, Gene smiled back and said, "I actually asked a big wig about it, once. I said I didn't want to be taking advantage. The big shot, he just looked right at me, and he said, *"Gene. I think your Blue contributes more to this establishment than half the men on my payroll. I think we'd be happy to cook a little extra bacon in the mornings for him.""*

I laughed out loud at that. Not much else was said between us as we ate our breakfast but I took two things away from our little exchange: First, if you want to get Gene to talk, just ask him about his dog. And second, this must be a damn fine place to work.

When I was heading out back to start sorting cattle for the day, a man fell into step beside me. He had a white, short-brimmed hat cocked over his right eyebrow and a big smile on his face.

"I heard we've got a new man on the payroll," he said to me. "Just wanted to say welcome to the joint."

I smiled back. "Mighty kind of you. I'm happy to be here."

"I'm Frank Keats. They tell me I'm in charge of the finances. Scary thought, ain't it?" he teased as he stretched out his hand. Frank kept a hint of a smile on his face the whole time he talked.

"Charlie Hyde. I'm not in charge of anything but they tell me to always stay on the good side of the man in charge of finances," I said as we shook hands.

Frank laughed a little and said, "Smart man, Charlie. You'll do just fine around here. Let me know if there's anything I can do for ya."

We parted ways and I watched Frank Keats walk away for a moment. He still had that same half grin on his face. He was the first man that had gone out of his way to introduce himself. A few people gave me a half nod while I waited for my breakfast but no introductions had been made. I had to admit, I was grateful to Frank for taking the time to say hello. I liked the guy immediately. And I liked his short-brimmed hat, too.

The rest of the day passed in a blur. There was more yelling than I had expected. Working on the farm at home was always pretty quiet. My dad could make your heart sink if he ever glared at you but he wasn't much of a yeller. Here at the Stockyards, it seemed as if everyone yelled. I noticed the cowboys made the most noise. They were constantly whooping and hollering as they moved pens. That wasn't the way I had been taught to move stock. We were always taught that the fastest way to sort animals was to do it quietly and slowly. But things happened fast in the back pens of a stockyard. I was going to have to change my methods if I wanted to fit in. By the end of the day, I was yelling just as I had heard others do. *"BRINGING UP 15 COW CALF PAIRS, YOOOOO UPPPP, COME ON GIRLS, EVERYBODY GOES."*

I met a few men as I worked. Mostly just in passing. I didn't think that there was enough time to visit. I just kept looking for the next job that needed to be done and then going ahead and doing it. I felt like I must've walked up and down those alleys ten thousand times that day. I had a short break for lunch and a shorter break for supper. It was dark by the time Rich and I piled back into my truck and I drove us home.

All I remember from that night is that Rich's couch sure was a lot more comfortable than it was the first night. I was asleep as soon as I laid down.

ticklish

It's funny how we don't truly know ourselves until we see who we are through other's eyes. In my first few weeks at The Stockyards, I got the reputation of being a hard worker. That always kind of surprised me. I'd never thought about the fact that I might work harder than other men. My mom and dad raised all of us boys to do what needed to be done. I never felt that I worked harder than my brothers. Certainly, no harder than Phillip – the gamey one of our bunch.

My parents were the real modest type. If they were aware of the fact that us boys worked harder than other people, I never heard them say it out loud.

That's why I was taken aback the first time someone said, "You wanna get wore out in a hurry, just try and keep up to Charlie when he's sorting pens."

Or, "Sum bitch, kid, what are you trying to prove?"

And my personal favorite, "That Charlie Hyde busts his ass around here."

I wasn't ever trying to outwork the rest of the crew. I just did one job as efficiently as I could and then I looked around for the next thing to do. Sometimes I would notice guys standing around and having a smoke. Plenty of guys took work breaks to play cards by the scale house. And by the end of the day, there would usually be a few beers around. But I never stopped to visit or smoke or drink until I couldn't see anything else that needed to be done. My dad was a man of few words and that taught me to be an independent worker. He didn't constantly tell me what I should be doing. He wouldn't stand over your shoulder and tell you each move to make. But Lord help you if he walked by and saw you standing around with your hands in your pockets when there was work that needed to be done. That's when he would let you have it: a harsh glare, some harsher words, or an ass whipping if he felt you deserved it. The truth of the matter is that his method of showing his disappointment was irrelevant. For a son, disappointment from their father is always punishment enough.

I also started to see myself differently when I visited the ladies in the front office. I tried to go out of my way to say hello to the secretaries because I'd been fond of them since the first day I'd met them. They worked harder than most the men in the back and I liked to show my appreciation. I would also be lying if I didn't say that I enjoyed the praise I received from them during our visits. They nearly always made a comment about my looks.

"Charlie Hyde, you are polite as they come and good looking to boot."

"Honey, with a face like that you won't be sorting cattle for long."

And my personal favorite, "Remember us if you ever become a movie star, Charlie."

I tried to keep in mind that the secretaries were overly polite to every person that came through their office. They lavished everyone with praise. They were like the proud aunts of the stockyards and every worker was her favorite nephew who could do no wrong. But even so, I began to take lingering looks in the mirror when I had the opportunity. I rubbed my hand over my jaw and chin and turned my head side to side. I had never really examined myself before. Staring at yourself in the mirror seemed like a feminine pastime and it wasn't something I was accustomed to. But after some time and deliberation, I decided that they were probably right. I was handsome. Maybe not quite Hollywood handsome but that was alright.

Within two weeks of working at the stockyards, I was known as the handsome kid that worked hard. And if you would've asked me to tell you about myself prior to that, "handsome" and "hard working" would have never made my personal list of adjectives.

Time was mostly passing in the same, uneventful way. I was meeting more of the men and I was enjoying the free food but I mostly just worked and slept for those first few weeks. It wasn't boring but it wasn't riveting, either. I'll never forget the night that all changed. It was my first taste of excitement at the Stockyards.

It had been a normal day up until quitting time. Usually, a few drinks were had at the end of the day but most everyone parted ways pretty quickly. We were either wore out from a day of work, going home to a family, or going to find a place with more excitement. But that day, something was in the air and no one was really wanting to leave. One drink turned into "one more" which quickly turned into "one more" and so on. Everyone was laughing and joking and there was just a contagious, good feeling spreading amongst us. Eventually, the idea of a poker game was brought up. Everyone was in agreeance that it was a good night for poker so we all had another drink to celebrate such a great idea being brought up.

Frank Keats finally took charge. I had spoken to Frank a few times since that first day when he took the time to introduce himself to me. I noticed that Frank always wore his short-brimmed hat and he always wore that half smile. I had yet to see him in a bad mood. It also seemed as if everyone was friends with Frank. Or maybe, as I remembered how Frank had taken the time to talk to me, it would be a better explanation to say Frank was friends with everyone. He could charm the secretaries in one beat, discuss God with a religious rancher the next beat, and then cuss an old bitch cow with the alley rat workers on his last beat. I figured that being so adaptable like he was probably helped him move up the ladder at the stockyards. He was the chief financial officer. He was in charge of loans, payouts, commissions, and all the money deals that I didn't yet comprehend.

Frank brought out a deck of cards and it seemed fitting that he gathered the money for the initial buy in. I opted out of playing in the game but I was sure interested in watching while I enjoyed a few more drinks. Rich decided to buy in. He was standing beside me and he leaned over and pointed a finger at me and said, "Shit, bud, don't you worry. I'll win enough for the both of us," which made us both laugh. Rich was well on his way to being drunk but he was the same good-natured, laughing guy that I had come to respect while we lived together.

A tall, scrawny American that I didn't know too well also decided to buy in. He said he was up here looking to buy black angus cattle for a big ranch in Bozeman, Montana and he'd been lingering around the last couple of days. If you weren't sure whether or not he was important, you only had to wait a minute and he would soon tell you that he was. The crew at the Stockyards liked to talk themselves up but it was always in good natured fun. When someone came around who was actually sincere in their arrogance, they quickly stood out and were ostracized.

A few of the cowboys sat down to play and they threw their money towards Frank. I had met most of them now and liked them all. They were always laughing and telling stories and they all seemed to have a rambunctious spirit. Of the group that bought in to the game, was one of the biggest men I'd ever met. Everyone referred to him as Lil' Joe. From what I'd gathered, he was somewhat of a rodeo star and had won a lot of money steer wrestling. Even with his broad shoulders, big strong grip, and swinging arms, I had a hard time imagining it. Lil' Joe seemed far too amicable and easy going to muster up the aggression he would need in competition. Of all the cowboys at the stockyards, Lil' Joe was the mildest one.

As Lil' Joe was sitting down at the table, he fondly put an arm around Rich and squeezed his neck and said, "Take it easy on me in the game, eh kid."

From a group of guys standing around watching, someone said, "Just keep an eye on his cards. Cheating is bred right into the boy."

My body instantly clenched at the comment. I looked at Rich. He was turning a deep red and he looked like he was ready to leap from his feet and fight the whole room. His anger was so intense and so automatic that I wondered how many times he had heard similar comments. I noticed Lil' Joe still had an arm on Rich's neck. But now it didn't seem to be a friendly gesture. It was a strong grip as he was holding Rich down in his seat, keeping him from standing up.

Frank calmly took control of the situation. He made it seem as if he was talking to himself but he spoke loudly and said, "All the jackasses standing around here can kindly keep their comments to themselves. And if you can't do that, you can put your money where your mouth is."

Good ol' Frank.

No one stepped forward to buy in to the game so Frank simply said, "That's what I figured," without ever looking in the direction where the comment had come from. It was the most non-confrontational way to confront a bad situation.

Then Gene stepped forward. I hadn't even noticed that he was still here. Sure enough, I glanced around and saw Blue sleeping ten feet away. Gene said, "Changed my mind. I think I will play. It looks too fuckin' easy to take money from this crew."

Gene wasn't laughing or smiling when he said it but everyone roared with laughter at the comment. Even Rich had a slight smile on his face as he watched Gene pull out his money. Frank had taken initial control of the situation but Gene had ensured that it wouldn't escalate any further. When Gene altered everyone's attention to himself, it was as if he was saying that whatever just happened no longer mattered. We were moving on.

Lil' Joe gave Rich a final, friendly pat on the back and pulled his arm away as Rich visibly relaxed. Everyone cut the deck to see who would deal first. Most of the bystanders either sauntered out the door, got another drink, or stood back just far enough that they wouldn't be able to see anyone's cards. I got a beer for myself and handed one to Rich and then pulled a chair up next to where Blue was sleeping. Blue noticed it was me and stood up to put his head in my lap. Most blue heelers had big, black beads for eyes. But right now, Blue's eyes were half open and half shut as I stroked his head. To be honest, I was using Blue as a distraction while taking a moment to myself to think about what had happened. While I sat there looking down at Blue, I made the conscious decision to not hold Rich's family history against him. I had no idea what that guy meant when he said *"cheating is bred right into the boy"* but I could make a few guesses that Rich's parents weren't exactly saints. And people were mad enough about it to confront Rich. Living and working with Rich for the past few weeks had been enough for me to make up my own mind in regards to Rich's character. And I wasn't about to let a jackass comment change that.

Most everyone ignored the game while it was in its first half. One of the cowboys was the first man out. He had bet wildly and they'd called his bluff but he just laughed as he threw his cards towards the dealer. Rich was the fourth guy out. He was playing too safe and his pile of chips just slowly dwindled down. As the game continued, the bystanders grew continuously rowdy. The night was wearing on and there wasn't a sober man left in the crowd. Finally, there was only Frank, Gene, and the tall American left at the table. This led everyone over to watch how it all would end.

Gene had been steadily sipping on beer all night but he didn't seem to be drunk. He was just the same, steady Gene. He made a good poker player because his facial expression never changed. And he wasn't much for chit chat. Frank and the American didn't stand a chance if they wanted to get a read on him. It showed too because Gene had the biggest stack of poker chips in front of him. Frank had a sizable stack to work with, as well, but the poor American was down to his last hope. He would have to go all in on this hand whether he had the cards or not.

Frank was dealing when suddenly he stood up abruptly. His chair pushed out behind him and fell over causing a loud crash that grabbed everyone's attention. Frank used his index finger to push his short-brimmed hat up and onto the back of his head, revealing his big, round eyes and raised eyebrows.

"Now, hold on a minute. Just hold on a minute, here," Frank was saying. Nobody moved. Frank was well-liked and respected amongst everyone. But, even more than that, he knew how to control a room. He had the whole place anticipating what he would say next. Finally, Frank settled his gaze onto the American.

"Son, I don't mean to accuse nobody of anything without a fair trial. I will let you speak your peace. But something isn't adding up here," Frank said.

The American instantly bristled up. But he didn't say a word. Frank continued, "Where'd that card come from, kid?"

Everyone looked in the direction that Frank had pointed with his index finger. Sure as shit, there was a card lying face down right by the American's foot. Someone crouched down beside him to pick up the card. They flipped it over on the table for everyone to see. It was an ace of diamonds.

That's when the American started to get loud. "I don't know NOTHING about that card," he proclaimed. "I didn't do a god damn thing. Never cheated in my life and I wouldn't start now with a bunch of men I don't even know."

Then he looked directly at Gene. "I work for THE DIAMOND N RANCH." He was a big man but his voice squeaked a little as he said *DIAMOND N RANCH*. It didn't do him any favors to come across as honest and believable. But he continued on, "Does anybody know who they are? Do you think they would send me up here if I was a cheat?!"

Gene was about to say something but by that time, it was too late. The American could've talked until his face turned blue. Our crew of guys had already made up our minds about him as soon as we saw that ace flip over on the table. Everyone was drunk and susceptible to believing that a man like him would be a cheater.

"Shit, son, I didn't know you worked for THE DIAMOND N RANCH," someone imitated. "Why didn't you say so earlier? You gotta let us know when you're real important like that."

"Yah, why didn't you just say so? I bet no one at THE DIAMOND N RANCH has ever tried to come out ahead in a poker game," someone else piped in.

"Maybe you can go home to THE DIAMOND N RANCH with a broken nose," another guy ventured.

The American stood his ground. "I'll fight the biggest bastard in here," he said. "And I'll do it because I didn't cheat. I'm not in the wrong here."

Everyone kind of laughed at that as all of our attention drifted to Lil' Joe. He was definitely the biggest bastard in the room. It was up to him what would happen next. Mild, soft-spoken, amicable Joe. I couldn't imagine him fighting.

But Lil' Joe knew he had to act. He strode right over to the American and they met in the middle of the circle. The American came in swinging. He was a big man and had a long reach but Lil' Joe ducked smoothly out of the way, popped up again, and grabbed The American by the throat. Then he stuck a leg behind The American's feet and tripped him down onto the ground. Before the American even knew what was happening, Lil' Joe was pinning him down with a knee on each arm.

No one ever could've guessed what happened next. And if I live to be 110 years old, I won't ever forget it.

The American was struggling like a tomcat in a sack but Lil' Joe was just calmly and firmly holding him in place. The American had his stomach on the floor and he couldn't get enough leverage to wiggle free of Lil' Joe's weight.

When Lil' Joe started to speak, his voice was as casual as if he was visiting about the weather. "Now, I've got a kid brother that likes to get in trouble and fight. He reminds me a lot of you when you said you'd fight the biggest bastard in here. All arrogance and no respect. I could've fought my kid brother many times throughout life and I could fight you right now. But I figure there's a better way to put you in your place and remind you who you're messing with when you come to the Stockyards."

No one dared breathe or move an inch while we wondered what method of torture Lil' Joe was about to employ on this cheatin' American.

Then Lil' Joe reached up two hands to the American's neck and started wiggling his fingers. "Tickle, tickle," he said.

No group of men have ever been taken by surprise more than we were. It only took a moment and then we all began to howl with laughter. I doubled over and slapped my knee, stood up and made eye contact with Rich and then doubled over laughing again.

The American was beat red and fuming but he couldn't escape Lil' Joe's grasp. He just laid there and sputtered and kept trying to wiggle free as Lil' Joe kept talking. "Come on now, little fellow, let's have a laugh. Tickle, Tickle," Lil' Joe mocked.

I can't imagine any better way to put a man in his place than what Lil' Joe did that night. Finally, Lil' Joe let the American up and those big, tall legs scrambled away from us as fast as they could.

"Tickle, tickle, you cheatin' son of a bitch," someone called out after him and we all roared with laughter again.

We took turns telling the story and retelling the story as the night wore on. Everyone had their own version and had something to add about the surprise of seeing Lil' Joe tickle a grown man. That story would be told many times throughout my life but it would never be as outrageous and as funny as it was to me that night when it first happened.

Finally, we were all out of beer and so drunk that we sauntered out the doors and stumbled into each other. Rich drove the two of us home. It's a miracle he stayed on the road as drunk as we were. But that's what we did in those days. Nobody ever worried about drinking and driving. Sometimes progress is a good thing.

I remember flopping down on to the couch and replaying the night in my head. I wondered what that big, lanky American's name was. Turned out it didn't matter because I never saw that poor soul again in my life. Before I drifted off to sleep, I wondered who ended up with all the poker money. In the morning, my head was too fuzzy for the thought to cross my mind again. It was a lot of years before I ever found out the truth of the matter. Sometimes I wish I'd never found out at all.

CHAPTER FIVE

indulgent

During those first few months I worked at the stockyards, I never worried about money. I had hardly anything and I was getting paid so little that I was beyond the point of worrying. What money I had went towards fuel, food, beer, and rent. That was all I needed to be happy. I was proud to be making an income and giving Rich a little to stay in his house. Looking back, I didn't pay him near enough. But Rich was only a year older than I was and neither of us knew what the going rate should be. I had yet to ask Rich about his family or how he ended up with his own house at 18 years old, but I was in no rush to talk about it.

That's the funny thing about young men. We're in such a hurry to prove ourselves but in no hurry to carry the burden of financial responsibility. We want to earn the respect of other men but we don't want to let those men know we crave their approval. And we want to understand the entire world around us but we don't want to ask our peers a personal question. A young man is a walking, talking contradiction until he becomes secure enough to set his ego aside.

And some men go their whole damn lives without ever reaching that stage.

At that point in my life, I was saving money for one sole purpose: to buy a mattress and bedspring. My young body could work all day, it could drink all night, and it could go on milkshakes all weekend until it was time to eat auction mart food again. But it couldn't handle the lumps in Rich's couch. I was ready to be off that thing.

One weekend when Rich asked if I wanted to drive to the movie theater, I balked. I'd only been to one movie in my life and that was a splurge from my Grandma during a trip we made to Edmonton. I didn't think I needed to see another movie very badly. But Rich talked and talked about the movie. *Rio Bravo* was playing and it was starring John Wayne. Tickets were a dollar. I looked at my measly savings towards my bed fund. I felt my sore ribs. But in the end, John Wayne won. We were headed to the movie.

Rich insisted that we drive my pickup. He said there was bound to be girls at the theater and they would notice us better in my truck. I thought of my kid brother Phillip saying Calgary women would surely love him when we last stood in the barn together and I felt a pang of homesickness. I didn't often miss home but when I did, it came in a sharp, surprising jolt. It always caught me off guard. I had called home a few times and talked to Dad. He seemed to speak to me differently during those phone calls. It was as if he could treat me as an equal now that I wasn't taking orders from him. Dad said more in those few phone calls than he did throughout the last entire year I had spent at home.

It all started when I asked how things were going and he said that Young Mare had died. She'd had trouble foaling, just as in the past. Her colt was coming out backwards. Dad wanted to pull the colt but he knew it would kill them both. His only option was to cut Young Mare open to get the colt out. After he did, he stitched her back up and thought she had a chance to survive. The colt was up and sucking and Young Mare was standing even though she was weak and sore in the back end. Both were shaky and Dad was weary by the end of it. At about 4 in the morning, he finally went to the house and crawled into bed, proud of the job he'd done. When he slept for a few hours and went back outside at 6, Young Mare was laying there dead. Dad said there must have been some internal complications that he couldn't see. Or an infection that acted quickly. Whatever it was, Dad was sure tore up about it. He talked freely about the guilt he had about going to sleep when he should've kept an eye on her.

For Dad, it wasn't about the money. Young Mare had given us enough colts that she had more than paid for herself. Dad would buy another mare to replace her. But he felt guilty about choosing his own sleep over staying with Young Mare. For my entire life, Dad seemed to carry a silent burden. It seemed to say *I should've done more.* No matter what the situation, Dad never quite felt like he was good enough. That's probably why he didn't take risks and buy more land like some of our surrounding neighbors. To buy more land and expand your farm, you had to feel as though you deserved to own more and be better.

In those phone calls with my dad during the first few months I moved out, I felt as though I began to understand him better than ever before. I respected him more. But I also began to understand the ways in which I didn't want to end up like him.

That was all heavy on my mind as I waited for Rich to quit staring at himself in the mirror before we headed out to the movie. It was a Saturday night and I was slowly sipping on a beer. I walked around aimlessly and occasionally looked out the windows onto the street. I still wasn't used to living so close to other people. I could see a lady out on her lawn. I was torn between walking outside and striking up a conversation with her or stepping back from the window and pretending like I hadn't noticed her. I chose the latter and started hollering at Rich.

"You can stare in that mirror all you want," I said loudly towards the bathroom. "But it won't change a damn thing. Let's get moving."

"Yeah, yeah. Easy to say coming from the guy with the movie star looks," Rich shot back. But he came out of the bathroom anyway and threw a jacket on. Rich wasn't bad looking. He actually was a fairly handsome guy. But I always felt like he had a forgettable face. Nothing about his looks stuck with you. I think it was because his personality was so big. You remembered everything he said and how he said it but you didn't remember what he looked like.

He grabbed a beer from the fridge and continued, "We haven't even so much as been on a date since you moved in. The problem is that I've been relying on your good looks to bring the girls in. That's proved to be pretty hopeless. So, tonight I'll start using my charm. Don't take it personal, Charlie. But I'm taking over."

"You couldn't pick up a radio station, let alone pick up a girl," I said.

Rich made a face in mock outrage. "I do believe you have me confused with someone else. Women really respond to me. Always have."

"Uh huh," I muttered with a smile as we walked out the door together.

"I'm serious," Rich persisted when we were in the truck. Then he started grinning and said, "In fact, why don't we see who the best man really is. First one of us that gets a girl to kiss him tonight wins. And the loser has to drive home. And also buy a case of beer."

I laughed out loud and then quickly stopped when I felt a pang in my ribs. Then I had an idea. "Okay, bud, I'm game. But let's up the stakes. Forget about driving home and the case of beer. How about the first guy who can get a girl to kiss him will get to sleep in the bed at home. Loser gets the couch."

"Shit, Charlie. What good does that do me? I'm already sleeping in the bed and I'll be sleeping in the bed again tonight after some lonely dame throws herself on me."

"If you're so confident, you've got nothing to lose. And bragging rights if you win."

Rich thought about it for a moment and then conceded.

"You're on," he said. Then we clinked our beers together and finished them off.

I slowed the truck way down as we pulled up to the theater. I felt that Rich had a point when he said my pickup was likely to get us some good attention so I wanted to give every opportunity for a pretty girl to see me drive in. It was a warm June night and people were spread out all around the theater. There were picnic benches in front of the theater and grass was surrounding the whole place. There was an ice cream store inside the theater and most people had scoops heaped on top of cones that they were licking. It appeared as though every girl I could see was more interested in her ice cream than she was in my truck. That was one of my earliest life lessons in understanding women.

We parked the truck and headed over to buy our tickets. We were there about a half an hour early so Rich grabbed us two more beers that he had packed along for the drive. We perched up on some grass a short distance from the bigger crowds of people. There were older couples, young couples, and plenty of groups of friends all mingled together. It seemed as though John Wayne brought together a wide array of fans.

I was surveying the crowd when I locked eyes with her. She was short, skinny, and staring right at me. She had a long, dark braid down her back. She reached back and grabbed the braid with her left hand and slung it over her left shoulder before she looked away. I kept staring for another beat. She was with two other girls that were both blonde. Her dark hair made her stand out. But it was also the way she was standing. The other two were busy chatting but she was a little more serious. She nodded along as if she was taking everything in but she also looked as if she was in another world. Her own world. At that point, I wasn't sure how long I had been staring and she glanced back in my direction. This time when I looked at her, I noticed how beautiful she was. She had a smattering of freckles across her tanned face and her sharp, green eyes looked like they never missed anything. I smiled and nodded and slightly raised my beer in her direction. She smiled back and nodded and raised her ice cream cone towards me.

Rich noticed what was happening and started chuckling to himself. "You know who that is, right?" he asked.

"Not a clue," I said as I started to walk towards her.

Rich followed behind me without another word. By the time we reached the three girls, they were all staring at us. The two blondes were giggling but my dark-haired beauty just kept a slight smile as she maintained eye contact with me. The closer I got to her, the more aware I became that I had no idea what to say.

"Hi," I said. There was more giggling from the blondes.

"Hi," she said back.

"Well, hello, Margaret," Rich said. I had nearly forgotten he was standing beside me and I was surprised to hear him call her by name.

She smiled fondly at him. "Rich Malaney, it sure has been a while since I've seen you!" she said. Then she gestured to the two blondes. "Do you know my friends? This is Pamela and this is Lorraine."

"Pleasure to meet ya both," Rich said with a crooked grin. I thought Pamela and Lorraine looked about identical but I didn't spend much time trying to remember the two of them. I was more focused on

Margaret. I think that became obvious because Rich spoke up again and said, "This is my friend Charlie Hyde. We're living together and working at the stockyards. He's new to the area."

"Nice to meet you, Charlie," Margaret said. Then she raised her eyebrows and glanced at my beer and said, "Leave it to two stockyards' boys to be drinking beer outside the movie theater."

I looked at the beer in my hand as if I was surprised to be holding it. The thought hadn't occurred to me that it might not be appropriate to drink beer while we waited for the movie to start. I was getting used to being around men all the time. I had to start remembering how my mother would want me to act.

It was almost as if she was daring me to say something sheepish in response but instead, I just handed my beer towards her and said, "Well, would you like a drink?"

To my surprise, she laughed. And I relaxed a little when she took the beer from my hand and took a long drink. Then I noticed the way her lips looked on the bottle and I felt nervous all over again.

I was more grateful for Rich in those next few moments than ever before. He casually and easily carried on the conversation with the three girls. I stood quietly and waited for the right time to jump back into the conversation. He may have been on to something when he said that charm gets the girls because I didn't think I was fairing too well. I still hadn't said another word when Margaret silently reached over, grabbed my beer, and took another drink before handing it back to me. That easy, silent gesture about did me in. I didn't know her last name, how old she was, or where she came from. But I was completely hooked.

Eventually someone suggested that we go into the theater and get a seat. I couldn't tell if it was Pamela or Lorraine. But I seized the opportunity and looked at Margaret.

"Can I get you some popcorn?" I asked.

"I would love some," she smiled back.

Rich piped up and said, "Pamela, Lorraine I'm buying us the biggest size they have. I'd be happy to share if it means I get to sit in between two pretty girls," which sent the two blondes back to giggling.

Rich and I headed to the concession lineup while the girls waited by the movie theater entrance. As soon as we were out of earshot, Rich started talking a mile a minute.

"Buddy, you're gonna have to say *SOME* words. You're killing me with the mysterious and timid act you've got going on. Seriously, my back will be sore by the end of the night from carrying this team. By the way, do you seriously not know who she is? Haven't you ever seen her at the stockyards?"

I shook my head no and was about to ask how Rich knew her but he fired up talking again before I had the chance to speak.

"That's Margaret Westerlund. Maggie, most people call her. As in John Westerlund's daughter. As in the biggest damn rancher in all of Alberta. Hell, he probably owns half of Alberta. I grew up with her, known her forever. She's always had that long, dark braid – it's her signature. I used to bug her about looking like an Indian. So, let me tell you right now, she's way out of your league. Even if you do have Hollywood good looks," Rich ranted.

I opened my mouth to say it was worth a shot but Rich was already talking again. He had glanced up at the menu and was now on to a new topic.

"I don't mind paying a little extra for popcorn if it means I've got double the odds to win this bet. You think those girls are competitive? I hope they are. Always been a dream of mine to have two girls fighting over me," Rich said and then laughed at his own joke.

That's when I realized that Rich was just as nervous as I was. He dealt with it by talking more and I dealt with it by talking less. I started laughing with him then, too. I wasn't laughing at his joke but at the whole situation. We had talked a lot of smack to each other on the drive in and now we actually had some girls that seemed to be interested in us. But neither of us could keep it together. I was thankful that we were about to sit in a movie with no requirement to talk and no pressure to put on the charm.

When Rich and I had our bags of popcorn in hand, we followed the girls into the theater. They picked out a row with five empty seats and I sat down beside Margaret. She fiddled with the end of her braid and then looked over at me and said, "So, Charlie Hyde, are you always this quiet?"

"Are you always this straight forward?" I asked as I forced myself to meet her gaze.

Her green eyes crinkled at the edges as she grinned and said, "I would like to think so. Life's too short to beat around the bush. Don't you agree?"

"Yup," I said. "Life's also too short to spend all your time talking instead of listening."

She looked thoughtful for a moment then just gave a short nod and said, "Amen," before taking a handful of popcorn and putting some in her mouth. I followed suit and started eating just as all the lights dimmed and the screen lit up.

Rio Bravo lasted for two and a half hours and I spent about two hours and twenty-five minutes trying to figure out how the hell I was going to kiss this girl. Not even John Wayne could inspire me to muster up the courage to make a move. We shared the bag of popcorn, we laughed together at the funny scenes, and we sat suspended during the shootouts. But I never so much as laid a hand on her. I did notice Rich wrapped around one of the girls with his head pressed up against hers at one point during the movie but I was beyond the point of caring about the bet.

After John Wayne and Angie Dickinson exchanged a sultry repertoire in the movie's final scene, I was ready to spring out of there. I wasn't used to sitting in one place for that long and seeing Angie Dickinson's figure on the big screen while a beautiful girl sat beside me about put me over the edge. The lights had barely come on in the theater when I was standing up and telling Margaret it had been very nice to meet her and I hoped to see her again soon. I was so nervous as to how to say good bye to her that I just avoided the scenario altogether. I practically pushed Rich towards the truck and gave a quick wave back to the girls.

Once we were loaded up, Rich started complaining. "What the hell was your rush? Things were just getting good. You sour that I won the bet?"

I shrugged him off and said I was just ready to go home. "Which one did you kiss, anyways? Was that Pamela or Lorraine?"

"Well," Rich paused and took a breath. "To tell you the truth... I have absolutely no idea."

We both sputtered with laughter at that and continued to talk about the girls for the rest of the drive home. Once we were safely distanced from the girls, our confidence returned and our stories grew bolder as we took turns retelling our personal versions of what had happened throughout the night. We also took turns talking about John Wayne and what a damned good cowboy he was.

When we got home, I flopped down on the couch for the night after enduring an endless stream of bragging from Rich. But it didn't bother me. It was the first time I had laid contently on that miserable, old couch. I was dreaming of other things. I had a girl with green eyes and a long, dark braid stuck in my head. I kept running the name *Margaret Westerlund* through my mind over and over.

I liked the way it felt to just lay there and think about her. It felt indulgent and sweet. And like I wasn't going to stop any time soon.

CHAPTER SIX

praise

On one particularly hot summer morning, I stepped in to the auction mart to get some breakfast. The sun was only going to get more powerful as the day went on but I didn't mind. When you grow up poor, you always welcome summer. Wealthy people have ways of avoiding the cold or at least making it more bearable. But the heat is an equalizer for everyone. Shade is free no matter who you are and in Alberta at that time, shade was the only relief from a hot day.

I got my usual bacon and eggs and then made my way over to Frank Keats. Frank and I had made a habit of eating breakfast together and chatting. It was always a good start to my day. Frank's positive, happy attitude was contagious. And he could spew knowledge on just about any subject. Frank always had a smile on his face and that short-brimmed hat on his head. I found comfort in the consistency of his character. Frank had become like family to me. Along with Rich and Gene and Blue. They were the first people that I had met when I came to the stockyards and I felt like that was God's way of setting me up with a good circle of friends. I trusted and respected all of them.

This morning, Frank and I didn't have a whole lot to say to each other. We were just eating our food and enjoying the easy silence. I put a half a piece of bacon in my pocket to give to Blue later that day. I had gotten in the habit of this after I saw Gene feeding Blue on my first day of work.

Rich was sitting with some rodeo guys at a table across from me when I could hear him bringing my name up.

"Charlie Hyde is your man! I'm telling you, he can get the job done," Rich was saying.

I perked my ears but didn't make any other movements. Frank had heard Rich's proclamation as well because he looked at me and said, "Got any clue what they might be talking about over there?"

"You never can be sure where a conversation will lead when Rich is involved," I said.

Frank chuckled and then looked up at the approaching men. Rich was leading a stout man with a dusty, old cowboy hat toward us. The man had a grim expression on his face and I couldn't help noticing his giant hands. They were cracked and raw and dirty.

"Looks like we're about to find out," Frank said before they reached our table. They pulled up two chairs beside us and Rich immediately started talking.

"Charlie, this is Arthur Langley. He's a chuckwagon driver and he doesn't live far from here. And I just got you a job with him," Rich stated proudly.

I just looked at Arthur in mild shock. Even though chuckwagon racing had been an event at the Calgary Stampede since the 1920s, I'd never seen it. My grandma was always saying she couldn't accurately bet on chuckwagon races because there were four horses per team. They were all hitched up to a wagon with one driver. She preferred races with one horse and one jockey because she felt you could read the horses better. With my little knowledge of chuckwagon racing, I had no idea what Arthur might be hiring me for.

The stocky man was looking me up and down with a frown on his face. Then he said, "One of my outriders broke his leg the other day. I need one more guy. For the Calgary Stampede. Which is in a couple weeks," he finished bluntly.

"What's an outrider?" I asked.

Arthur didn't hide his disgust. He threw his head back a little and said, "Jesus, Rich, I told you I don't need some farm kid who doesn't know what the hell is going on."

Rich shot right back and said, "Look, Arthur, I respect you but let's be honest. It doesn't take a damn rocket scientist to figure it out. I'll prep him and he'll be fine."

Arthur looked at me again and I was beginning to feel uncomfortable. Was I supposed to be offended? Then he finally huffed, "Be at my house tomorrow after supper. We'll see if this will work," and he got up and stalked out of the building.

Rich clapped his hands together in celebration and I just blankly looked at Frank and said, "Do you know what just happened?"

"It appears as though your friend just opened you up to a whole new world. Do you know how to ride well?" he asked.

I was going to answer modestly but Rich jumped in for me instead. "Does he know how to ride?! Frank, let me tell you a story. Charlie can ride the hide off anything you give him. It's probably how he got the name Charlie Hyde now that I think of it."

Rich proceeded to tell the story about the race my grandma lined up in which I ended up winning myself a brand-new truck. Rich's version of the story was a little more exciting than my own. He added harmless details that he had come up with himself. He talked about how mad the owner was at his own jockey after they lost to me. I never interrupted or said a word. One time I had asked Rich about his story telling and he just said, *"Charlie, I don't ever bother ruining a good story with the truth."* And anyone who knew Rich was fully aware that he liked to embellish things. I watched Frank as Rich told him the story. Frank nodded and raised his eyebrows and said a few words here and there. Frank would've known that Rich's story was all based in fact. You just had to sift through it a little to find the truth.

Finally, Frank looked at me and said, "Why didn't you ever tell me you were such a hand with a horse?"

"Guess it never came up in conversation," I shrugged. Most of mine and Frank's conversations had been me asking him questions and then listening. I learnt a lot from Frank during our talks.

Now that Rich wasn't the center of the conversation, he grew bored and drifted out the door. Frank was looking at me with a touch of fondness wrapped up in his usual smile.

Then he said, "Charlie, I hope you know the potential that you have. I think that you could go on to be successful at a number of things. You're probably going to achieve a lot more in life than just working the back pens at a stockyard or being an outrider for a chuckwagon driver. But for now, working the back pens and being an outrider is a damn good place to start."

I was shocked at the boldness in Frank's words. At that point in my life, I didn't think men ever praised each other in such a candid way. I'd never heard my dad speak to me or my brothers in that manner.

"Shit, Frank. Thank you. I really appreciate that," I mustered up the courage to say back.

Frank got up to leave then and I watched him go. His white hat always made him stand out amongst the other men. I could only see Frank's back but I could tell he was smiling at everyone he passed. I knew that Frank was a moment of happiness in everyone's day. All the men returned a smile or a respectful handshake.

I carried Frank's words with me throughout the rest of the day. I allowed his praise to wash over me. My grandma had often praised me but it always seemed different. She was related to me and therefore obligated to do so. Frank had no stake in the game. He simply said those things because he believed them to be true and because he was kind enough to say it out loud.

Frank's words that day changed the way I lived the rest of my life. I often made decisions about my career and took chances as if I was destined to be successful. As if life was already rigged in my favor. Sometimes it worked and sometimes it didn't. But I never quit trying. Frank said *I think that you could go on to be successful at a number of things*. And when he said that out loud to me, I started to think the same way.

I also took a note out of Frank's playbook and I started to speak more candidly. I began to realize the difference it could make in a life. I didn't immediately pick up this habit and it wasn't always easy for me to praise someone. But the more I put it into practice, the simpler of a gesture it became. I like to see the way someone's face lights up when you give them recognition. We don't realize how little credit we give to the people surrounding us until we see the difference we can make with a few words.

But, there I go, getting ahead of myself again. All this will tie together in time.

swirls

Rich was driving my truck like a bat out of hell. He was taking me to Arthur's place so I could try to prove that I knew how to ride a thoroughbred. Rich was shifting gears and grinning while the radio played. He was completely carefree and happy with the windows rolled down on another hot summer night.

"Man, did I ever miss driving a truck that has a radio player in it," he shouted over to me above the noise.

"When did you drive one before?" I asked.

He tensed up just a little at the question. It was as if he realized he had let his guard down and said too much. "Oh, another lifetime," he said with a chuckle. But the chuckle felt forced. As if he had just gotten a dream confused with real life and he was sheepish about it. I took the hint and dropped the subject.

My mind wandered back to chuckwagon racing. Rich had spent the entire night prior explaining it to me. The outriders played a more crucial role than I had realized. There are two outriders per each chuckwagon. The outriders race on their own individual thoroughbred horse and follow the chuckwagon around the racetrack. At the beginning of the race, we start on foot, hanging onto our horses' reins, as one outrider throws a symbolic stove into the back of the chuckwagon and the other outrider steadies the wagon team before we mount our own horses. Then we are required to give the chuckwagons the right of way around the track but must stay within 150 feet of the chuckwagon we are competing with. The first wagon to cross the finish line typically wins but there are a number of penalties that can change the outcome of the race. For example, a barrel can be knocked over in the initial figure eight pattern the chuckwagon completes before going around the track or an outrider can cross the finish line too far behind his wagon driver.

With all of this on my mind, I thought of Arthur. His enormous hands and stern disposition. I thought of what he would be expecting from me. And there was no way in hell I was going to be late crossing that finish line.

It was a forty-minute drive out to Arthur's place. He lived just north of Strathmore. When we went through the town of Strathmore, I was reminded of my own hometown. It was small and friendly. I was grateful for Rich's house but I began to realize how much I was missing the country life. This town seemed much more my speed than any city. When we eventually rolled up to Arthur's place, I could see a huge race track out in his field. It wasn't fancy but it looked like it was well used. I wasn't sure if Arthur had actually designed a track or if he had just followed his same path around the grass field enough times that the big, sandy oval had developed. There were thoroughbreds lined up everywhere I looked. Rich parked my truck in the yard and we started walking over to the track to find Arthur. As we walked through the field, mosquitoes swarmed all around us. Horses were stamping their feet and swishing their tails while Rich and I swatted ourselves and waved our hands about wildly. I watched Arthur as we began to approach him. He was calmly oiling some leather lines. He would dab on the leather and then rub it off with an old piece of cloth and repeat the process over and over. The surrounding mosquitoes clearly had no effect on him. I wondered if he had spent so many hours out here that he had grown immune to the bites or if his skin was so damn tough that a mosquito couldn't penetrate through. As we got closer and Arthur's hard disposition became glaringly evident, I figured either scenario could very well be true.

"Jesus, Arthur, you live in the middle of a mosquito nesting ground or what?" Rich said as we approached.

Arthur looked at both of us and although his eyes never changed, a small chuckle rumbled out of his broad chest. I got the feeling that he enjoyed watching other men squirm out on his track. I also got the feeling that he assumed those men were weaker. I made a conscious effort to stand with a little more composure.

Arthur fixed his gaze on me and said, "We'll be breezing all the backup horses tonight. It's a day off for my good team. You'll find everything you need in that shack. Go ahead and saddle the sorrel tied up closest to us. You can breeze that one while I finish oiling."

I didn't bother asking what bit to use or any other question. Arthur didn't seem like he wanted to bother with answering any questions so I decided to just go with my instincts. I made my way to the shack that Arthur had pointed at with his thick, gnarled finger and opened the door. The inside was spotless and everything looked as if it had its own place. There were brushes stacked up by the door, bits and blinders hanging neatly along one wall and saddle pads on top of three different jockey saddles sitting on homemade wooden saddle stands. I paused for a moment to appreciate the preciseness of it all. Then I grabbed a brush and headed over to the sorrel horse with a white blaze tied to the fencepost.

I eased up to the horse and began brushing along his neck. Although he didn't pull back, he was snorting and trying to step sideways away from me. I could see the white all around his eye. I kept making the same small brush strokes and started speaking deep and low, saying, "Whoa, son," and, "You're alright now." When I got up to his head, it became evident that I wasn't going to get anywhere near there with my brush. When he turned to look at me, I noticed two large swirls of hair on his forehead. My grandma was always a firm believer that the swirls on a horses' head could predict their personality traits. Some people thought it was just a myth but Grandma swore by the accuracy of it. Grandma would break it down to a science. She would talk about the placement of the swirl, the direction in which it circled, and the number of them. I couldn't remember all of the details but I did know what two swirls meant. A "double swirler" as Grandma said, meant that a horse had two personalities. One personality was good. The other personality was bad. This made double swirlers unpredictable and untrustworthy. But Grandma always said that often times the good personality was so good that it was worth putting up with the bad times.

I silently said a prayer asking if today I could get the good personality. But the sorrel horse continued to snort and round its neck as it looked at me with those big, wide eyes. I didn't think I was going to be so lucky.

After I had the horse saddled and bridled, I called over to Arthur and asked if he'd like me to breeze them with the blinders on. Blinders are like little cups that go behind a horses' eyes to keep their vision focused on what's straight ahead of them. It keeps them from spooking at things in their peripheral vision and helps them relax and go to work.

"Son, you'll likely need them," Arthur called back.

That's when I realized Arthur had picked this sorrel for me to ride first for a reason. He was testing me. I looked over at the three other horses I would be breezing today and they were half sleeping or lazily swishing their tails. Arthur wanted to see if I would scare off.

That wasn't going to happen.

Once I realized what was going on, a sense of calm came over me. My grandma always said that you had to take the emotion out of horse training. She said getting mad, frustrated, or upset rarely helped anything. I figured being nervous that I wouldn't meet Arthur's expectations wouldn't help much either. Besides, when you grow up on the back of a horse you understand that some things are in your control and some things aren't. I would just take my time with this sorrel and hope for the best. Striving for perfection just isn't realistic with every horse. And it ain't all that realistic with life, either.

When I hopped up on to the sorrel's back, I made a real effort to relax my body. I let out a deep sigh. I loosened my grip on the reins which had a domino effect. When your hands relax, your forearms and biceps and shoulders all release tension. This causes your back to loosen and you send a signal right down to the horse that everything is okay and there's no need to be tense. As I forced my body into a relaxed state, I saw the sorrel horse release a little of its nervous energy. Not all of it because nothing comes that easy and there's no quick miracles in horse training. But every little bit helps.

We began around the track at a trot. I figured I would do one lap at a trot, a quarter of a lap at a lope, and then let him go for the remainder of the lap to breeze at whichever speed the horse chose. When breezing a horse, you don't want to push them to give everything they have but you also don't want to hold them back and pull on their face. There was a middle ground in there that I was striving for.

The trotting went pretty well. We jumped sideways a few times but I just carried on and tried to keep him in the middle of my hands. I acted like it was no big deal when he spooked. I wanted to build his confidence and immediately reprimanding him for spooking didn't seem like the best method. I even reached down and patted his neck a few times to try and reassure him that we would be okay out here and I was on his side.

When I asked him to lope, he balked. He weaved side to side and it was his way of saying that he didn't want to go forward anymore. He knew we were near the place he'd been tied up and he just wanted to go stand there again with the three other horses. Now was the time for me to take action. I wanted him to know that I was on his team but at the end of the day, a horse still needs to respect that you're in charge. If you're not the one making the decisions, you're putting yourself and everyone else around you in danger. And you're not doing the horse any favors. A spoiled horse is like a spoiled child: nobody likes them.

When he was still weaving side to side and not wanting to go forward, I used my whip and cracked him once. It was good and hard. He shot forward into a lope. Once we were pushing forward in an easy, straight lope, I reached down and patted him again. "That's a boy, that's what we want," I said in the same low, soothing tone I had used while saddling him.

I was not ready for what happened when I asked him to breeze out. I dropped my reins and gave a light smooch and he took off like a bat out of hell. He gained speed so quickly that my weight shifted back a little and I had to use my core to bring myself up on top of him again. He stretched out so easily and beautifully that it felt like we were floating. It wasn't a thundering, hooves pounding, forced kind of run. It was a smooth, rhythmic, easy run. I was going way faster than I had intended but I never pulled up. I just let that sorrel horse do his thing. I was enjoying the ride and he was enjoying the freedom.

Every so often you get a moment of pure bliss on the back of a horse. There's plenty of happy moments but the feelings of pure bliss stand out. I will always remember the first moment I realized what that sorrel horse had to give.

Once we completed the lap, I started to lean back and pull on the reins. I resumed my same tone with him saying, "Whooaaaa now son, eassyyyyy boy, that's all now," and he surprised me by coming back down with the same ease that it took for him to gain momentum.

When he was down to a walk, I hopped off the side and pulled his reins over his head. I loosened his cinch and pulled his blinders off. I gave him a long, analyzing stare. He was impatient to keep moving and he let me know. He lowered his head down and pushed me in the side with his nose. I decided to let that one go and gave a little chuckle.

"You're something else, aren't ya?" I asked as we carried on and I walked him out around the track.

When I approached Arthur and Rich, the sorrel horse was relaxed and I was sweating.

Arthur barely looked at me and said, "We don't make a habit of spending 10 minutes to walk out the second-string horses around here."

"He sure didn't feel like a second-string horse to me," I said. I surprised myself with my boldness. So far, I had barely said any words to Arthur. And I definitely hadn't spoken my mind to him. To be honest, he scared the hell out of me. But I couldn't take back what I said so I just stood there and waited for Arthur to respond.

"Oh, trust me. He is sure as hell a second-string horse. But he didn't look like one with you on his back. Now let's see how you make out on the other three," Arthur said.

I figured that was as close as Arthur ever came to giving a compliment. I gave him a quick nod and headed over to the tie post so I could take the saddle off the sorrel horse. I tried to lead the horse forward but he stayed in the same spot and then stretched out both back legs and grunted before licking his lips and stepping into tow with me.

"Big day for you eh, DS?" I muttered to the horse under my breath.

I didn't think Arthur would have been able to hear me but he looked at me and asked, "DS?"

"Oh," I said. "DS as in Double Swirler." I was a little embarrassed that I had already given a name to Arthur's horse and I felt my cheeks redden slightly.

"You know that's all bullshit about swirls on a horses' head, right?"

"Maybe," I said and walked away. I wasn't going to argue with Arthur. That wasn't my way of going about things.

I carried on and rode three more horses that night. I took ten minutes to cool down each horse even though Arthur had said he didn't bother doing that for the second-string horses. None of the other horses showed as much try and ability as DS had. But they were all well-mannered and in good shape. Arthur clearly had a good program even if he didn't bother with a cool down.

When I was putting away the last horse, Arthur approached me.

He said, "I'm in a bind and you're the only option I've got. You did alright for being a farmer. I'll hire you to come out and ride every day leading up to the stampede. As long as it's going well, you can ride with me at the big show." He paused and added, "don't make me regret this."

"Yes sir," I said before leaving.

It was almost dark by the time Rich and I piled into the truck and pulled out. Rich was wanting to get every word in that he could on the way home.

"Man, what a mosquito infested hell hole that place was," he started. "Let me tell you, I won't be going back there again. You know your way now so you won't need me. And Arthur is about a miserable old bastard, isn't he? I tried to visit with him while you were riding and he flat out ignored me half the time. And he's hardly got a good word to say. The man needs to get laid more often or something. Life's too good to be that ornery."

I laughed along with Rich as I listened to him ramble. I agreed with most of what he said. Arthur was a little hard to take. And I was covered in mosquito bites. I could already feel my body burning with temptation to scratch everywhere.

But I didn't care about any of that. I was riding good horses. I'd found another way to make money. And I kept thinking about DS striding out. I couldn't wait to get back on him. My enthusiasm wouldn't be deterred by Arthur or mosquitoes or anything else.

CHAPTER EIGHT

The next two weeks felt like they went by in a blur. The auction mart was slower but steady. I woke up at 6 and went to work with Rich. Then I would head straight to Arthur's track. Arthur had plenty of jobs that he piled on me. I was cleaning tack, cleaning the barn, building pens, and helping him feed when I wasn't on a horses' back.

At some points, I felt like he was almost daring me to complain about the workload. But I never did. I'd usually keep my mouth shut and do what needed to be done and then ignore him once I started working with the horses. I was in a happy state of contentment when I was riding and I wasn't going to let anything bother me.

At the auction mart, Frank and Gene started asking me daily about my work at the track. They both seemed real pleased that I was going to be an outrider. One night, they even ventured out to Arthur's place to watch me ride. I never said much to them when they came out but I was downright proud to have them supporting me. And despite all of Rich's promises that he would never be back to that track, he also tagged along a few times. He claimed that he couldn't find another ride home from the auction mart but I suspected he just didn't like to spend too much time alone.

It only began to feel real on the day Arthur said we were loading up to head into Calgary. He said we would take the horses in a day early to get them settled in the barns. That's when I knew that I had to bring up something that had been weighing heavy on my mind and I wasn't sure how to best go about it. In the end, I settled for straight to the point. Arthur wasn't big on chit chat, anyways.

"I want to ride DS in Calgary," I blurted out. Over the past few weeks, my bond with the wild-eyed sorrel had grown stronger with each ride. He was by far my favorite horse on the place.

Arthur had been hunched over the trailer jack and cranking it ferociously as he hooked the trailer up to his truck. I saw him tense a little but he kept jacking the trailer and continued on with his job without ever looking up at me. I was unsure if he'd heard me at all and I was about to say it again.

But when he'd finished the task at hand, he straightened up and looked at me before saying, "I've got better horses than that counterfeit sorrel."

I was prepared for Arthur to say something along those lines. I had been going over a little speech in my head for the last few days and I laid it all out for him.

I took a breath and said, "I know you do, Arthur. But he's the fastest horse on your place; you know he is. And he's come a long way in the last two weeks. He trusts me and I trust him. That's the horse I want to ride. I can take your good bay horse in there, too. If things don't work out on DS, I'll switch."

Arthur mulled it over for a moment. I was happy that he was considering what I had to say instead of just dismissing me altogether.

"Fine," he finally agreed. "Hope you know what you're talking about. Hard to trust a damned farmer boy."

I didn't bother responding. I'd come to learn that Arthur would always throw a negative comment in to the conversation. I was working on the ability to block it out. Usually that meant ignoring him which was getting easier to do. And nothing that Arthur said could currently affect my mood. I was heading to the Greatest Outdoor Show on Earth on a horse that I had quickly come to love. Life was good.

I headed over to the barn to get a small scoop of grain and a halter so I could catch DS. In the last two weeks, his demeanor around me had steadily transformed. There was no more snorting or arched neck as I saddled him. He now stood quietly and let me run a brush over his whole body. I found that the longer I spent brushing him, the more relaxed he was when I got on his back. He would stand at the tie post and lick his lips as I found all his sweet spots with my brush. And in return for his good behavior, I would always let him run. That's when he was happiest. Sometimes when he would reach his flat-out speed, I had to resist the urge to try and pull him up. I was worried that I had lost all control. But after I felt he was satisfied with the length of his run, I would always speak to him in a low, soothing voice and he would always come down gently and easily. It felt like we had an arrangement on a subliminal level. I gave DS his freedom. DS gave me his respect. It was a mutual partnership.

The only drawback to DS was that he got really buddied up to other horses. If there were horses standing at the tie post, he would always try and get back to them. He would whinny at them or balk when I first tried to ride him away. In these moments, I would always need my whip. Usually, one or two quick cracks would return his focus to me and we could carry on. Some days it was a bigger battle than others but I never quit until I had won. That was something my grandma had taught me. She always said, *"don't start a fight with a horse that you can't win."* I had seen her go through a good deal of fights with some horses throughout the years. She was always quick and aggressive when she needed to get a point across to a horse. But no matter how long the fight took or how the horse initially reacted, in the end she was always the winner. The horse would give her what she had asked for. It didn't have to be perfect or anywhere near it. But the horse had to show a little bit of try and a little bit of respect.

As I continued to help Arthur load up everything into the trailer, my mind wandered between DS and my grandma and then eventually to Margaret Westerlund. Rich had helped me track down Margaret's phone number and I'd called her after our initial meeting at the movies. I always made my phone calls from the stockyards. There was an extra phone line that all of the workers used who didn't have their own office.

I had her number wrote down on a little piece of paper and I confidently stood in place, clutching the paper while I waited for the phone call to go through. I'd been rehearsing in my mind exactly what I wanted to say.

A woman answered and I asked to speak to Margaret. She told me to hang on and then I stood there waiting. It felt like forever. I was almost about to give up hope entirely when I recognized her voice as it flooded into my ear with a breathless, "Yes, hello?"

"Hi. Margaret. This is Charlie. Charlie Hyde. We met at the theater. The other day." I silently cursed myself for speaking in short, jerky sentences and vowed to calm down.

"Oh, hello Charlie. Yes, I remember who you are," she said. Her words poured out smoothly and I could sense a smile in her voice. I instantly relaxed.

"I'm glad to hear that," I said. "Look, the reason I was calling was because I'd like to see you again. I've actually just been hired on as an outrider for Arthur Langley… I don't know if you know who he is. But anyways, I'll be riding at The Calgary Stampede. Maybe I could take you out one night if you'll be there?"

The speech I had worked out in my head sounded a lot better than whatever just came out of my mouth.

But she replied with an easy, "It's a date."

"Wow. Great. That's real great," I said.

Then she cut me off, "Oh, and, Charlie?"

"Yes?"

"Everyone around here knows who Arthur Langley is. It's a tight knit community. Which is why I also know that you had no idea who Arthur Langley was when he asked you to work. You also didn't know what an outrider is supposed to do. But I'll be there to watch and I'll find you after," she finished.

I stood in place, dumbstruck. She spoke with that hint of a smile carrying through in her voice. It made it impossible to tell if she was mocking me or proud of me.

"Yup. You sure don't beat around the bush, do you?" was all I finally responded.

That made her laugh outright and she said, "I have yet to be called coy and I don't intend on it happening in this lifetime. Bye, now Charlie."

"Bye, Margaret. See you soon."

Then I hung up the phone and pressed my forehead against the cool wall next to the receiver. I didn't know if I had done well in that conversation or failed miserably but that girl had some sort of an effect on me. I didn't have time to process my emotions because Rich, the three secretaries, Frank, and four or five cowboys all started laughing and chuckling. I snapped my head up from the wall I was leaning on and whipped around. They were all staring directly at me. It looked like half the stockyards had been listening to my conversation.

Rich was the first one to break the silence as he mimicked, *"But anyways, I'll be riding at The Calgary Stampede."* That set everybody off laughing and my cheeks reddened and I headed straight towards Rich with a sheepish grin on my face.

"You hear that, boys?" Rich asked. "I line this fool of a friend of mine up with a job and it goes straight to his head. He's calling the richest and prettiest girl in southern Alberta just to brag about it. The nerve of this man…"

Rich's voice trailed off because I had swung my arm around his neck and put him in a good-natured head lock. Everyone watched and laughed and some of the cowboys joined in on the teasing. I took it all in stride. Leave it to Rich to make me laugh and get everybody talking about my personal business at the same time.

The conversation died down and everyone started meandering back to what they should be doing. I knew I had pens to clean and strode off to do it but Frank stepped in beside me.

"Say, Charlie, before you go. Just thought I should say. I grew up with Margaret's dad. John Westerlund. Real good family. And she's one of the good ones. Just something for you to keep in mind," he added before he tipped his hat at me and carried on to his office.

I didn't even have time to respond to Frank but his words echoed through my head. *One of the good ones.*

When Arthur and I finished loading the last horse on the trailer and I hopped into the passenger side of his truck, my mind was still meandering. I was thinking about riding DS at Calgary, I was thinking about my grandma's horse training advice and wisdom, and I was thinking about seeing Margaret Westerlund again. And the whole time, the same mantra was running through my mind.

One of the good ones.

CHAPTER NINE

blurry

I don't know what I was expecting before we pulled in to the Calgary Stampede, but I sure wasn't ready for what I saw. I'd never seen so many people and so much action all in one place. Arthur seemed immune to anything around us. He just kept his eyes straight ahead and slowly maneuvered the truck and trailer around to try and get parked beside the horse barns. But I gawked and stared and tried to comprehend it all.

The cowboys and cowgirls first caught my attention. I was mainly drawn to what they were wearing. The cowboys around the stockyards all seemed to take a certain amount of pride in their appeal because they never went anywhere without their hats, boots, and spurs all strapped on. But these cowboys took it to another level. They wore leather belts with intricate tooling. They had perfectly polished boots. Their hats were all shaped with an almost uncanny symmetry. And these cowboys clearly knew that their attention to detail in their attire was aesthetically pleasing because they all seemed to have a certain strut to their step. I wasn't much of a strutter. I never had been. But I did feel a tiny jealous ping in my stomach at how sharp they all looked.

The cowgirls were done up just as nice. Most of them wore dresses and skirts but I saw a fair amount in blue jeans too. They all wore one shade of lipstick or another and most of them had some sort of shiny silver jewelry that popped out and caught the eye. A few of the cowgirls had ropes in their hand that they twirled around effortlessly. I started to feel a little out of my element when I noticed that. What the hell was I doing at a rodeo? I'd never swung a rope in my life. These cowgirls and cowboys were going to spot me out as a phony as soon as I stepped out of the truck.

Just as all my worries were about to swallow me whole, I remembered to take a breath and center myself. I wasn't a cowboy. I was a horseman. There's a difference between the two and I wouldn't try to pretend I was something else just to fit in. The thought calmed me and my heart rate returned back to normal. I was Charlie Hyde, no better than anyone else here but certainly no worse. Surely that's about all the peace of mind we ever need to get through life's challenges.

All of these thoughts swirled around in my head but Arthur and I never said a word to each other. His wife was sitting in the back of the pickup. She was a quiet woman. I had offered her the front seat before I got in but she silently refused and crawled into the back. I had a feeling that when you lived with a man like Arthur, you got used to not taking up too much space.

We finally eased to a stop and Arthur turned off the truck.

"Get the horses put up," he said and he strode away without looking back.

I got out of the pickup and started looking around, wondering what exactly I should do first. The vastness of the barns and the stampede grounds left me a little lost.

Arthur's wife must have noticed because she said, "You'll have to go over to the front of the barn first. Tell them you are ready to stall Arthur Langley's horses and they will give you the numbers of the appropriate stalls."

I was about to thank her and carry on when she added, "Arthur just went to the main office to check in. That has to be done right away."

I wasn't sure if she added that for my benefit or hers. I just said, "No worries, Mrs. Langley. I'm happy to look after the horses."

She gave a small smile and I walked towards the main door of the barn. I was handed a piece of paper with my stall numbers and shown where they were located and then I was in a flurry of steady work. I unloaded horses from the trailer, walked them to the barn, put shavings in their stall, hauled water and feed, and then repeated the process over again until the trailer was empty.

Just as I was finishing up, a young guy approached me. He was thin and short and clean cut with jet black hair.

He stuck a hand out to me and said, "Charlie, I'm assuming? I'm Pat. I'm the other outrider for Arthur's team."

"Oh, good to meet ya. I heard you had to travel a ways to get here?" I asked.

"It was about a five-hour drive. I hopped in with some other guys so it wasn't bad," he paused and surveyed the boxstalls with the horses happily munching on hay before he added, "A little advice Charlie? Don't let Arthur take advantage of you. Most chuckwagon teams hire someone as barn help for the week while they're here. It's not really in our wheel house to be doing all of this for him. You get what I'm saying?"

"Sure. I guess. I don't mind the work," I said.

Pat chuckled a little and said, "I don't mind work, either. But not when it's unpaid and the guy making all the money is currently enjoying himself with a drink in each hand as he's posted up at the bar."

"I didn't realize that was the case," I frowned. "Thanks for the heads up."

Pat just nodded silently and started to walk up the alley way. He stopped at each stall and poked his head up close to have a look at the horse inside. When he got to DS, he had a long look and said, "Never seen this sorrel before."

"He was one of Arthur's second-string horses. He's got some quirks but he's the fastest sucker I've ever been on. I asked Arthur if I could ride him here," I explained.

"And Arthur went for it?" Pat asked me as his thick, black eyebrows shot up. "Well, Charlie, I might have mistaken you for a bit of a pushover earlier but, dang pal, you must have some balls if you could convince Arthur to do something your way instead of his. Come on, I'll buy you a drink. I think you're a guy I wouldn't mind getting to know a little better."

Pat and I meandered along on our way to the big building serving drinks. We made little comments to each other but didn't discuss anything of too much importance. I was still assessing Pat's character. His slick black hair made him come across as a little too smooth for my liking. And he claimed he didn't mind work but it sure was convenient how he appeared as soon as I was finished the hard stuff. I had a feeling that his clean clothes didn't often get too dirty.

When we got up to the bar, Pat bought the first round and we each started sipping on a beer. One of life's greatest little joys is savoring a cold beer after physical labor on a hot day. I was perfectly content to stand there and people watch but when I spotted Arthur, I knew what I had to do. I walked over to him and stood patiently to the side until there was a break in his conversation. He noticed me and gave me a slight nod.

"Get the horses taken care of?" he huffed.

That was exactly what I was hoping he would say. I seized the opportunity. "They're all good. Before the week carries on though, I was hoping you could tell me what I'll be paid for the barn work. Happy to do it, Arthur, just need to know we're on the same page."

To my surprise, Arthur threw his head back and laughed. I think it was the first time I'd ever heard a real laugh rumble out of his broad, stiff chest. I wasn't sure how much Arthur had drank but it must have been just the right amount to put him in a good mood.

"Alright, you'll get paid. As long as you do a good job of it. And I'll be the judge of that," he said.

I thanked him and turned to back away before I heard him mutter, "God damn farmers," under his breath with a small chuckle. I noticed that Mrs. Langley was nowhere to be found. I wondered where she had ventured off to and how she passed the time on her own before dismissing the thought and walking back to Pat.

The rest of the day carried on in the completely carefree, blurry way that only happens when alcohol is involved. Pat bought the second round again when he heard I'd gotten a pay raise. In his words, "Cheers to taking money from the tightest old bastard in the building." Then we took turns buying rounds and visiting with the people around us. Pat introduced me to plenty of the other outriders and a few chuckwagon drivers. It was good, simple conversation but a part of me wished Rich was there. I didn't mind meeting new people and I would visit with about anyone. But I sure preferred the company of a good pal that I knew I could trust. Rich had said he would be coming in to watch the races every evening and I was looking forward to having him here.

By the time Pat and I were both good and drunk, we decided it was our cue to leave. Pat had a tent set up for us close to the horse barns where a bunch of the chuckwagon crew had claimed camping territory for the week. I crawled into my bunk and tried to get comfy on the hard ground. It was only slightly more uncomfortable than Rich's couch.

I guess it proved how drunk I was because as I laid there and rolled over, the last words I muttered to Pat were, "Someday I'mma have the best mattress money can buy. Then there'll be no stopping me. No stopping me at all…"

memorable

That first day at Calgary passed by pretty smoothly. I woke up with a pounding head and sore ribs and vowed to not drink so much for the rest of the week. A little-known fact is that hard work is one of the best cures for a hangover. After the initial ooziness passed, I felt my body returning back to its old rhythm as I looked after all the horses. By the time I was finished with the morning chores, I was feeling ready for a coffee and some food. I tried to rouse Pat awake to see if he wanted to join but he just grunted and shook his head and returned to snoring.

After some exploring on my own, I found a big tent serving a complimentary breakfast. They had everything you could ever ask for: bacon, sausages, pancakes, eggs, potatoes, and more. But most importantly, they had coffee and that's where I started. I stepped in to the coffee line up behind two cowboys who were chatting away to each other animatedly.

I overheard the first cowboy say, "Oh and here's some information for you, too. Bet you haven't heard this one. The Queen of England is gracing us with her mighty presence tonight. She's gonna be perched up in the private suite to watch the whole rodeo and the chuckwagons, too-"

"- It ain't her *mighty presence*, it's her *royal presence*, you uncivilized hillbilly," the second cowboy cut him off. I chuckled a little to myself at that comment. Then the second cowboy added, "And I call bullshit, anyways."

"It's true! Swear to goodness. I heard it right from the General Manager himself – ol' what's his name? Maurice Hartnett, ain't it? He was proud as punch that we were going to have a queen here and he said we needed to give her a show to remember. Then he started rambling about how *the Calgary Stampede will forever be known as The Greatest Outdoor Show on Earth.* You know how he is," the cowboy finished.

The cowboys ambled away and I couldn't catch the rest of their conversation as I filled my coffee up. But it got me thinking about just how momentous this was for me. I was about to be amongst a group of men who were worthy of the queen's attention. I didn't know how I'd even gotten this far. Rich did me a heck of a favor when he pushed me into this gig and I intended to pay him back.

I was sitting by myself and mulling this all over while I finished eating my breakfast. Just as I suspected, a good meal and some coffee completely eliminated the last remaining traces of my hangover. Which was lucky, too, because then I saw a sight that almost made me wonder if I was still drunk. Sure enough, walking along at a brisk pace and chatting to each other as they went was my grandma and two of my brothers - Philip, and Walter.

I pushed up from the table and ran over to them with a wide grin on my face. They heard me stomping up behind them and all turned around to see who it was just as I approached them. Grandma was the first to act and she swallowed me up in a big, warm hug. She kept hanging on to me tightly and swayed back and forth a little. I could feel some surrounding eyes on us but, in that moment, I didn't care. I'd missed my grandma.

"What in the world are you three doing here?" I laughed as Grandma released me and I shook my two brothers' hands. Philip and Walter laughed too, proud to have successfully surprised me.

"We woke up bright and early to start our drive. Philip started chores at 3 am just so we could leave in good time," my grandma explained affectionately. "Honestly, Charlie, you didn't think we would miss your grand debut as an outrider for the chuckwagon races, did you?" she finished.

I surveyed them all and couldn't help smiling. That was just like good ol' Philip. A working fool and you'd never hear him complain about it, either. Philip had hardly changed a bit. Still wiry and strong and carrying himself with a happy go lucky attitude. And not that I like to pick favorites but, hell, I couldn't help it. He was still my favorite brother. Our bond was evident just in the way we grinned at each other, without saying a word.

And Walter was barely recognizable considering I'd only been gone three months. He had lost the round, plump parts to his body and they had been replaced with muscle. He was still thick but now he looked strong. It looked as though the extra weight he used to carry in his stomach had buffooned up to his broad chest. He carried himself differently, too. He had a smile on his face but he seemed to look more serious.

I couldn't remember if Grandma looked any different than when I'd last saw her. She was another example of one of those people you couldn't remember specific details of how she looked; only how she made you feel.

I led Grandma and the boys over to the complimentary breakfast. I grabbed myself another cup of coffee while they filled their plates and we all sat down together, catching up for lost time. The boys told me everything that was happening on the farm. I filled them all in on Rich, the stockyards, Arthur Langley, and DS. I didn't mention anything about Margaret Westerlund. I figured that was private.

Grandma mostly just sat and listened to us ramble on. Every now and then, she would reach on top of the table and pat one of our hands and give a quick squeeze. It sounded like Walter and Dad had been getting along real well. Walter talked about some of his ideas for making changes at the farm and how to expand. To my surprise, it seemed as though Dad was on board with Walter's changes. I always suspected Walter would be a good fit for taking over our farm once he grew into his potential. It seemed like things were headed in that direction.

I asked about Mom, Dad, and Grant. Dad didn't come simply because he was too stubborn and too settled to ever venture in to the city. Mom didn't come because she didn't go anywhere without

Dad. And Grant drew the short straw that left him at home to help with any work that needed to be done. Dad always liked to have at least one worker at home.

Finally, I commented on the change in Walter's appearance. "If we happen upon any drunk and disorderly individuals, it looks like we'll have some muscle to back us up," I said as I nodded my head in Walter's direction.

Philip jumped all over the topic. "Charlie, you ain't the only one who's noticing them new muscles! Walter puffed his chest up and strutted around so much while you were gone that he got himself a girlfriend."

Walter blushed just a little but didn't deny the claim. With some prodding and teasing, I finally discovered that Walter had been going steady with our neighbor girl. She was a year younger than him but always seemed like a sweet person. I thought it was a good pick.

In an effort to change the subject, Walter added, "As for the new muscles... I suppose I might not have realized how much you contributed around there until you left. There was just a lot of work to do," he shrugged.

After everyone finished eating and the conversation came to its first lull, I invited the crew to the horse barns to have a look at Arthur's team. They all eagerly agreed and we paced out together. I didn't realize how lonely I had felt in the city until I had my family beside me again. Any overwhelming concerns I had been dealing with earlier completely vanished. I felt like I could do anything simply because the people around me believed I could do anything.

When we made it to the horse barns, everyone quieted down and just walked slowly while peering in the stalls. Philip and Walter muttered small comments about Arthur's horses and how sleek and strong they looked.

When we got to DS, he stopped eating hay and looked at us with his ears perked forward. He wasn't spooking but he was definitely aware of what was going on. My grandma opened his stall door and slowly stepped in with him. She talked in the same low, soothing monotone that I had heard her use with horses throughout my whole life.

She put a hand on his neck and kept a steady stream of, "whoa son, easy boy, just coming in to check ya out, that's a good boy now," rambling out of her mouth while she ran her hands all over his body.

She was feeling his legs and checking his conformation. DS never shied away from her. He stood perfectly still and let her do her thing. Finally, when Grandma was satisfied, she stepped out of the stall and brushed her hands together to wipe off the dust and horse hair she had accumulated in her inspection.

"I believe you when you say that he can fly," she said to me. I just nodded so she added, "Good choosing, Charlie," and she put a hand up on my face and cupped my cheek affectionately.

The rest of the day passed in much the same manner. The four of us visited and explored and visited and relaxed and visited and ate. My first race was in the back of my mind all day but it helped to have a distraction. Eventually I told everyone I needed to head back to the barns and help Arthur get the team ready. They agreed and headed to the arena to watch some of the rodeo events while spewing a stream of well wishes and good luck to me.

At the barns, it was a blur of action between myself, Arthur, and Pat. Arthur gave orders and worked beside us as we hooked the team up to the wagon and saddled the outrider horses. Before I knew it, we were all heading towards the racetrack entrance and it was almost time to start the chuckwagons.

I was riding DS and when we got up close to the arena, I stepped off him. I led him to a panel and let him stand at the arena while I surveyed the crowd. I took it all in. I studied the people who were whooping and hollering and having a good time. I'd never seen so many people all in one place like that and it was a sight in itself. The July heat had been beating down on us all day but now it was beginning to cool off. Still, I couldn't help sweating. I wiped my forehead and then calmly placed my hand on DS's forehead. He seemed to be taking everything in just as I was. I said out loud, "Well, here we go," as I gave him one last pat and then Arthur was hollering at me to get on my horse and get behind the wagon.

I steered DS over to the wagon at a slow trot. Pat was on a solid, older bay horse that had been used for years as an outrider horse. I let DS idle up beside that bay to help us both relax. We followed Arthur and the wagon into the arena where four chuckwagons were taking their places at four different starting points.

Once Arthur was in his correct spot, Pat and I dismounted off our horses. We needed to throw the barrel and tent poles into the back of the wagon once the starting horn went off. I felt ready.

Then the horn went off.

And all hell broke loose.

I threw the tent pole into the back of the wagon with no problem and Arthur cracked his reins and smooched to his team. The wagon took off with surprising velocity. Pat showed his ability as a seasoned outrider as he swung a leg up on his bay and was a stride behind Arthur's wagon. But DS was losing his damn mind. I don't know if it was the horn or the crowd or the wild movements but it was all just too much for the sorrel speed demon that I had begged to ride. Every time I tried to step beside him to swing on, he pulled back. I had his reins in my hand and a firm grip on him but I still couldn't get close. He was backing away from me and jerking me along with him across the arena. At some point as I was trying to get close to him, I came to the bleak realization that I was the only person left in the arena. The four chuckwagons and all the outriders were already out on the track. My mind and my heart were both going a hundred miles an hour but somehow, I had enough presence of mind to know that I needed to relax. Or at least pretend to relax. I loosened the death grip I'd had on the reins. I let my shoulders slink back and down and I let a deep breath out.

"Whooooaaaaaaaaaaaaaaaaa," I said as low and as loud as I could. That did the trick because he finally relaxed enough to stop backing away from me. I seized the opportunity and hopped onto his back as stealthy as I could. But I guess DS needed to prove he wasn't going to be tricked that easily because he proceeded to rear straight up. He was standing on his two back feet with his two front feet pawing wildly through the air. In the moment right before he was about to lose momentum and come back down to the ground, I took my hat off and saluted it to a precise spot in the crowd. The people in the stands went completely nuts at that sight and started whooping and hollering.

When DS came to the ground, I dug my feet into his sides and smooched in his ear and we were gone. My grandma once told me that all four of us boys could ride like wild banshees. But I'd never rode as hard as I did in the first half of that racetrack. I asked DS for everything he had. And boy, did he give it to me. We were stretched out and flying so smoothly that it felt like his feet were never touching the ground. That was the closest I've ever been to being scared on the back of a horse. I'd just never known an animal to move like that. My eyes were squinted and watering but I just kept on asking him for more and he kept striding out. It seemed like each length stretched just a little bit longer than the previous one. The biggest crowd I'd ever seen was watching me go around that track but it felt like it was just me and DS, alone in the city.

Nothing else mattered in that moment.

I knew I was gaining ground insanely fast and I started to realize that I had a chance to cross the finish line close enough behind Arthur's wagon that he wouldn't be penalized for a late outrider. As the closely bundled group of chuckwagons rounded the last bend, I got a good enough glimpse to see that Arthur was in the lead. Whether or not I could catch up was going to be a make-or-break moment for me.

I started smooching more urgently to DS and I gave him a light tap with my bat. He seemed to understand and we both hunkered down for the final push around the track. Then I left the rest up to DS. He either had it in him to catch up or he didn't. I'd already asked him for everything he had and now it was his turn to decide how he wanted to finish this race.

When we crossed the finish line, we were right in line with Pat on the good bay and we were a stride behind Arthur's wagon. We were exactly where we needed to be. And Arthur had won the race.

I started asking DS to come back to me as I pulled on the reins. Just like always, he slowed right down and respected my hands. We eased down to a prance and both tried to catch our breath. Then I hopped off, swung my reins over his head, and stroked his pretty sorrel neck. I gave him a couple scratches and then walked towards Pat and his bay.

"Well, Charlie, I don't know what the hell happened out there but you sure like to make a grand entrance at the finish line, don't you?" Pat said to me with one black eyebrow raised high.

"Wasn't exactly my idea, Pat. But, damn, am I happy it all worked out," I replied.

Pat nodded slowly and said, "Mhmm," as he stepped off his bay and loosened the cinches.

"What?" I asked. I was afraid that maybe I'd still messed up. Maybe Arthur was still going to get a time penalty for something.

"It's just… nothing, really. But don't expect Arthur to praise you. A close call may as well be a bad call in his eyes."

"Oh," I said as I let out a breath and relaxed my shoulders a little. "I can handle Arthur. I'm not worried about that."

Pat and I made our ways back to the horse barns where we knew we would meet up with Arthur and help him unhook and put the team away. The adrenaline had been pumping through my body so intensely that I was still a little bit shaky but I tried not to let it show. DS walked behind me and occasionally threw in a little prance. He seemed prouder than punch about his performance. You'd never know that he had just been crawling out of his skin and nearly about to lose us the whole race a few minutes ago. I just shook my head at him. Typical double swirler.

I had just finished putting DS into his stall, when Arthur pulled the team up to the barn. I wanted to set to work right away but something stopped me in my tracks. I slowly looked up in to the wagon and met Arthur's gaze. He was glaring at me so fiercely that it formed a pit deep in my stomach. I wasn't about to back down. But I also wasn't expecting such a rage to be pointed in my direction. Then something caught Arthur's attention and his eyes flickered away from me. His stance changed and the deep, thick creases in his forehead went away. I didn't understand what was going on until someone was right beside me.

"There you are! Just who I've been looking for. The man of the hour, let me tell you what. I came to shake your hand," the stranger grabbed my hand and smiled at me as if we were long lost friends.

I had no idea who he was or what he was talking about. I was a little startled but tried not to show it. "Uh, yes sir, thank you very much," I said as I eyed him up.

He was dressed to the nines. Everything about him shined from his boots to his buckle to his personality.

"That was some move you pulled out there, kid," he said with approval. "I couldn't have planned it better myself! And that's saying something considering I'm pretty good at planning." He laughed at his own joke.

I tried to chuckle along with him but I still wasn't quite sure what he was talking about. He sized me up and down with the same smile still on his face.

"So, what's your name and what's your story? The newspapers will be wanting the information, of course. I'll happily pass it along and be your representative, if you don't mind me doing so," he said.

"That would be… fine," I managed. "My name is Charlie Hyde. I'm from Lacombe and living in Calgary. Just started working for Arthur Langley. This is my first stampede." I thought the last part seemed pretty self-explanatory. But the stranger just nodded along as if everything I was saying was overly fascinating to him.

"Charlie Hyde… first stampede… perfect, that's just perfect," he said with his head bobbing up and down. "Okay, then, happy to have met you and thank you for your memorable performance out there. Outstanding to see, just outstanding. I'll talk to you again shortly," he said as he trotted off.

I barely had time to register the conversation when someone else came up behind me and slung their arm tightly around my neck. Except this time there was no mistaking who it was.

"Calgary is crawling with girls and you're all over me. Let me go, ya needy bastard," I said with a half-smile.

Rich laughed out loud and tightened the headlock he'd wrapped me in just to show me who was boss before releasing me.

"I bet you haven't even got a clue who you were just talking to," Rich said.

I didn't want to admit that he was right but I also didn't know how to talk my way into convincing Rich otherwise. I just shrugged and said nothing.

Rich feigned distress and sighed. "You see, Charlie. You need me."

"Save the dramatics and tell me who he was," I laughed.

"Maybe you've heard of him? Maurice Hartnett. He's only the man in charge of the whole damn stampede. You better believe he makes a pretty penny. I think he's a good guy. Have you seen his wife? What a looker she is…" Rich trailed off.

"How does everything relate back to women with you?" I said as I gave another laugh. It sure felt good to have Rich here and get back to our familiar banter. "He told me I was brilliant and said something about being in the newspaper."

"It figures I'd line you up with a job that eventually leads to your fame and fortune. Remember me when you've made it to the big time," Rich said.

Our conversation was cut short when I saw Grandma, Philip, and Walter approaching. They walked up to us and I instantly introduced them to Rich. My grandma embraced Rich in a tight hug. She was funny like that. Soft and affectionate one moment, tough and demanding the next moment. I figured that type of versatility might be what made her so special.

After Grandma released Rich, she turned to me, "Quite a show you put on out there," she said with a soft smile and a wink.

"I really thought DS was ready to handle it all. I don't know if I pushed him too early. But I think he'll be better now that he's got a taste for it. He sure loves to run."

Grandma nodded and considered this. "I would give him one more chance. At least now you know that he can make up for a blunder with his speed."

While Grandma and I had this quick exchange, Rich and Philip were talking to each other a mile a minute as if they were long lost friends. I knew the two of them would hit it off. Both of them had the same vivacious attitude towards life. They were bouncing off each other with quick witted observations while Walter listened and smiled.

I suggested we all walk over for a beer but Grandma declined. They were going to make a late-night drive back to Lacombe. I wasn't ready to see any of them go but I knew that chores would be waiting for the boys in the morning. Life on the farm was a constant supply of work. I was grateful to them for making the trip to watch me when they had to sacrifice so much sleep and time.

Our goodbyes were a round of handshakes and hugs after Rich and I walked everyone to the pickup truck. I sent my best to Mom and Grant and Dad.

Rich shouted to Philip, "Hey, little brother! You come see us anytime, alright? I'll kick Charlie off the couch for you," as they were all climbing in the vehicle.

"You can count on it but I may never leave," Philip retorted.

We watched the pick-up pull out of the parking area and Rich gave me a sideways glance. "Well, Charlie. Should we go have ourselves a beer?"

"Rich. We would be absolutely crazy not to," I said.

Which led to me doing exactly what I had promised myself earlier that morning I would not do.

I got drunk. Again.

forgiving

I didn't know what time it was or how many beers I had drank, but I knew it was time for me to stumble my way back to the horse barns. I felt warm and fuzzy all over. Between the booze and the laughs and the win in the first heat of chuckwagon races, I was pretty damn content.

Rich had been on a roll all night. He kept drawing in new crowds of people with his exuberant stories and jokes. I was mostly just along for the ride and kept him supplied in beverages but I added in when I could. I felt like his color commentary man for the night. I'd let him take the main stage but I was ready to fill in the blanks or add something if I was needed.

Eventually Rich started aiming his stories purely towards pretty girls. He began to charm one girl so thoroughly that his story telling redirected itself to a one-on-one conversation with her. It happened slowly but the two gradually parted from the crowd as they became more engrossed with one another. When I could no longer hear what they were saying, I knew it was my time to leave. Sometimes a guy has to go to the biggest party in the city just so he can get a little privacy and intimacy with one girl.

Instead of walking straight to the tent to pass out, I decided to head in to the horse barns. I wanted to check on all the boys but I also just wasn't quite ready to lose the good feeling I was carrying around with me. I wanted to hold on to it a little longer before sleep would lead to an inevitable hangover.

I was in the horse barn when I heard the first crack.

Whack...

Followed by two more.

Whack... Whack...

It had a steady rhythm and a sharp emphasis. I sobered up a little as I stopped and listened. Then I followed the sound as it led me directly to the stall DS was standing in.

I stopped and stared inside the stall. Arthur was holding my leather reins in tightly clenched fists. I could see veins popping at the back of his neck and every bone in his body seemed tense but he kept the same smooth repetition as he continued to hit DS in the head with the reins. DS was pushed up against the corner of the stall and shrinking back more every time the reins connected with his hide but he never moved forward or backwards.

I wasn't sure how long I stood there before I said, "What are you doing?" My voice was more even and calm than I had expected which was probably from the booze. But I said it loudly and firmly which was probably from the rage gathering in the pit of my stomach and working its way towards coursing throughout my entire body.

Arthur turned towards me slowly. He never met my eye but he never cowered or showed any trace of shame. He turned his head to the left and spit before slowly wiping his forearm across his forehead where beads of sweat had gathered. Then he methodically coiled up the reins in his hand and stepped out of the stall. He secured the latch and stepped towards me as I braced for what was to come.

Arthur pushed the reins directly on to my chest. "I was doing what you should've done right after the race. I told you this sorrel was a counterfeit piece of shit," he said as he walked away.

I stared dumbly at him until he disappeared. Once he was out of my sight, I realized I was still holding on to the reins against my chest. I slowly dropped them down and studied my shirt where they had been. There was an outline of blood.

86

I threw the reins in the closest garbage and grabbed a bucket to fill with hot water. I rummaged around the barns until I found a clean rag and I dropped it in the bucket with the hot water. When I stepped inside DS's stall, I gently set the bucket on the ground and let out a big sigh. I tried to let out the frustration that had been building ever since I heard that first *whack*. DS stepped out of the corner he had retreated to and walked right up to me. That beautiful, forgiving damned sorrel horse stepped up to me as if to say *don't worry, it will take a lot more than that to hurt me.* I wanted to kiss the goofy sucker. But instead, I just brought the rag up to his head and slowly started wiping down the cuts and welts that were forming. He occasionally jerked his head away when he didn't like something but I just kept repeating the process over as I started to talk to him in the low, soothing monotone I reserved especially for him.

I stood in his stall and let the hot water drip down my arms as I raised my hands up to his head. The bucket turned a pinkish red color as I rinsed the rag out. I continued to wipe him down long after the cuts had been cleaned. There were no eyes on us. No cheering crowd or rambunctious fans. But there was a disheartening world outside this stall. There were people that I couldn't begin to understand and there were hurtful actions that I couldn't stop.

Once again, none of it mattered. Just like when we were on the racetrack, it felt like the rest of the world disappeared and it was just me and DS.

I knew me and him would be alright.

CHAPTER TWELVE

easy

The next morning, I felt groggy and irritated. I had stayed awake with DS long enough to sober up and save myself from the more severe hangover symptoms but I still wasn't feeling like myself. I had no idea what time it had been when I finally crawled into the tent but I knew I hadn't slept long when the sun woke me. After fighting an internal battle about whether or not to go back to sleep, I pulled myself out of bed to begin the morning chores. I wasn't quite ready to face the day and everything it entailed. Truthfully, I just didn't want to see Arthur. But the horses would be hungry and that trumped my personal issues.

I threw everything some hay, filled water buckets and rationed out grain according to each horse's personal needs. Lastly, I stepped inside the stall with DS and applied some salve to his lashings. His head looked a lot better in the morning light. No deep damage done and it would heal easily with time. DS seemed to have forgotten the whole scenario because he impatiently turned away from me as I tried to apply the salve. Eventually I had to put a halter on him and tie him up just to get the job done while he restlessly stamped his feet and flicked his tail. I began to wonder if last night had really been a bonding moment between the two of us or if the alcohol had just made me think it was something special.

Regardless of my new perspective on the severity of the wounds, I knew my opinion of Arthur had forever changed. It wasn't so much what he had done; it was how he had done it. A senseless, cruel beating that wasn't for the betterment of training. It was just for a man's personal reasons and his own demons that he dealt with in the middle of the night.

I shook it all out of my head as I walked towards the same breakfast buffet I had ate at the previous day. I couldn't believe only 24 hours had passed since I first spotted Grandma and my brothers. It felt like a lifetime ago.

I stood in line, once again, as I first got myself a coffee. I wanted to sit and enjoy the hot coffee before dishing up for breakfast so I meandered back to the entrance and found an empty bench. I had just sat down ready to enjoy my own company when I saw the most beautiful girl I'd ever seen walking towards me. Her thick, black braid was slung over her left shoulder in what I had come to recognize as its usual resting place.

"Hi, Margaret," I said as she approached the bench and sat herself down beside me.

"Good morning, Charlie. Please just call me Maggie. It suits me better, don't you agree? *Margaret* sounds like a prude who enjoys staying in the house all day and darning a gentleman's socks or buying new dresses. I am, in fact, none of those things," she finished with a small laugh and a big smile directed at me.

I liked the way her ramblings put me at ease. She was so comfortable and so unapologetically herself; an open book. "Maggie it is, then," I said as I returned the big smile.

"So, Charlie, you've taken me by surprise. I took you for the quiet, humble type and here you're actually a boisterous showman. A man of the people!"

I gave her a dazed look and tilted my head to the side a little. "I'm generally pretty quiet and humble," I said.

"Oh my gosh, you don't even know, do you?" she asked.

"Know what? You're going to have to help me out a little here," I said as I tried to piece together the puzzle Maggie seemed to be speaking in.

"Oh, what a riot this will be," she teased as she popped straight up off the bench. "Wait there, I'll be right back."

I was perplexed as to what was going on but I stayed put on the bench and watched her bounce away; happy to enjoy the view. When she came striding back shortly after, she was clutching a newspaper in her hands. She had a secretive little grin permanently plastered on her face. I became much more interested in watching her behave in this giddy manner than whatever might be inside the newspaper. She seemed like an entirely different girl than the one I had met at the movie theater. The serious edge had completely vanished.

She placed herself beside me on the bench, a little closer than the previous time. I felt the newspaper spread out on my lap and she gave it a light tap with her index finger as she said, "Ta Da!"

Reluctantly, I tore my eyes off of her and glanced down at the paper.

"Holy shit," my eyes widened once I realized what I was looking at.

This brought her great delight. She hunched over in a fit of laughter as I just kept staring. Right there, splashed across the cover of the Calgary Herald, was a giant picture of me and DS. It was the moment he had reared up after I'd finally settled him down enough to get on. DS was picture perfect as he stood perfectly erect on his hind legs. I was leaning into him and tipping my hat precisely into the crowd. The headline read, **Stampede Salutes Queen** and below the picture was a small description saying *First time stampede competitor, Charlie Hide, makes grand debut as he tames an outlaw horse and wins over Queen Elizabeth in same act.* I studied the picture a little closer. I followed the direction my hat was pointing to and, sure enough, there was Queen Elizabeth herself. Prince Philip was sat right beside her with a white cowboy hat perched on top of his head. They both looked in awe but the Queen was beginning to break into a wide smile. She was inched towards the edge of her seat and peering down at me with regal anticipation.

"See what I mean, now? A man of the people!" Maggie nudged me slightly with her elbow.

I started to chuckle and then laugh out loud and then gradually succumb to a full-blown howl. My eyes watered and I dabbed at the corners and shook my head while I continued to laugh. I was putting the pieces together in my mind and everything began to make sense. That big shot tracking me down after the race, saying he couldn't have planned it better himself; everything was adding up.

I knew I should let Maggie in on the joke. "Let me show you something," I said. I grabbed her hand and brought it over to my lap. I enclosed my fist over hers and pulled out her index finger and then placed it on the paper. "This is me," I said as I put her finger directly on my outstretched arm pictured. "This is where it looks like I'm pointing," I traced her finger slowly and deliberately along the paper towards the Queen. "And this is where I'm actually pointing," I brought her finger straight down. Directly below the suite was a small spectator bleacher. It was perfectly positioned to allow people sitting in it to have a full view of the racetrack. It was a good viewing spot for a true fan or a real horseman who cared about the whole race and not just the beginning and end. "You can barely make them out," I said. "But that's my Grandma and two brothers sitting right there," I explained. "I scoped them out before the race started so I knew that's where they were. I think I just tipped my hat to them as a way to let them know I was going to be alright."

Now it was Maggie's turn to laugh. She peered down closely at the paper and then laughed again, a little louder.

"Do things always seem to work out in your favor like this?" she asked.

"Not always," I said. "But sometimes a guy just gets lucky." As I said that, I squeezed her hand a little tighter. I had yet to let go of it after using her finger to trace the diagram of my salute. She didn't say a word but she smiled and squeezed my hand in return with downcast eyes.

I don't remember how long we sat on that bench after that. She chattered away and started asking me about my family. I was an open book and gave her detailed explanations of everyone. Time seemed to pass breezily by us and it wasn't until she heard my stomach start to rumble that we decided to go eat. Maggie knew every nook and cranny of the stampede grounds so she led the way to a burger spot. She explained to me that she had been coming to watch the stampede every year of her life. It was a tradition for her family to come in to the city. Her father gathered around with other ranchers to partake in an abundance of well-meaning smoking and drinking meetings while her mother attended elegant banquets for the ranch wives. She spoke of the traditions surrounding the stampede and she became downright sentimental.

That's when she stopped and looked at me. "Of course, I see the humor in how you landed on the cover of the Calgary Herald. But it's still something special. You're a part of history now, Charlie. The stampede isn't just about winning. It somehow manages to bring people together. You made a simple gesture when you tipped your hat to your grandma but that gesture will now impact hundreds and maybe even thousands of people. You made the queen of England smile, sure, but you'll also leave an impression on every single person who sees your picture in the paper." Then she gave a little shrug and started walking again as if she hadn't just made an impassioned speech.

I tried to keep up with her natural rhythm of bouncing between casual and profound conversation topics. We spent the entire day together but I wasn't ready to part ways when it came time for me to prepare the horses for the night's race. I reluctantly told Maggie I needed to carry on. She thanked me for the burgers and milkshakes I bought and I was about to walk away when she said, "Are you honestly not going to kiss me? After a day like that?"

"I- I didn't know," I stammered. That girl damn well knew how to take me by surprise. I felt a rush of nerves pass through me but I knew it was time to man up. I put one hand on the back of her head and the other hand on the small of her back. She slipped her fingers into the two front pockets of my pants and pulled me closer. It was a slow, easy kiss but it was enough to make my heart pound and my adrenaline race. Somewhere near us, I heard someone let out a cat call and a low whistle but I didn't care.

You just don't worry about things like that when you're kissing the most beautiful girl you've ever seen.

tough

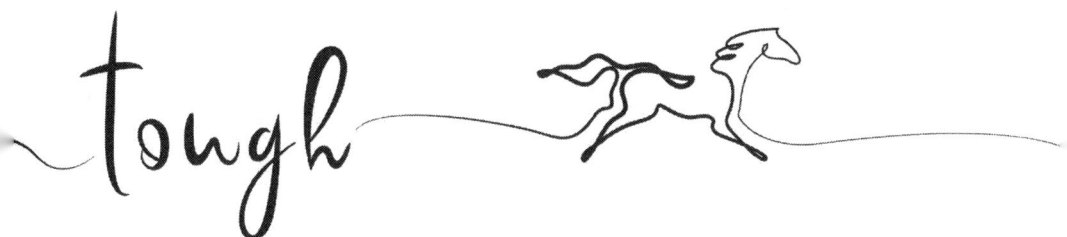

The rest of the stampede passed by in a comfortable, uneventful manner. I continued to ride DS. He became accustomed to the loud noises and chaos at the beginning of the race just like I had hoped he would. There were several times that I had to ease him down around the track or he would have passed by Arthur's wagon. He always came down when I asked him but I think both of us felt a tinge of regret each time. It wasn't in our nature to back off.

I never spoke to Arthur about the night he whipped DS. For one, Arthur never gave me much of a chance to have a conversation with him. He barely acknowledged me let alone spoke to me. For two, the cold facts were that Arthur was the boss and he owned DS. I simply had no say in the matter.

Maggie and I continued to meet up each day. There was more talking and plenty more kissing. We both became emboldened after that first kiss and began engaging in regular public affection. I often slung my arm around her shoulder and played with her thick braid that was part of her everyday attire. She was never around when the races were over because her parents wouldn't allow her to go out at night. They said it wouldn't be proper for her to be *galivanting around.*

Rich came in and watched a few more nights and we always proceeded to drink a few beers but never got completely carried away again. Rich had latched on to the girl he met the first night. She seemed just as infatuated with him and they always slowly slipped away in the night. We would start in a group conversation and then the two of them would become more enthralled with each other before disappearing.

A highlight for me was when Gene and Frank came in to watch. The two guys that I had first befriended at the Stockyard's were continuing to support me. They tracked me down before the race and Frank said, "We've got your picture from the paper cut out and tacked up right at the Stockyard's main entrance," with a puffed-up chest. I was real proud to hear that. Gene didn't say much, as per usual, but it meant a lot just to have him there. I realized that it was the first time I had seen Gene without his dog Blue being somewhere close by. It didn't feel right to see him without his dog; like the energy was off.

On the last night of races, it was determined that Arthur had a fighting chance at winning the aggregate which was the biggest cash payout. There was a lot of buzz surrounding the final race. Anything involving that much money is going to include some hype. But it was easy for me to stay centered because I was paid the same wage whether Arthur won or lost. And since the night in the stall with DS, a wedge had been firmly driven between Arthur and me. I felt completely indifferent towards his success.

The last race gave the people something to cheer about. Arthur ended up neck in neck on the final length of the track with the man leading the aggregate. I knew he would have to pull ahead by half a length to win everything. I kept DS on the outside of the track and watched the two men. Arthur was shaking the reins at his team and yelling with a deep, loud booming voice. ***"HEEE-YAW, HEEE-YAW, HEEE-YAW."*** He reminded me of John Wayne riding into a fight scene. He was completely fearless and a touch reckless as he shook the reins at his horses as if this last race was a matter of life and death. Arthur pulled ahead and was going faster across the finish line than I'd ever witnessed his team go. He won the $5,000 in prize money.

He simply wanted it more than anyone else there.

When the races were over and the excitement had died down and all the horses had been looked after, I began to look for Rich. He had my truck and the two of us had agreed to go home that night. After one week of being at the stampede, I'd had about all the fun I needed to. I was ready to go home and get back to my regular routine. I was also ready to start including Maggie into that regular routine and the thought made me smile to myself.

I was walking a lap around the horse barns when I finally spotted my truck. Rich wasn't sitting in the driver's seat. Oh great, I thought, *he's probably socializing and we're never gonna get outta here.* When I walked closer, I peered at an unfamiliar lump in the passenger seat. I couldn't figure out what it was until I jerked open the door and stared a moment.

"Rich," I managed to choke out as realization and fear merged together. "What the hell happened?" I crawled into the truck and gently pulled his sagging shoulders up to inspect his face. His right eye was completely swollen shut. It looked like his nose was probably broken. There was a slow trickle of blood coming out of a gash by his right ear.

Rich was only semi-conscious but he still tried to let out a small chuckle. It came out sounding more like a wheeze. He clutched his side and I imagined he might have a broken rib. "Y'know the pretty lil' girl I been hangin' with all week?" he asked. His words came out in a slurred, hushed jumble.

"What about her?" I said.

"Well, shit… Turns out her dad did a lil' business with mah dad… Guess he didn't like how it all turned out."

I wasn't exactly sure what Rich was talking about but I'd put enough clues together to get the main gist. I didn't ask him any more questions. I just silently pressed the clutch down and turned the key. When the truck rumbled to life, Rich perked up a little bit. "Better take me home, Charlie… You're a real pal."

The rest of the drive was silent. When we pulled up to our house, I rushed over to the passenger side and put Charlie's right arm around my shoulder. He winced as I drug him out of the truck and helped him into the house. "I think that big son of a bitch might've broke a few ribs on me," Rich said.

"And how did he look after the fight was over?"

Rich turned solemn as he said, "It's not much of a fight when only one person is partaking. My dad did a lot of folks real wrong, Charlie. He doesn't deserve my defense on his behalf." I let that soak in a moment before the old Rich was back. "Besides," he added with a half grin, "I liked the shit out of that daughter of his."

After I got Rich situated in the living room, I filled an ice cream pail with hot water and grabbed a facecloth. Then I sat down across from Rich and started washing off the gash in his head. Rich never protested. He just accepted the help and leaned back into his chair. Then he let out a deep sigh and started talking.

"I grew up with money. A lot of money. We were so rich that I took ballroom dancing lessons as a kid. I never questioned it much. Why would I, ya know? My dad worked a lot and I'm an only child so that pretty much just left my mother and I to preoccupy our time by spending as much money as we could. We had some good times doing that." A soft smile spread across his face. "But when I was 16, everything changed. Dad came home one day with sweat dripping off his forehead and shaky hands and he told us we had to run, we had to get the hell out of Canada, and it was all over for us. My mom wouldn't budge. She stayed put and kept demanding to know what was going on. I just watched the whole thing wordlessly. Eventually my dad just gave up and said he didn't care anyways. Said he would go by himself and that Mom always had been a stupid bitch. He packed a suitcase and left and never said one word to me. I'm not exactly sure how far he made it before the cops caught him. To be honest, I hope it wasn't very fucking far."

Rich took another ragged breath in and let out a deep sigh as he paused to collect his thoughts. I had remained wordless the whole time. He gave his head a slight shake before he continued on.

"Dad was an investment banker. Growing up, I thought he must be the smartest man in Alberta. We were never close but I was still proud of him. Turns out he was just really good at embezzling money. Until he got caught, anyways," Rich shook his head again. "My mom and I just found things out slowly from the lawyers and the newspapers reported on it a fair bit, as well. My mom never went and saw him once. Can't say I blame her much for that. I haven't seen him since the day he came home in a panic."

Rich seemed to trail off at that point. "Where's your mom now?" I asked.

"She's living in Toronto. She's got family out east. The whole deal was pretty hard on her. This house was in her name and it's about the only thing that didn't get seized. She tried to talk me into moving away with her but I couldn't imagine it. The last thing she did before she left was transfer this house into my name."

I nodded along. I'd been wondering what Rich's story was for quite some time now. The funny thing was that it seemed to be a big secret but now that I knew, it didn't change a damn thing. I wasn't going to hold it against Rich but I also wasn't going to give him any pity or sympathy. We would just carry on -exact same way we'd been doing.

As I finished cleaning up the last bit of Rich's wounds, I realized it was the second time in a week that I had played the role of caretaker. First with DS and now with Rich. Both of them had been trapped in a corner that they couldn't see any way out of so they took a beating. But I also figured that both of them were tough enough to handle it.

That's one of the things about life. Sometimes it knocks us down for no reason other than to see if we can get back up again.

1981

"I hope you live a life you're proud of. And if you find that you're not, I hope you have the strength to start over."

~ F. Scott Fitzgerald

CHAPTER FOURTEEN

uncomplicated

Walking through the pens at the Stockyards, I strummed my fingers along a wooden plaque as I passed by the brand inspection office. I had a habit of doing that each time I passed by. I always liked to feel the deep grooves in the wood that spelled out *Here Lies A Damn Good Dog*. I think it was my way of giving Blue a symbolic pat on the head.

It's been fifteen years since Blue died, but I still remember how hard it was on Gene – one of the first men I'd met at the Stockyards, a true friend to me, and a damn fine brand inspector. For a lifetime bachelor like Gene, a dog is the closest thing he had to family. Gene grieved the loss of Blue in his own way. He didn't say much or show much emotion in front of the crew at the stockyards. But the morning after we buried Blue and nailed up the small plaque, I walked past to find a piece of bacon sitting on the freshly dug up ground.

Now Gene was becoming an old man. He was still working and still sharp as a tack. But his face had become weathered and worn. He had deep creases and he often went weeks without shaving so he had become scruffy and unkempt. He went through a few dogs after Blue died before he found the perfect match. It was a red heeler named Hank. Something about a heeler seemed to match Gene's disposition. Maybe it was the fact that they tended to be all business. Or maybe it was that they were loyal right up until their dying days.

I carried on walking past Blue's resting place to make my way to my office. I had some papers to sign. A part of me missed the days when I would spend all my time in the back pens. I missed the sorting and the satisfaction of a hard day of physical labor. I missed the laughs when a mean ol' mama cow would get on the fight and run a couple guys up the fence. I also missed the reckless freedom that came with being the low man on the totem pole. I just did the best job I could do every day and I never had any skin in the game so I never had any real stress.

Now stress seemed to be a constant burden that I carried with me. Cattle prices were down. We'd had a dry summer and that's always hard on the agricultural community - no matter what sector you're in. It's particularly stressful when you're an auctioneer trying to catch bids. It took a heavy toll on me when I'd conclude my rambling with a definite "SOLD" and I could understand full well that the price I'd just sold the cattle for wouldn't be enough for the rancher selling to make ends meet. I never thought of any of that when I started messing around, practicing auctioning things off. After hanging around the market long enough, I started to get the rhythmic numbers spouted off by auctioneers stuck in my head. With a natural knack for it and a lot of practice, I'd been working as an auctioneer for the last seventeen years.

I meandered past the secretaries at the Stockyards' entrance just slow enough to peer in and give them a smile and tip my hat. They all returned a smile or a wink back at me. Then I bounded up the stairs, taking two at a time, before coming to my office. I settled in at my desk and plucked a cigarette out of a pack to puff on before going over my paperwork. As I leaned back in my chair and exhaled a long cloud of smoke, I looked at the picture framed on my desk. It was Maggie and I on our wedding day. She had brought the frame in the day I became chairman of the feeder finance program and moved in to my own office. *"This is so you can always look at us to remember where we started now that you're a big shot,"* and she'd kissed my cheek gently after she said it. Her father had given us 4 quarters of land with rolling pastures and a four-bedroom log house but Maggie always somehow

104

managed to make me feel like I was accomplishing something instead of being handed everything.

I was on the last drag of my cigarette when my younger brother Philip and old pal Rich walked into my office. They slunk down into their usual spots in the two chairs across from my desk. Usually once a day we would all congregate in my office to bullshit.

Philip started coming to the stockyards as often as he could when he turned 16. He would stay with me and Rich and he would work in the back pens like he had been there all his life. He never was the nuisance kid brother that seems to be the stereotype. We were all close and I liked having him around. Philip had an uncanny instinct of being two steps ahead of everyone else. He was foreseeing problems and solving them before the cowboys working in the back pens had even started on a task. Philip thrived at the stockyards. Everyone took to him immediately because of his simple, genuine charm. At 32 years old, he was currently the foreman of the back pens. I know some folks raised their eyebrows at a man that young being promoted so quickly but the truth of the matter is that Philip had been working in the back pens for half his life. He was a natural born stockman but he also knew how to motivate other workers with his zest for life. To me, it seemed that Philip being the foreman was the most logical progression in his life. If there was another man that I thought could do a better job, I would have said so. But I'd yet to meet a harder worker than Philip.

Maggie had become fixated on finding a woman for Philip. He had built himself a successful life but had never settled down. Philip had constructed a little guest lodge on mine and Maggie's property that he currently resided in. He'd started picking away and buying his own cow herd and he ran his cows with Maggie's herd. As long as Philip had been living next to us and working with us, I'd never heard him and Maggie exchange a cross word. Maggie had a soft spot for Philip and he had the same for her. They had worked together for so long and become so in sync that the two of them could work cows without barely even communicating verbally. They simply knew where the other one would be and what needed to be done and things would carry on seamlessly. I often joked that the two of them had the happiest cow herd in North America but there was an underlying truth to it. They both loved their cows and worked them stress free and it showed in the quality of their cow/calf production.

Rich was an order buyer. That basically meant that he drove all across Canada and talked to farmers and ranchers for a living. Just like Philip, Rich was perfectly suited for the job he held. Rich didn't just buy the right cows for the right ranchers, although he was awfully good at that, too. Rich took his job one step further. He developed deep, lasting friendships with the ranchers he bought cattle for. He managed to remember everyone's name, the name of their wives, their kids, their dog, and their childhood best friend. He took a vivacious approach in keeping up with how everyone was doing. And it worked. The ranchers loved Rich because it was obvious that he truly cared.

Sometimes that's all we ever need. Someone who cares.

Rich was married to the petite, pretty thing he had met the first year I was at the Calgary Stampede. Her name was Georgia. I'll never forget how she came marching up to our door the day after her dad nearly beat the life out of Rich. A lot of girls would have come crying and begging for forgiveness or they would have followed their father's wishes by never speaking to Rich again. Not Georgia. She came with her head held high. I opened up our front door and she looked right past me to see Rich propped up on the couch. They never said a word to each other. She stood there for a moment as they gazed into each other's eyes and then Rich lifted up an arm and motioned for her to come sit beside him. She rushed over to him and curled up beside him. I left the house and went for a milkshake to give them some privacy but when I returned, they were still in the exact same position. Rich was lightly stroking her hair and Georgia was crooning in his ear. That looked about as good of a sign as any that the two of them were going to wind up together.

Rich and I both got married in the same year and we stood up as each other's best man. Seven years after we got married, Maggie and I had our first and only child. A boy we named Jake. He was now 15 years old and starting to get a little lippy. I needed to work on that.

About the same time Maggie and I were expecting Jake, Rich and Georgia started telling us about their complications. I lost track of the number of miscarriages Georgia had before they gave up on ever having a child.

Maggie was an only child and she wanted to have a whole hoard of children. I loved having three brothers and a big family so I was on board with the idea. But when she had Jake, she lost a lot of blood.

She was hospitalized for three weeks and the doctor warned us that another birth could be even more damaging. We both agreed after that scare that Jake would be our only child.

I knew part of the reason that Jake was becoming borderline mouthy was because he had been undeniably spoiled. He knew his parents had money and that his grandparents (on his mother's side) had even more money. He had been given everything he ever wanted growing up. Rich and Georgia loved Jake as much as they would have loved their own child. They were at his beck and call as a way to show that love. He often accompanied them on trips to the movie theater or the zoo or to fast food restaurants – which were his current favorite. Rich would always laugh about that and start to tell Jake stories about how often *"your dad and me used to go for milkshakes."*

I was snapped out of my daydream and brought back to the moment by Philip raising two fists in the air and chanting, "Ali, Ali, Ali, Ali." Rich laughed freely at the spectacle and I felt a smile spread across my face. The sports section of the *Calgary Herald* had just announced that Muhammad Ali would be retiring from boxing.

"Good riddance," Rich muttered. "Never seen a man so full of himself as that – "

"RIGHTFULLY full of himself after 56 *wins*," Philip cut him off.

Rich and Philip had always disagreed on Muhammad Ali's career. Philip loved him and loved all his antics. Rich hated him.

"Okay, Charlie, you never have actually told us what side of the Muhammed debate you're on. The man is retired now. Time to give us your opinion," Rich urged.

I leaned back in my chair, pondering. Once they were both looking at me and I'd built the suspense, I pounced forward, up on to my feet, and slugged Rich in the bicep. Then I imitated a boxer's side to side dance with my fists up in front of my face. "Float like a butterfly, sting like a bee, baby," I said.

Philip howled with laughter and slapped his knee. Rich good naturedly rubbed his bicep and shook his head in mock disgust.

In that moment, I didn't worry about the paperwork on my desk. I didn't worry about cattle prices. I wasn't thinking about how to be a good father and how to raise a good man. I was just laughing with my pals and bullshitting about things that really didn't matter. In that moment, I wasn't a 39-year-old husband and father and head of the Calgary Stockyards Feeder Finance Program. I felt like the 17-year-old kid again who believed everything about life was blissfully uncomplicated.

CHAPTER FIFTEEN

passions

I pulled up my long, winding driveway. My favorite sight in the world was coming home to see our log house with the expansive front porch and lilac bushes planted on either side. Everything about our place was seeped with Maggie's style and taste. She'd built her dream home and set up her idyllic lifestyle when she planned our log house and started her cow herd. As I shifted my pickup down with dust blowing up behind me, I looked out into the pasture east of the house. I could see five or six thoroughbreds standing together. The rest were probably over the hill. They were my wagon horses. After spending years as an outrider and slowly building up my own herd, I'd started driving chuckwagons and entering when I turned 30. I thought I would miss being on the back of a horse but there was something beautiful about helping four horses work together at the same time to accomplish a task. I'd grown to love wagon racing more than anything else I'd ever done. It was my true passion and purpose.

Besides loving on Maggie. I was pretty passionate about that, too.

I parked my truck and walked up to the front door. Even before I turned the knob, I could hear the T.V. blaring inside. I was instantly peeved. I knew I would find Jake propped up on the couch in the living room. He wouldn't acknowledge my coming home or say hello. He would just sit there and stare intently at what was happening on the screen. Like a damned fool.

I stepped inside and glared in Jake's direction. His back was to me so I pulled off my boots and placed myself in his peripheral view, still glaring. He was zoned in on the television set, just as I'd imagined. I finally looked at the screen. He was watching his new favorite show *Dukes of Hazzard*. He'd become obsessed with it recently and I never understood how a person could just enjoy sitting so much. When I was his age, I barely ever sat. I was always working or riding or goofing off with my brothers.

I was about to open my mouth and say something when Daisy Duke appeared on the screen. She came strutting along in cowboy boots and short shorts. I mean *really* short shorts. Jake never moved from his seat on the couch but his eyes got a little bigger and his head moved forward towards the television as he ogled. My anger dissipated and I almost had to suppress a laugh.

"Didn't know it was legal to dress like that on television," I said.

Jake never looked in my direction, his eyes were locked on the screen, but he quipped, "It's the '80s, Dad."

I nonchalantly made my way to the TV and reached down and hit the power button. Daisy disappeared and the screen went black.

"Let's go grain the thoroughbreds," I said.

Jake visibly stiffened and a light scowl flickered across his face but he knew better than to say anything. We both walked towards the front door, pulled our boots on, and headed to the grain bin. Jake began scooping grain into three buckets and I backed the farm truck up to the bin. Then we dropped the tailgate down and loaded the buckets into the back of the truck before coasting towards the east pasture. Jake hopped out and got the gate and we were driving towards the back of the pasture before either of us said a word to each other.

"Pretty day," I said breaking the silence.

"Yep," Jake replied.

When the horses heard the rumble of the truck, they started running towards us. They knew the old feed truck driving out in the pasture meant there was a good chance they would be getting some oats. I watched the horses run and prance and toss their heads in the air. I noticed each little idiosyncrasy. It was important to note which horses were the ring leaders or the boss of the herd out in the pasture because those were the ones you'd want as your lead horse on the wagon. It was also important to note their character. Some were tough as nails and responded better to dominance. Others were flighty and sensitive and needed a lot of reassurance.

I was in my glory. This was my element; observing a herd of horses and looking after them. The oats they were about to eat would not only help their coats shine and help them gain a little weight but it would also allow them to perform their best. I was lost in my own world of contentment with a dozen thoughts bouncing around in my head but then I glanced over at Jake. He looked utterly bored.

I finally parked the truck and we both got out and grabbed a bucket. We each poured out a bit of grain on the ground and then moved a few feet away and poured another batch. Eventually every horse was standing at their own pile of grain with the exception of a few who would pin their ears as they moved from pile to pile. I threw the empty buckets into the back of the truck and sat down on the dropped tailgate. I was in no rush to get back to the house where Jake would inevitably return to the television. He followed suit and sat beside me.

One horse stood out as the most aggressive. He could run any of the others off and have his pick of whichever grain pile he preferred. I smiled softly as I watched him. His age was starting to show but he was still a big, beautiful sorrel and the double swirls on his head still stood out sharply.

"DS has gotta be over 30 years old now. Can't believe how good he still looks," I said to Jake.

Jake searched the herd before his eyes landed on DS and he nodded, "Yah. He does look good."

"I'd like old Arthur Langley to see him now. He might not even remember him."

Jake had heard the story plenty of times before. He knew that DS was the first horse I ever owned myself. He knew that the first year I was an outrider, I rode for Arthur Langley. After the Calgary Stampede was over and done with, I went to Arthur's house to be paid. He handed me some cash for our agreed upon price and then I asked him how much he wanted for DS. He said, *"DS?"* all confused. I clarified that DS was the sorrel I'd been riding at Calgary all week. Then Arthur threw back his head and gave one of his rare laughs and said, *"Farmer, you can have him. I don't want him."*

"You know, ol' DS didn't have a very easy life before I owned him," I said to Jake. He lifted an eyebrow at me but remained silent, so I carried on. "Arthur was a bit of a cruel bastard. Probably still is, to tell you the truth. I saw him whipping on DS one night. Just whipping him on the head, over and over. It nearly broke my heart to witness such a senseless act... And Arthur lived in a mosquito infested swampland, on top of that. All his horses probably spent half the year feeling itchy as hell." I paused a moment because I wanted what I was about to explain to Jake to really sink in. "Sometimes I wonder if all that didn't help make DS so great. I don't condone any of it but somehow DS ended up being this tough, willing, superstar of a horse with a huge heart. He wasn't always granted an easy life but it made him a fighter. I never saw a horse that loved to run as much as that sucker and he was guaranteed to put his whole heart into it."

I trailed off unsure of whether I had properly conveyed the lesson to Jake that I was trying to place in the back of his mind. I wanted him to know that being handed everything in life doesn't leave much room to develop a strong character in a horse or in a man. That we need some obstacles to develop grit.

Jake hopped off the tailgate and eased towards DS. He approached him steadily but slowly and talked to him the whole way up. I noted Jake's mannerisms around a horse and thought they were just like mine, which were just like my grandma's. The Hyde family horse training gene was deep rooted.

Jake scratched DS in a few sweet spots and the two of us made small talk about all the horses before we headed back to the house. It was a pleasurable, relaxed evening. I knew it was getting close to supper time before I finally mentioned to Jake that we should head back to the house. He agreed but didn't seem desperate to leave.

Progress.

Maggie had supper cooked and was waiting when we walked in

the front door. She took note of the easy conversation still transpiring between Jake and I and she never mentioned a word about waiting on us. The good feeling between all of us lasted through supper and we had a few good laughs. When we finished eating, Maggie leaned over my shoulder to grab my dinner plate and start clearing up the dishes. I seized the opportunity to wrap my arm around her waist and pull her in to me and kiss her. She laughed after returning the kiss and standing back up again. Jake rolled his eyes.

"Hey, how about a Monopoly game tonight?" Jake asked. I was about to protest but Maggie had already answered, "Sure thing, hun."

Jake was instantly on the move. "I'll go ask Uncle Philip if he wants to play," he hollered as he barreled out the front door. I knew he would hop on his bike and pedal as fast as he could toward Philip's cabin. I also knew that Philip would agree to the Monopoly game without question. Philip never said no to Jake.

I stood up and walked towards the sink where Maggie was already elbows deep in hot water and soap. "I hate that damned board game," I said.

"You hate it because you never win," she said with a sly smile over her shoulder.

I stepped behind her and grabbed her sides, poking her gently in the ribs where I knew she was the most ticklish. She tried to shoot forward but had nowhere to go so she tensed and squirmed between my hands. "You know it's true!" she said.

"Maybe so," I responded as I softened my hands and slid them down to her hips. Then I stepped closer and said in her ear, "You know Jake and Philip aren't going to be coming in the house for at least another ten minutes. Maybe longer."

"Charlie!" she said. But she never disagreed. I kissed her neck and she never protested, just slightly moved her head to the side. I seized the opportunity and scooped her up into my arms and started walking towards our bedroom.

As I mentioned earlier, I had two passions in life...

celebrating

"God damnit," I muttered. I'd just rolled the dice and landed myself on Kentucky which was owned by Philip and had three houses on it. My stash of Monopoly money had already dwindled down to close to nothing.

Philip, Jake, and Maggie could hardly contain themselves. They were sputtering with laughter. I tossed the remainder of my cash and the two railroads I owned in Philip's direction. "I'm out," I said.

"It really wouldn't be a Monopoly game unless Dad is the first one to go under," Jake said, and they all laughed again.

"This game has no real-world applications. You can't just buy everything with no backup or savings – " I began but my rant was cut short by the three of them unanimously telling me to save it.

I eased out to the porch and lit a cigarette. I took turns breathing in a puff of smoke and breathing in the scent of Maggie's lilacs. Crickets were chirping loudly in the night and the coyotes were beginning to howl. I could hear roars of laughter or heated debates pouring out of the house in random outbursts. I sat patiently on the deck; perfectly content to just be in the moment.

Eventually Philip came sliding out the front door and plopped down on a chair beside me. "Your wife is a cut-throat businesswoman," he said.

I nodded my head in agreeance, "She comes by it honestly," I said. Both of our minds wandered to my father-in-law who had made millions through land, cows, and oil. Mostly oil but the other two didn't hurt.

"What are you going to do when you inherit all that money?" Philip ventured. We normally kept the topic of Maggie's money off limits. But something in the night air was whispering that it was okay to talk about it.

I took a deep breath and blew out an exasperated sigh with puffed out cheeks. "I honestly haven't got a damn clue," I admitted. It felt good to say that out loud.

Philip laughed a little but kept his non-judgmental demeanor. "Too much money ain't necessarily a bad problem to have," he commented.

"No. It isn't. Could you imagine if Dad ever heard me worrying about money in that way?" I raised my eyebrows high at the thought. Although our dad probably couldn't even fathom how much money Maggie's family really had. "I worry about Jake more than anything," I continued to Philip. "He's handed everything, and he knows he's already got it made for the rest of his life. How do I keep him grounded when everybody around him puts him on a pedestal? How do I keep him humble while he lives such a privileged life?"

Philip didn't dismiss me entirely but he did stiffen a little. "Shit, Charlie. Give the kid a little credit. He's just a boy but he is doing a lot of things right. He'll probably make a few thousand more mistakes, but hell, we all did."

"I suppose," I said.

Philip retreated a little and gently said, "Have some faith in him. And have some faith in your parenting, too."

I gave a lopsided grin. Leave it to Philip to put things in perspective. We continued to sit on the porch and amicably discuss life. We discussed some of the cowboys working in the back pens for Philip. We labeled some as stockmen and some as lazy. We talked about my wagon horses and the upcoming season. Lastly, Philip asked to borrow my truck for the night because his wasn't running right. He said he needed to take it to the shop tomorrow but he wanted to go into town tonight. "See if I can't rustle me up a pool game or two," he winked.

"Keys are in it," I said as I nodded toward my pickup.

"Alright, I'll say goodbye to Maggie and Jake," he said as he slapped his hands on his knees and then popped out of his chair. I got up more slowly, reluctant to let the good feeling and easy conversation die away.

As we walked through the front door, we witnessed the final blow to Jake's Monopoly crusade. Maggie had built herself an empire with hotels everywhere. Jake had just landed on Park Place which must have been Maggie's property judging by her squeals of delight. Jake leaned back in his chair and threw his head back and groaned. Maggie soaked in the sight of defeat on Jake's face and then she stepped on to her chair, moved up on to the table, scattered a few pieces about, and did a victory dance.

"Winner, winner, winner, winner," she kept repeating as she clamped her hands together and shook her fist on either side of her head as she wiggled her body about.

Jake watched the whole scene sulkily. Philip was halfways shocked. And I roared with laughter.

"Does she come by that honestly, too?" Philip leaned towards me and asked as Maggie climbed down off the table.

"No," I said wiping at my eyes, "No, that's pretty much all her. Sometimes just a little too spirited for her own good," I quipped. I never took my eyes off her as she stepped down and when she glanced in my direction, I gave her a small wink.

Philip said his goodbyes with a squeeze on Jake's shoulder and a kiss on Maggie's cheek. Then he was out the door in a hurry.

"See you in the morning," he called. Light rain started tapping on the roof as he ran to the truck. I knew the clouds had been building and swirling. We were probably in store for a classic Alberta thunderstorm tonight.

We cleaned up the Monopoly pieces and Jake retreated to his bedroom. I was walking around the house and shutting all the lights off when Maggie followed me down the hallway towards our room and slipped her hand into the back pocket of my jeans.

"You know what I like about Monopoly?" she asked as she sidled up close to me.

"What's that?" I looked down at her with a raised eyebrow.

"The celebrating." She grabbed my hand and tugged me into our room.

When we were done celebrating, I decided I might like Monopoly after all.

CHAPTER SEVENTEEN

froze

    I woke up the next morning as the sun was beginning to shine into our bedroom window. I laid in peace for a few moments and glanced at Maggie in bed. Her back was to me and her long, black hair was tumbling all about her pillow. She still wore it in a braid nearly every day but I liked it best in the mornings when her hair looked as wild as she was. Eventually I pulled myself out of bed and headed toward the kitchen to put the coffee pot on.

    I stood at the coffee pot and peered out the kitchen window. My truck wasn't parked in its usual spot. I silently cursed Philip for driving it to his cabin instead of returning it back to my yard. I looked out the window for a few more moments before something else came into my vision, just barely noticeable at the end of our long, curving driveway. I walked over to the front door and pulled on my boots. I had blue jeans on but no shirt yet and I didn't bother to put on a jacket. The cool, damp morning air hit my chest and goosebumps crawled all over my skin as I stepped outside. I started walking down my driveway and then jogging and then sprinting as I began to realize what I was seeing.

My truck was on its side and laying on top of our broken fence. I could see tore up grass and tire tracks in the grass between our driveway and where the truck was. There was broken glass everywhere.

I reached my truck, heaved the door open, and froze for a split second. Then I reached inside, pulled out a lifeless body, and hugged it to my bare chest.

Philip was dead.

CHAPTER EIGHTEEN

salute

When your world comes crashing down, you'd expect to feel an unbearable amount of pain. When you lose your favorite person in the world, you'd expect to cry and rage and sob. When you find your dead brother, you'd expect to call someone for help.

I did none of the above.

I was numb to the point of not even being present in my own body.

Maggie informed me later that I carried Philip all the way to his cabin. I laid him down on his bed and she eventually found me there. I had filled a bucket with hot water and I was gently using a rag to wipe the blood and wounds clean. I have no recollection of any of this, but I suppose I was caring for my little brother in the only way I really knew how.

I do remember glancing in Maggie's direction at one point and seeing her hunched over on the floor. I stared at her a moment, wondering what she was doing, before I realized she was crying. Some voice in the back of my head tried to tell me that I should go over to her. That I should wrap my arms around her. That I should cry with her. But instead, I continued to dip the rag in the water and clean Philip off; slowly, methodically, absently. Eventually, Maggie wasn't in the cabin anymore, but I never heard her leave.

An ambulance came out to the cabin and men I had never met before eased in and cautiously explained to me that they were going to take the body. I just nodded and wished they would quit tip toeing around. When I finally returned to my house, Maggie and Jake were wrapped together on the couch. Maggie was softly patting Jake's head and rubbing his hair to the side. They both had red, puffy eyes. Again, I had a small, nagging sensation telling me that I should go to my family. But I only glanced at them before heading into my bedroom and shutting the door.

The next few days were filled with phone calls. Maggie would walk me over to the telephone, tell me who I had to call and what I had to say, and I would do it.

"Charlie, call your brother Walter. He can get your parents and Grant together to tell them. Your mother shouldn't hear this news over the phone."

I dialed my brother Walter's phone number from memory. He answered happily and all I responded was, "Philip rolled my truck last night. He didn't… make it." I couldn't recognize the sound of my own voice as I spoke.

I repeated that sentence over and over. *He didn't make it*. Every time Maggie wanted me to call someone, I told them that Philip had rolled my truck and he didn't make it. The phrase began to confuse me. Philip didn't make what? Then I would remember. He didn't make it out alive.

I was told about the funeral arrangements, but I had nothing to do with organizing them. Philip would be buried in our hometown - next to my grandmother. The funeral was going to be in four days. Maggie and I were driving up in three days. The pastor at our family church was going to speak. The men from the Stockyards had planned a tribute.

I still felt nothing.

I would find myself in situations and couldn't remember how I got there. I was standing out in the east field graining my chuckwagon horses but I couldn't remember filling the buckets up with grain. I was laying in my bed at night but I couldn't remember how the day had passed.

Eventually I found myself standing in the family room at the funeral chapel in Lacombe. There was a tray of food on a small table in the middle of the room surrounded by comfy chairs and couches. I looked at the food, wondering when the last time was that I had ate. I couldn't remember.

Maggie was standing in the corner of the room talking to our pastor. Her black braid blended in with her black dress. She had no make-up on and her eyes were still red and puffy. She was clutching a Kleenex tightly in her hand. I heard her say my name. "Charlie is… not quite… processing all of it yet," she said softly. I didn't listen to the pastor's response.

The funeral began like any other. The pastor cleared his throat and spoke words that were supposed to bring comfort but that generally went over people's heads. At that point, I wanted to stand and shout. I wanted to scream that Philip was unlike anyone else who had ever lived. He deserved a funeral that stood apart and had the same vibrant, outgoing nature that Philip embodied. But I stayed in my seat.

When the pastor called on Jake to speak, my head snapped up. For the first time, I noticed that Jake was holding pieces of paper tightly in his hands that were filled with his chicken scratch writing. Jake stood and walked up to the front of the room. I stared blankly as he approached the mic.

"My Uncle Philip – " Jake began and his voice cut in two. He inhaled sharply and held back the sob that was caught somewhere in his chest. He paused, took a few breaths, and began again.

"My Uncle Philip was the best man I ever knew. He was everybody's favorite person. He had this incredible knack of working you to the bone but you had so much fun being around him that you never realized how wore out you were." A few chuckles in the crowd broke out and Jake seemed to find his confidence. He stood a little taller. "I remember one time Uncle Philip and me, we were shoveling out boxstalls in the horse barn. He told me that if I could clean my boxstall out before he had his cleaned out, he would take me to town and buy me a burger and fries. I went as hard as I possibly could and I had horse shit flying everywhere but I never stood a chance against Uncle Philip. He cleaned his out and then he helped me finish mine… And he still took me to town for a burger and fries. That's just the kind of guy he was.

Uncle Philip had endless amounts of energy. He could work at the Stockyards all day and night, being on his feet and running around, and then he could come back to our house and still have energy to hang out with me. He taught me how to play pool and poker and 21 hold 'em. He taught me that the fastest way to sort cows is to go slow. He taught me about Muhammad Ali and why he's the greatest boxer of all time. Uncle Philip taught me how to work and how to have fun and how to do both at the same time.

Uncle Philip was everybody's favorite person. He could sit on the porch and have a smoke with my dad, help my mom clean up the dishes, and then watch Dukes of Hazzard with me. And somehow during each of those things, he would make each of us feel like the most special and important person in the world.

My family is never going to be the same without Uncle Philip. I am never going to be the same without Uncle Philip." Jake's voice broke again. I could hear sniffles and muffled sobs coming from the people surrounding me.

"But I am a better person today because of knowing Uncle Philp," Jake continued. "His influence will carry on in those who loved him. He lived largely and we can all do the same as we remember him..."

Jake's voice trailed off. Then he shuffled his papers together, cleared his throat and stepped back from the mic before receding back to his seat. I couldn't quite tell if that was where his speech was supposed to end or if he simply couldn't take standing up there any longer. Maybe he decided he had said all he needed to. Jake sat down beside Maggie and she patted his knee tenderly. Jake held his head up proudly and he seemed to jut his chin out in determination. I reached my arm around Maggie and squeezed Jake's shoulder. Jake glanced in my direction and nodded his head at me. We never spoke a word but I wasn't sure if we had ever communicated better than we did in that moment.

I closed my eyes a moment as the pastor began to speak again. An overwhelming feeling of comfort washed over me. I let out a deep breath. The source of comfort was a thought that had just been planted in my mind. I don't know if it was my subconscious speaking to me or God or, hell, maybe it was Philip. But it said, *The great man you lost was just replaced by another.*

Jake had stood up and faced his grief in the bravest way a person ever could. He leaned in to it and he spoke his truth while honoring his uncle. You could never hope for a son to be more of a man than that.

The rest of the funeral proceeded without any noteworthy moments. I was ready to get the hell out of that building. When the last hymn had been sung, I guided Maggie and Jake towards the door and we were one of the first families to step outside. To my surprise, Maggie was just as eager to get out of the funeral chapel. As the flow of people steadily increased outside, I began to realize why.

The men from the stockyards were trailing about 40 head of cows right down the street in Lacombe and in front of the funeral home. I recognized the brand on the cows; it was Philip's. His cows were bawling and mooing as the men guided them along in the best damn funeral procession I ever saw. At the very front of the herd, I saw Gene and Frank striding along on two good looking bay horses. Both men were over 70 years old and they looked as comfortable on top of a horse as most people looked sitting in a rocking chair. Gene's dog Hank was working the cows, keeping any strays in line and bringing them back to the herd. Gene was keeping an eye on him and an eye on the herd. Frank was keeping his eyes peeled ahead and making sure traffic was moving to the side of the road. He spotted me standing there watching and he took his white hat off and tipped it right at me. I raised a hand back in salute. That was all we needed to say.

Maggie watched Philip's cows ease in front of us with her eyes glistening. "Did you have anything to do with this?" I asked her.

"Maybe," was all she responded.

I didn't smile but it was the first time since I'd found Philip's body that I felt a spark of joy.

My little brother got the vibrant funeral he deserved.

CHAPTER NINETEEN

coincidental

Ten days after Philip's funeral, I was due to head to a northern rodeo for a chuckwagon race. It wasn't the biggest one of the year, but it was a good warm up before Calgary Stampede. I thought about turning out and staying home before ultimately deciding that it would serve me better to be with my horses and clear my head on the long drive. The night before I was going to leave, Maggie laid in bed beside me and tossed and turned.

"Are you sure you want to go?" she finally asked.

It took me a moment to realize what she was talking about.

"I'm sure," I said.

She was silent and I thought the conversation was over until she spoke up again and gently said, "I think Jake and I need you home right now. It feels too soon to leave. We need to be together as a family."

"Well, we're not together as a family because Philip isn't with us," I said. My tone came out harsher than I had intended. I almost retracted my statement, but it was truly how I felt so I left it hanging between us. It was a truth that I still didn't want to face, yet I could think of nothing else. I felt like I was at war with myself and my grief.

Maggie chose to rise above my harsh tone and my lack of empathy. I could almost feel her withdrawing into herself. Then, with her voice barely above a whisper, but with a croaky determination, she said, "Charlie, you're not the only one who lost a brother you loved."

I laid perfectly still for a moment. Then I rolled over to my side with my back facing towards her and never said another word. We remained that way for the rest of the night; side by side in our bed, feeling more alone than ever before.

I barely slept and was outside by 5 am, catching horses. I talked gently to each horse as they came up to the grain piles I had distributed while calling them into the catch pen. I stood a moment with each horse and let them get a few mouthfuls of grain as reward for coming running into the catch pen. I patted DS on the head a few times, even though I didn't need to catch him. He was long retired from being a wagon horse but I still felt a tinge of guilt when I would catch all the younger horses and load them on the trailer. DS would always stand with his head over the fence and his chest pushing against the wooden rails as if to say, "Hey, notice me. You're leaving your best horse behind." Then he would take off running and kicking and swinging his head. Probably showing off.

To my surprise, at about 5:30, Jake stepped out of the house and walked over to the haystack and started throwing square bales into the back of the truck. It was a brand-new pickup that had been delivered to my door a few days after Philip's death. Becca's father had handed me the keys and said, "*Not a damn thing I do or say is going to make any of this any better or any easier. But here's one less thing to worry about.*"

Jake noticed my raised eyebrows at his early rising hour and said, "I couldn't sleep."

"Been having the same trouble myself," I said.

"That's obvious. You look like shit."

I snapped my head in his direction and was about to give him hell before I saw the look on his face. There was kindness in the crinkled, sleepy edges of his eyes and a goofy, half grin waiting to erupt into a full smile.

"I'm still better looking than your ugly mug," I said and Jake let the smile spread across his face before he heaved the last bale into the bed of the truck.

"Take care of your mom while I'm gone," I said to him as he wiped the hay off his clothes.

He nodded and said, "Hope you win this one. For Uncle Philip."

I stepped into the pickup and slammed the door shut. I tried to swallow the lump in my throat down as I waved to Jake. I managed to keep the tears at bay until I reached the curve in our driveway where I had found Philip. Then I stopped the truck and choked out a loud, heaving sob. I cried the tears that I had locked inside myself for the past 11 days and they came out in a ferocious outpour. I cried for Philip, I cried for Jake, and I cried for Maggie. I cried over the stupid, God damn curving driveway that I had once loved so much. I cried because it felt good and I couldn't stop even if I had wanted to. I laid my head against the steering wheel and I cried for my mom who had to bury a child – a pain no person should ever go through. I cried for allowing Philip to take my truck and not having the sense of mind to tell him he didn't need to go to town and get drunk. I cried because I was angry with God for the first time in my life. I cried because Philip was too good for this world. I cried because it should have been me.

And when I couldn't cry anymore, I wiped my eyes and blew my nose on the long sleeves of my shirt. I put the truck back into gear and I headed out to a chuckwagon race simply because I didn't know what the hell else to do.

I pulled into town and eased the truck and trailer into my usual gas station to fill up with diesel. I noticed a parked truck sitting by the pumps that I recognized. Georgia was sitting behind the wheel and Rich was in the passenger seat. When they saw me pull up, Georgia gave a smile and a wave and Rich hopped out with a duffel bag. Georgia peeled out of the parking lot before I had even turned the keys off in my ignition. Rich came walking up to my truck, yanked open the back door, threw his duffel bag in the back seat, and said, "Morning. Mind if I tag along?"

"Maggie called you, I'm assuming?" I asked. Rich knew me better than anybody but him waiting patiently at the fuel station at the correct time was a little too coincidental.

"Ah, maybe she did, maybe she didn't," Rich evaded the question while simultaneously confirming my suspicion. Then he hopped into the passenger seat and looked over at me for the first time. "Jesus," he muttered. "You look like shit."

I couldn't help but smile, thinking of Jake. "Yah," I said. "So I've been told."

CHAPTER TWENTY

We pulled into the rodeo grounds around 4 pm. The rodeo performance started at 5 and the chuckwagon races were to follow. Chuckwagon races were becoming a popular entertainment attraction for the drinking crowd. People liked to enjoy some beverages and bet amongst themselves on the winner. They liked to cut loose and holler and cheer for the horses to run faster. I had grown out of the stage in my life where I partook in the party scene. I had been hungover enough times as an outrider that I had it out of my system as a driver. I'd also seen what happens to drivers who indulge in too many drinks. The difference is sometimes unnoticeable but a disadvantage slowly starts to seep in and drivers will verge on the edge of being sloppy, tired, or reckless.

Also, my first experience with chuckwagon racing was with Arthur Langley. Although he was a winner at times, I firmly resolved to myself to be the exact opposite of him. Arthur loved going to the rodeos and getting drunk. The only time his wife tagged along was at Calgary and, even then, he largely ignored her and spent his free time posted up at the bar. I'd seen Arthur fall in to every different kind of mood when he drank. He could become happy and buoyant which was the most at odds with his sober personality. But he could also become angry, bitter, and aggressive. That was his most common drunken display. One time, I walked Arthur away from the bar and back to his sleeping quarters while he tried to fight off an overwhelming sadness. "I'm not a good person," he slurred repeatedly. I never disagreed with him.

"You ever hear from old Arthur Langley?" Rich asked me as we maneuvered our rig into the area where the rest of the chuckwagon racers were setting up camp.

"Shit, I was just thinking about that old bastard," I chuckled. "Nope, haven't talked to him in ages. I don't really go out of my way to see him, either."

"I guess he brags you up every time you win," Rich informed me. "He'll be around town or around the stockyards saying that he helped you get going and he taught you how to drive a wagon."

"His main critique was always to call me a stupid farmer," I said. Rich laughed and I added, "But he did give me DS. I never paid a dime for him. And I suppose he's right, I never would've gotten into this world if he didn't hire me to be an outrider." I gave my head a small shake. "Still think he's a goofy old prick, though," I concluded.

"Won't argue with you on that one," Rich said.

Rich and I had conversed in an easy, light-hearted manner for the entire drive. We bullshitted about cattle prices and what was going on at the stockyards. I hadn't been to my office since Philip died so Rich filled me in on the goings on. We also enjoyed long moments of silence where we would roll the windows down and smoke and get lost in our own thoughts. Amicable silence is the true marker of a real friendship.

Now we stepped out of the truck and simultaneously stretched our limbs out after the long drive. Then Rich stepped into the horse trailer, untying one horse at a time and handing them to me on the ground. I would tie each horse to the side of the trailer, leaving the lead shank long enough that they could reach their heads down and get a few bites of grass. When all the horses were unloaded, I set off to find a water hose and fill up my buckets. I made three trips back and forth, carrying buckets and setting one down in front of each horse. I then studied each horses' flank area to see if they were ganted up at all. If they looked tucked up, I would throw them a flake of hay. It is a continuous process trying to keep weight on a thoroughbred horse. They have to be in good enough shape to stretch out and run but they also need the strength and the muscle to have stamina enough to be a chuckwagon horse. It is a fine line that chuckwagon drivers need to balance in order to keep their horses at peak performance and health. I ultimately decided that they all looked full and content and I would wait until after the race to feed them.

Once the horses were looked after, I realized I hadn't ate or drank anything all day. I had been forgetting to eat regularly since Philip died and now I barely noticed when I was hungry but Rich was probably starving. That's when it fully dawned on me how much Rich was doing for me by coming on this trip. He was here 100% for me and whatever I needed at the moment. No complaints, no requests. Just a friend staying beside a friend in a time of need. I didn't want to admit it, but I was sure happy Maggie had called Rich and asked him to go with me.

"You want to get a burger?" I asked Rich as he patiently leaned against the hood of my truck.

"Thought you'd never ask," he said and we walked together towards the arena to find a concession stand.

Nearly everyone I saw stopped me to offer their condolences. Although Philip wasn't involved in rodeo, plenty of people knew him. The agriculture community in Alberta is tight knit between the rodeo cowboys, the ranchers, the farmers, and the horse trainers. Each discipline seems to overlap between the others. Philip left an impression on nearly everyone he came across so even if people had only briefly met him before, they took the time to stop me and say a kind word about their encounter. I had never been more grateful for the kind souls that encompass the agricultural world. The majority of them truly were some of the most compassionate people in the world and we were a tight knit group. No one said anything that made me feel better but when Philip was at the forefront of my mind, it was nice to know that he was on other people's mind, too. Hearing his name openly praised was all the comfort I could ask for before I got ready for a race.

Rich and I ordered some cheeseburgers and sat down on a picnic bench beside the arena. The stands were filled with cheering people of all different ages. A rodeo clown was in the middle of the arena performing a dance that was making everyone laugh and clap. The night air was starting to settle in around us and a generally good feeling was coming with it, as all of the surrounding people enjoyed the rodeo atmosphere. Rich and I bit into our cheeseburgers and watched the rodeo progress. The Saddle Bronc Riding was about to start – one of my favorite events to watch. You might not expect a reckless cowboy on top of a broncy, snorting horse to be an event of beauty, but that's certainly what it is. A good bronc ride almost always turns into a thing of rhythm and symmetry; instead of the horse and cowboy working against one another, they end up moving together and they both put their entire hearts into the ride. There is a contrasting sense of freedom and sense of security in a bronc ride. Freedom comes from the bucking horse doing what comes most naturally to them. Security comes from knowing that they will do that same thing every single time and you can always respect the effort.

Rich and I made small comments to each other as we watched. "Nice horse," he would point out. "Dang good spur ride," I would say.

After the last bite of my supper, I wiped my hands on my pants and got ready to stand up. "I'd better go start getting ready. Meet you after."

Rich just nodded. "I'll be here," he said. "Might even have myself a beer or two."

"Wouldn't expect you to pass the time any differently," I returned as I started to walk away.

I got back to the trailer to find my two outriders already brushing off my horses. I shook hands with them both and patted them affectionately on the shoulders as I did so. Craig and Cody Lockett were two young brothers that had been outriding for me the past couple years. They were good boys – young men now. They always traveled to the chuckwagon races by themselves and brought their own outrider horses. They would switch their horses out quickly in between heats and work for as many drivers as they could. They were dependable, hard-working, and easy to get along with. The very first time they raced for me, Craig noticed one of my horses had over reached while he was running and nicked himself on the backside of his front foot. Both of the boys helped me hose him down with cold water and walk him out until we were all confident it was nothing serious. I gave the boys a bonus when I paid them that night for being so attentive and helping out. They had been loyal and riding for me at every single race since then.

"You guys don't have to do this," I motioned my head to my horses. I knew they had a full workload just getting their own horses saddled and warmed up. I usually got my horses ready and hitched up to the chuckwagon by myself.

"It's no problem," Cody shrugged.

"How are you doing?" Craig asked. I knew by the tone of his voice that he was asking how I was holding up after Philip's death. I figured Craig and Cody might have more empathy than anyone. You rarely ever saw the two brothers apart. One always came with the other. They had a bond that was strong enough to notice in the small exchanges they made with one another. You could see how close they were by the unspoken words, the glances they shared, and the easy energy that always surrounded them. They reminded me of Philip and myself.

"Oh... I'll be alright," I said. I knew I didn't have to lie to them.

They both nodded but neither of them said a word. They didn't need to.

"I still get goosebumps thinking about the Stockyards crew running his cows down the street. I don't know who planned that but it was sure as hell a good way to honor a guy," Cody said.

I smiled then, recalling the memory. I was grateful that I was able to associate a good memory with that day.

"Shit, I didn't know you boys were there. Sorry I missed you," I said.

Craig gave me a funny look as he squinted his eyebrows while turning up the corners of his mouth in a half smile. "We wouldn't have missed it," he said. Then he carried on getting my horses and team ready – going above and beyond his paid duties just to show support in the best way he knew how.

CHAPTER TWENTY-ONE

brutal

My horses moved and swayed but remained in their spot in the arena. All four of them were ready to run but they respected my hold on the reins and never took a step forward. I spoke in a low monotone, just loud enough for them to hear. "Eassyyyyy, boys," I repeated.

We were on Barrel 1 which meant we were closest to the racetrack entrance. I loved being on barrel 1. We would swoosh through the required figure eight pattern as smoothly as possible and then we would take off towards the track and hopefully earn a spot on the inside rail. The three other chuckwagons were lined up to my right on Barrels 2, 3, and 4. I was up against a tough heat. I knew I was going to need the advantage of being on Barrel 1 if I wanted to win this one.

I tightened my grip on the leather reins as I braced for the horn to go off which would start the race. Before the horn had a chance to blow, the horses on Barrel 3 lunged forward. The driver had lost control of his wagon, which can easily happen. I tried to let my horses and my body relax as I waited for wagon 3 to reposition his horses after he slowed them up. In a tough heat like this one, everyone wants their horses to be on the muscle and ready to go. The driver on Barrel 3 probably pushed the limits just a little too much. When your horses already naturally want to run, it's a fine line when it comes to preparing them for a race. I tended to lean more towards the other side. I would let my horses relax as much as possible before a race. I trusted that their conditioning, their feed program, and their experience would all kick in when the horn blew. But it was always personal preference and each driver had to find what worked best for their style.

The lunge forward on Barrel 3 had given time for the suspense and anticipation to build. The announcer used the opportunity to talk up each of the four drivers. Many of the party crowd that hadn't been paying attention earlier were now focused on the arena, curious as to what was going on. Energy is always contagious in an atmosphere like that. I could feel the hairs on the back of my neck begin to stand up.

This was going to be a good one. For Philip.

The horn blasted through the air and my horses responded with a lurch forward. I guided them through my two barrels in the figure eight – one turn to the right and then one turn to the left. Tight enough to not take up too much time but wide enough to keep the barrels standing and avoiding a penalty. My horses moved swiftly and I gassed them towards the track entrance after completing the pattern. The wagon whipped out as the power of my horses increased at my command. I was sure that I would be heading for the inside rail but the wagon coming off of barrel 2 was already beating me to it. I knew I was going to be pinched off and forced to take second place on the inside rail. I eased my horses up as slightly as possible but they didn't want to slow down. They wanted to be in first place just as badly as I did. I was forced to pull hard on the reins. Running too close to another wagon is a safety hazard and there are unwritten rules of respect out on the track. I looked over both shoulders to gauge the position of the other two wagons. The wagon that came off barrel 4 was only slightly behind me and the wagon from barrel 3 was nowhere to be seen. He must have had more problems at the figure eight.

I decided to make my move early to win this thing. I steered my horses away from the rail and put them in a position to pass the wagon in the lead. We were just rounding the first corner of the track. When the track straightened out, I asked my horses for the big push that we needed to move up beside the lead. They all visibly stretched out and buckled down, happy to do what I asked. We steadily gained speed and moved up beside the first wagon, inch by inch. I squinted my eyes to properly see as we flew through the air. All I could hear was the rushing wind and the clanging of my wagon. My favorite sound in the world.

Just as the horses in the back of my team were approaching the front of the wagon to my left, I heard a loud crack. Then another crack followed almost simultaneously. My horses suddenly and drastically slowed which caused my wagon to wobble and shake. The wagon almost flipped completely over as I felt the back wheels coming up off the ground. I was propelled out of the front seat and went shooting through the air, slamming roughly on the soft ground of the track ahead of my team which were now completely stopped.

I laid on the dirt, quickly realizing that I couldn't breathe. I still couldn't breathe. What was happening to me? I was almost about to reach a state of panic when my breath came back in a loud, sucking noise as I gasped for air, trying desperately to make it reach my lungs. The wind had been knocked out of me.

As my breath returned, my mind turned to my team. I slowly stood up and surveyed the mess behind me. My horses were all staying put in one spot, even though a few were fidgeting and spooking. I silently sent a prayer up, thanking God that they were as broke as they were. My wagon was no longer behind the horses, as it should be, but it was swayed out to the side so that the horses and the wagon formed a 90-degree angle. All of the safety straps that hooked the horses up to the wagon must have broke on one side. But they did their job; they kept the wagon from flipping over.

The other wagon – the one I had just been trying to pass - wasn't far from my horses. It was still hooked up but the wagon was slanted and crooked. It looked like a wheel was missing.

I started to walk towards my horses just as all of the safety riders were approaching. The safety riders were men on horses who stood around the outside of the racetrack. They were called upon for many different things. They acted as judges because they had a close view and could make sure no rules were broken out on the track. They surveyed the races. They also went riding head first into any wrecks to try and sort things out. They were mostly fearless and they all had good horse sense.

I was just about to reach my team and pet my lead horse on the forehead when one of the safety riders approached my horses from the opposite direction and muttered, "Son of a bitch."

I was still a little out of it but I heard the despair in his voice loud and clear. I hustled over to his view point and saw what he was looking at.

My heart sank. My stomach tightened in a knot. I thought I might be sick.

I had found one of the spokes from the missing wheel on the other wagon. It was lodged directly into my horses' lower hip. Lower down from the spoke, my horses' leg was dangling at a strange angle. I knew it was broken.

I could feel the eyes of the safety riders on me as I walked up to my horse. He was a big, black beauty with only a small white star on his forehead. I called him Hubba Bubba – Bubba for short - because the man I'd bought him from had been chewing Hubba Bubba nonstop and I always laughed to think about the grown man popping the pink gum in his mouth and blowing bubbles. I approached Bubba slowly and avoided his back leg. I went to his head and softly stroked his neck.

"It's okay, Bub, you're gonna be okay," I told him. I let the words fall out of my mouth and I repeated them over. But even as I said them, I knew they were a lie. From the moment I'd seen the broken leg dangling, I knew what the outcome was going to be.

I wanted to cry. I wanted to forget about the rest of the men standing around me and just lay my head in my hands and weep. I also wanted to scream and fight. I wanted to slink over to the chuckwagon driver at the broken wagon and knock his front teeth out for being stupid enough to race in a wagon that was on the brink of falling apart. I wanted someone to pay for what had just happened. I wanted to pinpoint it on a singular person who was to blame. My horse was about to die and I wanted it to be anyone's fault but my own. It couldn't be my fault. I'd needed to come here; I had to race for Phillip. Chuckwagon racing was the only thing in the world that could save me and make me feel like myself again. For a brief moment, I wondered what God was doing.

But I didn't fight anyone and I didn't get down on my knees and pray. Instead, I did what I always do. I softly tried to comfort the injured.

The safety riders were unhooking my team of horses. Everyone was easing around gently and making small movements. No one wanted any of the horses to spook or move. My outriders – Cody and Craig were beside me. They never spoke to me but instead focused on Bubba. "Easy now, Bubba, that's a boy," Cody said as he unhooked his harness.

Rich was there next. He had drove my truck and trailer over and slowly backed it up to my horses, as close as he could get.

I remained with my feet rooted firmly beside Bubba's head as the slow hum of activity continued on around me. Finally, Rich laid a hand on my shoulder. "I got directions to the vet clinic. Let's load him on the trailer," he said. When I met Rich's eyes, he startled a little bit. "Are you alright?" he asked me in a low tone.

I turned away from Rich's gaze without saying a word. It was all I could do to just stay on my feet. I felt like death was swarming all around me and I couldn't get away from it. Couldn't make sense of it. Couldn't feel what I needed to feel because a hundred eyes were on me. Even though Bubba was at the forefront of my mind, I was still strangely aware of the crowd of people who had paid money to come to watch the chuckwagon races. I noticed that the safety riders and numerous other people had all stood in a broad circle around Bubba, but tightly grouped together to try and block the viewpoint of the spectators. Everyone wanted to stop the crowd from seeing a horse with a broken leg. We were supposed to pretend that everything was under control. I wanted to push them all aside. I was losing a great horse; wouldn't the crowd understand that my heart was broken? Wouldn't they have sympathy? Certainly, this was more terrible for me than for any random person in the crowd. I was the one who had trained and cared for Bubba for the last 6 years of his life. They didn't even know this horse – would never understand his idiosyncrasies, his heart and his try. They had never appreciated how strong and sleek he looked in the summer time or how he always leaped on to the trailer like he couldn't wait to get where ever it was we were going. Why was everyone acting like his imminent death needed to be concealed from the crowd but it was something I should be able to handle?

Above all else, I wanted the crowd to know that death was an unavoidable part of life. Best to be aware of that lesson now. Because sooner or later, we're all confronted with the brutal god damn reality of something or someone dying.

This race was supposed to be something great; I was supposed to win for Philip. I could've handled losing. But this was all too much. I felt like if I wasn't careful, death was going to swallow me whole.

CHAPTER TWENTY-TWO

desperate

I gripped the steering wheel and kept my eyes planted on the road ahead. Rich and I were about 6 hours in to the 8-hour drive home. We were carrying one less horse in the trailer than we'd had on the drive up.

Rich had offered to drive but I knew that I needed the distraction. I wouldn't have been able to sit in the passenger seat without feeling the weight of the world pushing in on me. The drive had been mostly silent. We exchanged a few words but I couldn't bring myself to talk much. I just wanted to be home.

"There," Rich pronounced, breaking the silence. He held up the piece of black mane that he had been fiddling with for the last couple hours. It was braided into a fancy, four-piece braid with a leather string wound through it. Rich then leaned over and used the leather string to tie the braided mane onto my keys.

I reached up and touched it, running the braid through my fingertips a few times. The coarse black hair felt like a source of comfort. When the vet had confirmed what we already knew about Bubba's fate, Rich had the presence of mind to pull his knife out and gently cut off a piece of mane. I felt an overwhelming rush of gratitude for everything Rich had done throughout the whole process.

I kept toying with the braid and cleared my throat. "Thanks," was all I managed to say. I had been trying to keep myself together. I'd cried enough in the last few days. It was time for a man to start acting like a man.

"No sweat, pal," Rich said lightly.

I thought we were going to return to silence but then Rich piped up again, "I've been thinking," he said. I had known Rich long enough to understand that when he said that phrase, he was preparing to dive into one of his infamous monologues. Rich could still out talk most anyone I knew.

"That right?" I asked as I looked over at him with one raised eyebrow.

"Yup. I've been thinking about Philip... Can't seem to think about anything else, actually. When I got the phone call about what happened, all I kept saying over and over to Georgia, was *how could this have happened? How could he have wrecked that bad in the driveway?* I've been racking my brain, wondering what happened and wondering what you or me or anyone else could have done to save him... Have I told you that I was there playing pool with him in town on that last night?" Rich asked.

That shocked me. "No..." I startled, "I never knew that."

Rich scratched his chin as tears pooled up in the corners of his eye, but he carried on talking. "Well, I was. We played three games against some hay farmers. We won a game, lost a game, then won the tie breaker," Rich said, causing us both to smile a little. "But neither of us was drunk. We were just sipping on some social beers, having a good night but not getting carried away. I would've told him to come stay on my couch instead of driving home if I thought he had drunk too much. I know I would've."

I wasn't sure if Rich was trying to convince himself as he told the story but the pooled-up tears had begun streaming down his face. His voice remained fairly steady as he sniffed a little, gathered his thoughts, and continued, "Philip said he was ready to go home because there wasn't a girl in sight in the whole bar. I told him he oughta think about settling down so that he'd always have a good woman to go home to, like I did. He laughed me off and waved goodbye and said, *I live too damn fast for settling down*. I watched him climb into your truck when I was walking to my own vehicle. Those are probably the very last words he said."

At this point, tears were running down my face, too. I never wiped them away. Just let them pour out of me while I relished in the strange solace washing over me by the words Rich spoke.

"When I was trying to make sense of things, I kept telling Georgia that I shouldn't have let Philip drive home. I kept saying to her that I should've made him stay with us. But even in all my grief and confusion, I knew that wasn't right. I couldn't have ever stopped Philip from *living fast*, just like he said. Living fast was exactly Philip's fate. That's how God designed him. Every single person at his funeral said something about it. It's how he was known, how he was loved, and it's who he was meant to be. Philip became exactly who God wanted him to be. That's what made him so genuine and so powerful all at the same time."

I nodded along at this point, knowing that Rich was speaking the truth. Every word was resonating within me. I felt it deep in my bones, in my soul.

"And I guess the reason this is all making sense to me now is because of what happened to Hubba Bubba last night. I know you feel responsible, like you should have been able to save him or somehow keep him safe. Hubba Bubba's accident was just as much a freak fuckin' deal as Philip's accident was. The only way we could've kept either of them safe would have been to stop them from living the way God created them to live. Hubba Bubba would still be alive if he hadn't been on that racetrack last night. There's no denying that. But that horse loved nothing more than to run. Anyone with any horse sense at all knows that. To keep a thoroughbred from running would be one of the cruelest acts we could ever do. That would be like keeping a bird in a cage all its life. Just wouldn't be right; it goes against nature."

Rich gave his head a slight shake, gathering his thoughts. "And Philip would still be alive if you hadn't let him go to town or if I hadn't let him leave town. But doing that would've been just as cruel and no way for a man like Philip to live. Philip liked to live just as fast as Hubba Bubba, DS, and every other one of your thoroughbreds." Rich paused again, building up for the final comment of his speech. "And who the hell would we be to ever try and stop them?"

I had known Rich for 22 years before that moment. We remained friends until our dying days as old, worn-out men. But in all that time, I never heard him give a better monologue than that.

I finally wiped away the tears on my cheeks. We rolled down our windows and each savored a cigarette. Death was still swarming around me but I no longer felt like it was going to swallow me whole. I felt better than I had in weeks.

When we finished the last few drags on our smokes and rolled the windows back up, I started talking. I didn't speak as eloquently or poetically as Rich had. But I spoke my truth. It came out in halting, jarring puzzle pieces. I talked about my last conversation with Philip and how we had been discussing Jake. I said that Jake's speech at the funeral had made me prouder of him than ever before and how Jake had come outside to work at 5:30 yesterday morning. I said I couldn't quite place my finger on it, but I thought that maybe Jake was becoming a new man and if he wasn't, I was still going to try to be more patient with him as we went along because that's what Philip had wanted. I also spoke about Maggie's father giving me the keys to a new truck. I said I couldn't quite understand why a generous act had left me feeling so worthless. We debated this topic for the remainder of the drive. Rich had a complicated past in regards to money. He had grown up wealthy without ever questioning it until it was all taken away. Rich's fortune had been seized by the government when his father was found guilty of embezzlement. My fortune was going to be handed to me one day through inheritance even though I had done nothing to earn it except fall in love.

Money was nothing more than a matter of circumstances in both mine and Rich's lives. It came and went as easily as the seasons. We couldn't control it any more than we could control the weather. I think that's what made both of so apt to try and control what we could in our lives – which was working hard and being good men.

Rich never showed an ounce of jealousy or envy when I talked about Maggie's family money. He was as carefree and easy-spirited as ever. At one point, he nonchalantly added, "Speaking from personal experience, it's true when they say money can't buy happiness. But it damn sure can buy a nice truck," and he tapped the dash of the pickup.

When we finally made it home, I found myself looking forward to seeing Maggie's face. I knew I had been distant with her and I knew she was verging on the edge of desperation. She was trying to clamor back into the place of my heart that she was used to. I don't know why I had been reluctant to let her in. I was trying to numb the pain of losing Philip and I knew that she was the one person in the world that could evoke deep feelings out of me. She sparked more emotion in me than I had ever known. If I let my walls down around her and let the pain flood in, I wasn't sure I could handle it.

We eased the truck and trailer to a stop by the barn. Georgia's car was parked up by the house. She was waiting for Rich to give him a ride home. Rich had called both Georgia and Maggie from the vet clinic to explain what had happened. I hadn't talked to Maggie or Jake yet. I was too focused on Bubba to think of anything else so I let Rich handle it.

I walked back to the trailer door and swung it open. I felt the uneasy pang in my gut once again when I saw the empty spot in the trailer. I swallowed it down to focus on the horses in front of me. They were still alive and well and they needed looking after. Life carries on. Rich helped me unload everything and tie them to the trailer. I hosed down all of their legs with cold water and then got a spray bottle filled with witch hazel to apply to the wet legs. All of the horses stood patiently; they knew this routine well. I always did this when I got home from a race to help their bodies adjust after the trailer drive and the running.

Rich stood off to the side and watched me work. Jake had come out of the house and they were chatting easily. I couldn't hear most of what they were saying but Jake was smiling and laughing and I liked the look of that.

Georgia came out of the house next, followed shortly after by Maggie. Her hair was tangled and whipping around in the breeze. I vaguely wondered why it wasn't braided.

Georgia and I approached Jake and Rich about the same time. Georgia smiled and gave Rich a light peck before coming over and giving me a hug.

I was about to suggest all of us eating supper together but Georgia cut me off before I had the chance. "Rich, hun, we'd better get going." Then she caught the look in his eyes and added, "I left the crock pot on high at home. Our pot roast will be dried right out if we don't get back soon."

"Can't have that, can we? Nothing worse than a dried-out pot roast," Rich said somberly enough for everyone to know he was being sarcastic.

That's when Maggie reached our small gathering and I realized for the first time how pissed off she looked. Her hair was a mess, she had no make-up on, and her arms were crossed. She didn't speak as she walked up. Rich's social graces never failed him and he smoothly reached an arm around Maggie, giving her a half hug while her arms remained firmly planted across her chest. Rich told her that he was sorry they had to leave so soon and we would get together later this week. Maggie shook out of her trance enough to softly thank Rich and Georgia and say good bye but she never smiled.

Before Rich and Georgia had even begun pulling out of the yard, Maggie turned to face me.

"You never called," she said in a flat accusation.

I looked at her a moment, not sure how to proceed. Jake was still standing close by and listening. "That's what you're so mad about?" I finally asked. "Rich told me that he talked to you about everything."

She grew visibly angrier, scrunching her face up. "Oh, come on, Charlie. Don't pull that on me. Don't act like it isn't justified for me to be upset. Don't make me seem crazy," she sputtered. She was talking fast and shaking her head. I couldn't help thinking that she was, in fact, acting crazy.

I threw my hands up in an exasperated shrug. "I don't know what you want from me at this point. Just calm down a little," I said.

Apparently, that was the wrong thing to say. She rolled her head back and started in on me. "We BOTH know that you would've called before. You ALWAYS would have called. You're pushing me AWAY. Why are you doing this?" Her voice escalated and teetered towards shrill. My heart softened and I knew I needed to apologize. I was about to say all the words that would have made things between us better when she threw the dagger.

She looked directly at me and said, "I told you not to go. But you still had to get away from me. And Bubba was killed because of it."

All of my tender feelings and hopes of reconciliation immediately dissipated. I couldn't bear the weight of hearing that a horse died because of me. It didn't matter if it was valid or justified. It was too much for me to cope with and I couldn't confront my own shame. I had always considered myself a horseman but if doing what I loved caused a horse to break a leg, what did that make me? The peaceful feeling that Rich brought about in his monologue was completely gone. It was now replaced with a hot, thumping rage that I felt deep in my chest.

That's how easy it is for a divide to come into a marriage. A wedge can be drove between two people so quickly that they don't even have time to stop it. My disengagement towards Maggie in the aftermath of Philip's death had the process in motion. Her words had just delivered the final blow. She stood in front of me with neither of us saying a word. I stared at her with squinted eyes and a clenched jaw. She looked as if she might speak again but I didn't want to hear whatever it was she might say. I spun on my heels and walked toward my truck. I heard nothing but the sound of the crunching gravel underneath the leather soles of my cowboy boots. The same thumping anger was still coursing through me. I got in my truck and slammed the door shut as hard as I could before driving off.

I was too lost in my own world to hear Maggie's soft, desperate voice when she said, "Charlie. Wait."

CHAPTER TWENTY-THREE

disapproval

When I returned to work at the stockyards, I was going through a rollercoaster of emotions on the inside. On the outside, I was keeping my same calm, relaxed demeanor that I had become known for. I was like a duck sitting on water. Calm and cool on the surface with my feet flapping a hundred miles an hour below the water.

Every day, I felt stabbing tinges of pain during the moments when Philip would have been present. The chair Philip used to sit in at my office remained overwhelmingly empty. I think people were avoidant of taking Philip's place – as if that chair had a sacred power now. I wanted to tell everyone that I would feel better if they'd just sit the hell down and talk about Philip instead of attempting to honor him by standing up and not mentioning his name. But, of course, I remained collected.

As much as it hurt to be at the stockyards without Philip, I still preferred it to facing Maggie at home. I began working longer hours, consumed with the paperwork at my desk. The steady drone of numbers, loans, payments, and applications was a welcome numbness. When I was home, tension between Maggie and I was at an all-time high. We barely spoke to each other and when we did, it came out in sharp, accusing tones which was different than we had ever spoken to one another throughout our entire marriage. We did our best to be pleasant in front of Jake but we each began spending more time with him one-on-one as opposed to being together as a family.

When I finished a long day inside my office, I would wander to the back pens and help where ever someone was needed. The physical work cleared my head. Then when there would be no more work to do, I would find myself with anyone who was having mixed drinks or beers. The alcohol blurred my mind again before I returned home. On several occasions, I would drink enough to pass out in a chair for the night without returning home.

The only three people who truly knew me and understood me during that time in my life were Rich, Gene, and Frank. The three of them took turns periodically checking in on me. They were the only people who would speak freely about Philip and not tip toe around me.

People have a funny reaction to grief. When you first lose someone, everyone you know offers their condolences and their regrets. Even people who had never met Philip were expressing their sympathy for my loss. But after a certain amount of time, it becomes taboo to mention the name of the person you lost. All of a sudden, no one spoke about Philip. No one asked me how I was doing. Because after the initial grieving stage, you're supposed to be a man. You're supposed to be strong and stoic and no one dares to mention grief in case of accidentally revealing that you might not be as strong as you are pretending to be.

Often times, Rich would have one or two mixed drinks with me at night before attempting to gently coax me into going home. Sometimes I listened and sometimes I didn't but he never pushed or judged no matter which way I went.

Gene would bring his red heeler Hank into my office or ask me to take Hank out back for a while to work cows. He would groan and complain about his joints and say he needed to take ten in my office and that Hank needed to keep working. I always took him up on these opportunities. I would affectionately pat Hank on the head and admire how he could turn his aggression on in an instant when we began chasing cattle.

Frank was retired but he still found reasons to come to the stockyards on a regular basis. When I took time off after Philip's crash, Frank took over for me. He never bothered me with a single question or concern during that time. He handled all the work seamlessly and figured everything out in his own way if he ever had any problems.

I was currently sitting at my desk and looking over a ledger filled with Frank's neat, precise handwriting. One of my favorite characteristics about Frank was how he always had time to visit and get to know everyone he came across. He also always had the time to make his paperwork perfectly meticulous. All of his numbers were straightly aligned. He put a short dash through every number 7 that he wrote down – a habit that always stood out to me because I had never seen anyone write a line through their 7s. I asked him about it once and he laughed and said that how someone wrote a 7 was a dead giveaway for what generation they were from.

Frank was heavy on my mind as I looked over the paperwork on my desk so it startled me when his face popped in my door.

"Hope I'm not bothering you," he said after noticing the look on my face.

"No, not at all. I was actually just thinking about you," I said.

Frank let himself into my office and stood inside the door. He still wore his short-brimmed white hat. When I had first met Frank, he oozed charisma. Now old age had softened him a bit. His walk had more of a shuffle in it than a swagger. But he was still good, ol' Frank. He could charm anyone just by being himself.

"I thought I would stop in to have a visit with you in your office but I think we may have more excitement out back," Frank gestured his head towards the sorting pens and motioned for me to go with him. "That is, if you aren't too busy at your desk," he added.

"Oh, I can probably manage to tear myself away," I said as I got up and we walked to the door that took us on a catwalk outside. The catwalk was high enough above the pens that you could see a long distance out but low enough that you could get a good look at the cattle in the nearby pens. The catwalk was mainly used for order buyers or ranchers coming to scope everything out and take a look at what they might buy. The catwalk was also used for tire kickers who would never actually raise their hands and bid on anything but still congregated at the stockyards to see what was selling.

As soon as Frank and I stepped outside, the low, constant mooing filled my ears. That sound had become as familiar to me as my own breath but it still filled me up every time I immersed myself in the back pens. As we walked along, it didn't take me long to realize what Frank had been so eager to watch.

"Henderson's brought their heifers in, did they?" I asked.

Frank nodded and smiled. We didn't need to say much else to each other because we both understood what that meant. Henderson's had a big ranch south of Calgary and they had become famous at the Stockyards. They were good people and they raised well-built stock but that didn't have anything to do with their notorious last name. The Henderson's reputation preceded them because every year when they brought their heifers in to sell, all hell broke loose. They raised some of the wildest, snortiest, chase-you-down, hook-you-while-you're-down, cattle that you ever did see. The Henderson's owned more land than they needed to for the amount of cows that they ran. Because those cows had so much space, they didn't often see human lives. And if a cow has never seen a human before, they can be awfully scared of 'em. For whatever reason, Henderson's heifers always got on the fight. Maybe it was the water out there or maybe it was a bad line of genetics but you could guarantee that their heifers would cause some ruckus when they came to town. Luckily, Henderson's sold their bull calves privately so we never saw them come through the auction mart.

Frank and I found a good view to watch the goings on and we perched up with our arms leaning against the top rail and our heads peering down below. A group of men slowly convened around us. We all muttered a few remarks to each other but mainly waited in anticipation and passed a pack of smokes around.

Finally, a young buck that hadn't been working at the Stockyard's too long came strolling up. I couldn't remember his name but I knew he was a nice kid, if not a touch on the lazy side. I smiled as I had a good idea of what would soon happen.

"SENDING UP PEN 12," he hollered.

"SEND 'EM UP!!" an unknown voice hollered back.

The youngster swung the gate open and turned around to chain it up so that the pen opened up into the alley. Normally, he would chain it up and then walk into the small holding pen to chase out whatever was in there and continue to chase them up the alley towards the sale ring. But this time, with his back turned to the pen as he ran the chain through the latch, a black heifer came straight towards him with her tail in the air. He might have heard her blowing air through her nose or maybe his instincts kicked in but he looked over his shoulder, saw what was coming, and attempted to crawl up onto the fence in a flustered scramble. The heifer caught a piece of him and pushed her head into the back of his knees, slamming into the fence in the process.

"Whoa, you crazy bitch!" the young kid yelled as he finally dropped down onto the other side of the fence and limped around in a circle, rubbing his knees and cursing.

The peanut gallery surrounding Frank and I roared with laughter. I sputtered out a few chuckles, sending cigarette smoke out into the air. The kid looked up at all of us watching. He knew better than to throw fuel on a fire with this crowd – it wouldn't do him any good to get mad. Instead, he let out a small laugh and said, "Guess it would've been too much for you gentleman to offer a warning, hey?"

Frank was the first to respond. He said, "Son, it wouldn't be a proper initiation ritual if we gave you a warning. Welcome to the Stockyards!!" He opened his arms out wide and proud as he smiled down at the kid.

"Yah, alright," the kid muttered as he still rubbed his knees. Then he stood up, gave us a wave and a half-hearted tip of his hat, and said, "Happy to be here," with only a touch of sarcasm seeping through his voice.

I laughed and nodded at him which was my way of giving my approval for the way he handled the situation. "Son, I hate to break it to you but that's just the beginning of it. Henderson's bring in about 80 head and they're all the same." Then I threw down the package of smokes that we'd been passing around earlier. He caught the little carton and looked up at me questioningly. "That's for when you need to gather your composure. Sometimes with cattle you gotta know when to keep working 'em and you gotta know when to sit back and have a smoke," I said.

"Thanks, Mr. Hyde," the boy said as he gave me a little salute before carrying on.

We all watched him go and then I turned towards Frank and said, "It seems like I've barely blinked and I went from being the boy working down in the alley to the man standing and watching and being referred to as a Mr."

Frank raised his eyebrows at me and said, "It's even more of a shock when you become the old, retired man that people offer their seat to and take pity upon."

"Never known anyone to pity you but I can quit giving you a chair when you come to my office to sit down if that makes you feel any younger," I said.

"Never mind, now. Speaking of old men, where's Gene?" Frank peered around and then we both began to scan the alleys before we spotted Gene's stiff figure. His red heeler, Hank, was crouched down right in front of him.

"Hank will have his work cut out for him with these heifers today," I commented. Then Frank and I both parted from the other men and moved along the catwalk to get a better view of Gene working his dog.

They often say with dogs that their bark is bigger than their bite. That wasn't the case with Hank or any working heeler dog that I'd ever seen. Hank's bite was definitely bigger than his bark. But if you think about it, that's the way it needed to be. A cow or heifer or steer is a lot bigger than a dog. Aggression is the only way a dog is going to over-power a cow. To some people, it might seem slightly vicious to watch a dog bite a cow's heels in order to chase them forward. But to me, it was just animal nature. And to watch a good dog work was a sight of beauty. A good dog is nature's finest example of how animals establish a pecking order. The dog is smart enough to understand what the task at hand is. The dog knows that the cow needs to go forward down an alley. When the cow doesn't understand what the task at hand is or is just refusing to cooperate, a dog can come make it clear to that cow. We can't talk to the animals we're working with every day but we sure can communicate with them in our own ways.

And, let me tell you, Hank was making himself real clear to those Hendersen heifers.

They were kicking at him and trying to hook him but Hank just kept moving in circles around them and then darting in behind them at the right time to shoot them forward. He would bite and growl. His lips were raised, showing his teeth. Then Gene would call him back and Hank would sit contently at Gene's side and raise his head to feel the quick strokes that he knew would come from Gene's calloused hands.

Frank and I watched the whole goings on with an easy conversation bouncing back and forth between us. We laughed at the close calls between the heifers and the men working and occasionally called down smart remarks. We admired the men who handled the heifers efficiently and occasionally yelled down words of praise. But mostly we just admired the day and spoke softly to each other.

Eventually, I said, "Ya know, the only thing missing right now is a couple ice cold beers. Why don't I run downtown and pick us up a case?"

I tried to ignore the brief look of concern that flashed through Frank's eyes. But he agreed with a slight nod of his head, "Sure. Sure, I'd have a beer with you."

I eased down the catwalk and jogged down the stairs to start walking towards my truck. The beer store was only a short drive away. When I walked in, I headed directly to the 12 packs of Alberta Genuine Draft and reached my hand out to grab a case. As my hand was in midair, I noticed a tremble and shake before it made contact with the handle of the beer case. I paused a moment with an uneasy feeling in my stomach. Frank's look of concern and the tremble in my hand were hard to ignore. But I gave my shoulders a slight shake and picked up the beer case and drove back to the auction mart while pretending not to notice how intensely I wanted to crack open a beer for the short drive.

When I saw Frank standing in the same place, I handed him a beer first and then cracked open my own and took three long, slow drinks. I felt my body relax just a little bit. Frank's eyes were on me but I never looked in his direction.

Then Frank clinked his beer can against my own. "I was going to give you a *cheers* but you started drinking before I had the chance." There was no judgment or sarcasm in Frank's voice. He just stated the facts.

"Yah. I guess I was thirsty," I said as casually as I could.

Frank knew that he had made his point and he changed the subject in his diplomatic way. We chatted a while longer before Frank glanced past my shoulder and nodded his head towards something. "You expecting company?" he asked. I followed Frank's gaze and saw Maggie walking towards us.

"No… I wasn't," I said. Maggie approached us with a warm smile and a hug for Frank. We would never speak rudely to one another in public but the energy between us was still noticeably tense.

"What are you up to?" I finally asked.

"Oh, I just decided to stop in on my way to get groceries. I haven't swung by in a while. I already chatted with all the ladies in the office. They told me I could probably find you up here," and her eyes dropped down to look at the beer in my hand but she didn't say anything else.

Frank asked her about Jake and her cows and all the usual topics that they normally discussed. Then he finished the last drink of his beer, poured the remaining foam down on to the ground, put the empty can back in the case, and excused himself.

An uneasy silence built between Maggie and I after Frank left. She let out a big sigh and brushed the loose strands of hair away from her face and then turned towards the pens to watch the men working. She leaned against the rail with her hands hanging down.

"I've never told you this. But I saw you quite a few times before we ever spoke to each other for the first time at the movie theater," she said without ever turning to look at me.

I had no idea why Maggie had showed up at the Stockyards or what she was going to say but I certainly wasn't expecting that. She still had the innate ability to surprise me in a conversation.

"What do you mean?" I asked as I leaned against the rail with her so that we were standing shoulder to shoulder.

"Well, I used to come to the Stockyards with Dad all the time. He would sit by the ring to bid on cattle or watch or visit with people. Sometimes I sat with him but most times I would wander around and I'd usually tour about on this catwalk." She patted the steel rail a few times. "I remember the first time I saw you… You were so focused on what you were doing. You hustled but it was in your own smooth way so you never seemed like you were trying too hard. I stood up here and watched every move you made and admired the way you worked. I kept waiting for you to look up so that we could make eye contact. But you never did. You just kept working. Eventually, I grew embarrassed and gave up hope of trying to catch your eye. I came back a few more times and always saw you but never could get you to notice me."

This was a revelation to me. She had never even mentioned any

158

of this. We had often fondly recalled our first meeting at the movie theater but Maggie had somehow always managed to leave this part of the story out. I looked thoughtfully down at the men working and tried to imagine Maggie as a young girl, looking down at me all those years ago.

"How come you're telling me this now?" I asked. She glanced over at me and it was only when I saw the hurt in her eyes that I noticed the blunt, accusatory tone I had used. That had become the rut we were in. Speaking to each other without the compassion we were accustomed to and only realizing it after the words had been said out loud.

I took a breath and started again. "I just meant… How come you never told me before? I kind of like the idea of you watching over me." I bumped her shoulder a little bit and I could see the relief wash over her face. We smiled at each other for the first time in months.

"I guess I've just come to the conclusion that you can be a little clueless in my attempts to get you to notice me. But maybe it's because my attempts aren't that noticeable. I've just been in my own head a lot and I wanted to stop in and let you know that… I'm here. And I'm trying." She let out another deep sigh and her shoulders dropped down and her body loosened as if she was physically releasing something that had been building up inside of her.

Without consciously making the choice to do so, my own body loosened beside hers. In our marriage, it had often felt like we shared the same energy. In that moment, I was convinced that we did. Together, we let go of the anger and the disconnect. We just stood side by side and decided to love one another again.

It was that hard and it was that easy.

I reached over and grabbed her hand that was still dangling loosely above the rail. I pulled it towards me and brought it up to my mouth and softly kissed her fingers. We'd had such little physical contact since Philip died that the small gesture felt electric. I wanted to pull her whole body close to mine but I was still aware enough to remember where we were and I refrained.

She must have read my mind and been feeling the same type of way because she gently cleared her throat and said, "Perhaps Jake should spend some time with Rich and Georgia tonight? I'm sure they'd all like that…"

"Never heard a better plan," I said without taking my eyes off her.

She was the first to break eye contact and she looked down at the beer case and the half drank beer I was still holding in one hand. "Charlie – " she began. I braced for what was to come. With Frank's recent disapproval still fresh in my mind, I knew I deserved whatever it was. I knew I needed to make some lifestyle changes. I was also very aware of the fact that those lifestyle changes weren't going to come easily to me at this point. How did I get here? I wasn't a drunk. But I sure had been acting like one lately.

Then Maggie reached across me, gently taking the beer from my hand, and brought it up to her lips. She drained a half a beer without stopping. She took steady gulps until her head was tilted all the way back and she tapped the beer with her finger a few times until she was sure that it was empty. When she was done, her eyes watered a little and she stifled a cough. At this point, my eyes were wide in surprise but I never said a word. She gave a little shrug and said, "Guess I was thirsty."

I laughed out loud. I had just said the same words to Frank but now they had a completely different context and meaning. "Is that right?" I asked.

"Well," she paused, testing the waters between us and our newly rekindled energy. It was as if she didn't know how far she could push her luck. "Maybe now you can drink half a beer less today than you normally would have?"

She was taking on a little piece of my burden. She wasn't judging or accusing or demanding change. Just like she said earlier, she was here and she was trying. I loved her all the more for it.

We were both shook out of the bubble we had built around us and brought back to our surroundings when right below us, the kid who had gotten smacked against the fence earlier yelled loudly, "I GOT YOU BITCHES LINED OUT NOW."

I had to stifle a laugh. I was assuming he would be watching his language if he knew my wife was right above him but I couldn't blame him for not being aware. Apparently, I had been in the same situation myself many years ago. I also knew what it was like to spend a full day working with animals that were trying to get you in any way they could. He had been bringing up snorty, wild heifers which meant that his fight or flight instincts would be in full effect. I remembered the feeling. It took a lot of years of practice before I could handle every type of livestock while still remaining calm. It was a learned practice.

"Hey, kid," I called down. He finished latching a gate and glanced up at me; immediately looking sheepish when he noticed Maggie standing there. She reassured him with a smile. "Almost done for the day," I said. "How was your Henderson heifers initiation?"

"Let's just say I'm glad I had the pack of smokes," he tapped his front shirt pocket where he was keeping the carton.

"How about a case of beer now?" I asked. I reached behind me and picked the case up that was only missing three beers. I didn't wait for him to respond before I reached it down as low as I could and dropped it to him.

He looked up at me as if I had just given him the most precious gift of his life. "You're my damn guardian angel today," he said without an ounce of sarcasm. His genuine appreciation made me laugh.

"I remember what it's like to be where you are. Just promise me you'll split the case with a buddy," I said.

He gave me a salute for the second time that day and said, "I sure can do that!" and he carried on happily swinging the beer.

"For the record," I said to Maggie, "That's the way beer is supposed to be drank. When you're young and you earned the right to cut loose after a hard day. Not when you're an aging man who has a wife and kid waiting at home. And drinking to try to feel better about yourself."

CHAPTER TWENTY-FOUR

judgements

Jake hopped up in my truck and slammed the door behind him. He barely had the door closed before he started talking. "Don't take this personal, Dad, but I am really looking forward to when I don't have to get picked up by you from school."

"No offense taken," I said. He was going to be getting his license soon and I could hardly believe he was going to be old enough to drive himself. "To tell you the truth, I'm looking forward to not sitting at this parking lot and waiting on your slow-moving ass."

"It's the girls, Dad. They flock around me so much that it's hard to break free from them," he retorted.

I snorted and shoved him in the shoulder. "That sounds exactly like something Uncle Philip would have said."

"I know," Jake smiled. I glanced over at him and smiled, too. There's no other man that I would rather have Jake trying to live up to.

"I'm taking you to Rich and Georgia's, if that's alright with you. Sounds like you guys are gonna have a game night," I said.

"Oh. Cool. That's good with me," he said. We drove in silence a moment before he asked, "What are you gonna be doin'?"

"Not much. I'll head to the house after I drop you off."

Jake raised one eyebrow. "So just you and Mom home alone tonight?"

That question and that raised eyebrow said it all. We can fool ourselves into thinking that teenagers are living in their own world. We think that our problems aren't their problems. But it doesn't work that way. Our kids are always affected by what's going on with their parents.

"Yup. Should be good," I tried to keep my tone as casual as I could. I could've tried to explain the situation but sometimes less is more. This never should've been Jake's burden to bare and I wasn't about to unload more on him than we already had.

"Cool," Jake nodded.

I dropped him off at Rich's house and then I carried on to my next stops. I hadn't been fully truthful to Jake when I said I was going straight home after this. There were a few things I needed to buy for my night.

When I finally pulled up to the house, I parked my truck in its usual spot and I walked up to the door carrying a few bags of supplies. The closer I got, the more I realized how nervous I was. For one, I'd drank about six less beers than I normally would have if I had stayed at the Stockyards and proceeded in the same manner I had been recently normalizing. For two, I wanted to get this right. There's a lot of pressure involved when you're restoring a marriage.

When I stepped in to the house, I caught a waft of a familiar tangy aroma. As I moved to the kitchen, I realized what it was. "You made ribs?" I asked Maggie as she reached up to a cupboard to grab some plates.

"Your favorite," she smiled. I met her at the table where she set the plates down and we embraced. I put a finger under her chin, lifted her face up to mine, and kissed her.

When I pulled away, I let out a little laugh and said, "Now tell me why I was almost as nervous to do that as I was the first time we ever kissed."

Maggie winked at me and said, "Could've fooled me, baby." I didn't know if she was telling the truth or not but I appreciated her saying it, either way.

We sat down to our meal and fell into conversation. I told her about Jake's comment regarding girls swarming him when I picked him up from school. She laughed but she also vented about how she knew it was actually quite true. She said Jake was going to need a serious talk from me soon. It felt so good to open up about our worries and our day-to-day concerns. I hadn't realized how much I held inside when I wasn't talking to Maggie.

When we finished eating, she stood up and began clearing our plates. I didn't offer to help with the dishes; I had to move on with my plan. I went over to the bags I had left laying by the front entrance and brought them to the living room. I pulled some candles out of one and placed them around the room, lighting them as I went. Then I took a cassette tape out of the other bag and put it in the tape player. I walked back to the kitchen where Maggie was putting leftovers into the fridge. I cleared my throat, held my hand out, and said, "How about a dance?"

She looked at me and looked at the hand I was holding out and then back up at me. "Oh. Now? A dance?" She seemed dubious.

I didn't reply and instead led her into the living room, clicked the play button and pulled her in to me. The music filled the room and we started to sway in perfect timing; the way that only a couple can do after they've been dancing together for twenty years.

Willie Nelson's melodic rasp was coming from the tape player. I had picked this song specifically for us. I held Maggie tightly to me and let Willie say all of the things that I couldn't. We moved around the dim living room as Willie sang.

And maybe I didn't hold you

All those lonely, lonely times

I guess I never told you

I am so happy that you're mine

Little things I should have said and done

I just never took the time

You were always on my mind

You were always on my mind

When the song was over, Maggie pulled away and looked up at me. Her cheeks had tears running down them. I reached up and wiped them away with my thumb.

"I'm sorry," I said. "I know that losing Philip was just as hard on you. He loved you. He… really loved you."

She nodded as more tears poured out of her eyes. "I'm sorry it all got so messed up. It was never your fault that Bubba died," she said. She sniffed and wiped her eyes. "How about one more song?" she asked.

"We can do this all night, if you want," I laughed.

"Oh, I've got a few other things that I'd like to do tonight, too. But first, let's just dance."

I smiled and took her hand again as we resumed our sway. I lost track of how many songs we danced to. I figured we had some time to make up after the last few months so I succumbed to Maggie's wishes and danced with her until she'd had enough. And just as she promised, she eventually showed me what other things she'd had on her mind.

When we woke up in the morning and returned to the kitchen, there were dirty dishes still scattered about. Maggie had a personal rule of never going to bed with a dirty kitchen but I was glad that last night she made an exception. We were wrapped up in each other just like when we were kids. As I helped her clear the remaining dishes and got the coffee going, my mind drifted to Philip – as it often did.

"I'd like to put Philip's cow herd into Jake's name," I said.

She thought about it a moment before nodding. "I love that idea."

I paused a moment to admire her. She was always beautiful in the mornings. She seemed to rise with the sun and it accentuated her best qualities. In the mornings, she was free and light and happy.

I walked up to her and gently kissed her on the forehead. "Your man loves you," I said.

She wrapped her arms around me and squeezed before replying, "I love you… And I love Willie Nelson, too."

I laughed and squeezed her back before letting her go. "I'm going to head out and pick Jake up and tell him the news about his new cow herd. Then I might take him to the Stockyards, if you haven't got anything else planned? He can work and I've got some paperwork to catch up on that I didn't do yesterday."

"Sounds good to me. I've got a full day here. We can all eat supper together at 6:30? Leftover ribs sound okay to you?" she asked.

"You know I'll never get tired of your ribs," I winked.

We parted ways. I was already dressed so I poured a cup of coffee to go and headed to the door. Maggie headed to our room to get herself ready for the day before she went outside. I knew she would check the cows, roll out a bale or two, haul out some grain, check my thoroughbreds. Those jobs would take the better part of a day but she would somehow still manage to find a countless number of other little projects to complete along the way. Then she would have supper on the table at 6:30. Our morning had been an easy-going, small exchange but it felt like a huge relief. It felt like we were back to our old selves. We had made a huge decision about Jake's life but it was so easy for us. We were on the same page again and, god damn, it felt good.

I pulled up to Rich and Georgia's house and turned the truck off. There was no sense letting it run because there was no such thing as a short visit with Rich. I let myself in their house and Rich was waiting for me in the kitchen, ready to top up my coffee cup. Jake was in the back yard with Georgia where she had him busy helping her with a few projects.

"Morning," Rich said as he filled my cup. "Well, you look awfully chipper," he added as he eyed me up with the slightest bit of a smirk tugging at the corners of his mouth.

"Me?" I feigned surprise but I knew exactly what he was hinting at. A night of reconciliation with your wife puts a bounce in your step. Rich knew it as well I knew it and every other married man knew it.

"Uh huh," Rich murmured. "Happy to have you back to your old self, anyways. I was beginning to get a little worried about you two."

"We were overdue," I agreed and then not another word was mentioned about it.

Eventually, Georgia and Jake stepped into the kitchen. Jake had a bit of white paint splattered on his sweater.

"Morning," I said to him. "Been hard at it?" I asked and nodded at the paint splatters.

Georgia piped up before Jake had a chance to talk. "I told him not to worry about it this morning. But he insisted! Got all my wooden lawn chairs touched up for me." Jake sat down in a kitchen chair at the table and Georgia affectionately stood behind him and squeezed his shoulders as she spoke. It always tore at my heart strings a little to see Georgia and Jake together. She loved him as much as she would've loved her own child and I hoped Jake was aware enough to know how lucky he was to have her in his life.

"Glad he made himself useful," I said, downplaying how proud I was.

We chatted easily and I smiled as I listened to the three of them debate who the actual champ of game night was. When I was done my coffee, I told Jake to gather up his things and we headed out the door with a wave.

We climbed into the truck and I settled in before asking Jake, "How do you feel about working at the Stockyards today? It will be a full day of loading liners."

"Sure," Jake shrugged. I was unsure what his response would be. I thought he might have preferred to spend his day off from school differently.

"I'm glad to hear that," I said. "Because you're going to have to get used to working cattle in your spare time… Your mom and I were talking this morning and we decided we would like to put Uncle Philip's herd in your name."

Jake sat back a little further in his seat. He didn't say a word – only looked at me. I wasn't sure if he was happy or frustrated or if he even understood me.

Then with that same mischievous glint in his eye that I had seen the previous day, he asked, "So you and mom were actually talking to one another?"

I reached over and thumped him in the shoulder, just as I had the previous day. "Smartass," I said before breaking down and smiling.

Jake rubbed his shoulder with a proud smirk, clearly happy with his level of sarcasm. Then he sobered a little while he considered the situation. Eventually he asked, "All 200 head transferred into my name?"

"Well, you'd take over 200 head of the cow/calf pairs. But Uncle Philip owned half the bulls, too. So, there'd be 10 bulls in your name."

Jake leaned back in his seat as he seemed to weigh this information. "Will I have to contribute to feed costs?"

I was pleasantly surprised that this was one of the first questions a

168

fifteen-year-old boy would ask. I put my chin in the palm of my hand and rubbed my face as I mulled it over. Maggie's cow herd had always been prosperous because we were lucky enough to have no real expenses. Her dad gave us the land, he set her up with her cows, and he even bought us our first tractor that Maggie still feeds with. Maggie was handed so many things but she still worked harder than most women I knew. I think the main reason she remained so grounded and disciplined was that she was handed opportunities instead of being handed an easy way out. I took all of this into account when I said, "I think your mom and I can cover the feed costs for the first few years. We can maybe re-evaluate that once you turn 18."

Jake nodded somberly. His disposition allowed me to believe that he was understanding the magnitude of this.

"But there will be a few conditions," I continued. "First, you're going to be expected to bust your ass helping your mother. I'll pitch in, too. But you know I'm busy at the Stockyards and gone a lot during chuckwagon season. Your mom and I have always kept our work lives separate. If you start helping her out, that will mostly remain the same."

"I know. I want to do the work," Jake said.

"Good. The other thing is that we will still be in control of the money when you sell your calves. It's your money and it will be in your bank account. But I'd rather make sure you're saving it for a truck and a college education than God knows what else you'd spend it on."

"You had me when you said *truck* and then you lost me at *college education*."

"I'm serious," I said without smiling at his joke. "Nothing turns a man into a damned fool quicker than giving him the opportunity to have a little extra spending money. You're going to have to learn how to be smart about this. I expect you to be the first Hyde to go to college."

Jake fired right back, "Why would I need to go to college if I'm being set up with a cow herd and…" he trailed off. But I knew what he was leaving unsaid. Jake was still well aware of how much money his grandparents had and that he was an only child.

I wanted to lose my cool on him. I wanted to say that him relying on his grandparent's money was my biggest fear. But instead, I took a breath, thought of Philip, and exhaled loudly. "We'll talk about it more with your mom tonight, alright?"

"Sure," Jake replied, clearly relieved that nothing turned into an argument or, more likely, a one-sided reprimanding for him.

We pulled up to the Stockyards and I walked Jake towards the back pens. We meandered into the brand inspector's office. Just as I suspected, Gene was sitting in the office and looking at his little brand inspector notepad, going over the numbers from yesterday's sale. Gene nodded a hello at me and then shook hands with Jake. "Good to see ya, young fella." He spoke in his usual gruff tone but I knew Gene well enough to know how much that handshake meant. He really liked Jake.

"Hey, Gene," Jake replied as he glanced around the brand inspector office.

I walked over and crouched down to pat the red heeler Hank on the head. "You had a big day yesterday, didn't you, ol' buddy," I spoke softly to him as he lay there with half closed eyes.

"He worked as good yesterday as Blue would've," Gene stated matter-of-factly. I could see the pride in Gene's eyes. The closer I had become with Gene, the harder it was for me to remember that everyone else thought he was just a tough, ornery old man. I always saw the softer side of him.

"I thought Jake could give you a hand today," I said to Gene as I gripped Jake's shoulder. "I've got a good stack of office work to do but I can help out a little too before I head up there."

"You think I'm getting so worn out that I need two of you helping me do my job?" Gene accused. Then he turned to Jake and said, "It'd go smoother without your dad in the way, anyways, wouldn't it?" He jerked a thumb in my direction. "Me and the boy will do just fine on our own."

Jake laughed and agreed and we all walked out the door together. Jake and Gene split off from me. I decided to go to the stairs and walk up on the catwalk. I could head into my office that direction and I could also get a good look at what was going on. When I reached the top of the catwalk, I took a look out at all the pens. Something made me stop to appreciate the vastness of it all. I really did love this place. It was easy to get caught up in the stress of my job. But moments like these always made me stop and appreciate the enormity of it. It was the biggest auction mart in Canada. Cattle ranchers depended on this place to market their cattle and make a living. People depended on cattle ranchers to provide food and feed their families. Sometimes I had to slow down and take a moment to appreciate my role in all of that. It felt good.

As I stood in place on the catwalk, Jake and Gene moved below me. Gene was speaking so low that I couldn't hear what he was saying. But Jake was nodding along and taking instruction. I stopped myself from walking into my office. I was curious to keep watching to see how Jake would do.

Gene pointed down to the cattle liner at the load out chute and Jake nodded again. They were both leaning on their sorting sticks as they appeared to make a game plan. I couldn't hear what Gene was saying but I could guess. I knew that there were about 30 head in the pen and I knew they all needed to be loaded on to the liner. Jake and Gene would have to bring five head at a time. The cattle were loaded into the liner in compartments to make sure that the animals had enough room and didn't all crowd into one area of the liner. It was also the only way to push the heifers up to the front of the liner.

Jake would have his hands full loading the Henderson heifers for two reasons. First, it would be hard to cut out five head at a time. And next, it would be hard to take five head all the way up and into the liner. I was hoping that Gene had explained to Jake to keep his head up around these heifers. Jake had been around cows his whole life but he was still only 15 years old. When I came to the stockyards, I was 17. I began to feel a tightening knot in my stomach as I considered how Jake would manage. I watched as Jake slowly eased into the pen. He looked wary as he moved towards the herd but he was standing in the correct spots. He cut into the herd to push some heifers towards the gate. One, two, three, four, five black heifers pushed past Jake and ran towards the gate. He darted behind the fifth one to chase her up the alley and stop any other heifers from following with. Jake moved quickly and slammed the gate shut behind him as he left the pen. He attempted to chase the group up the alley but the heifers balked. The first one slowed and the rest followed suit. Then, as is always the case, the heifers turned around to try and go back the way they had come. Jake didn't hold his ground for long before one, two, three, four, five black heifers rushed past him with their tails in the air. They all crashed to a stop at the gate Jake had closed.

Gene had been watching the whole time and now he stepped out to Jake and spoke loud enough that I could hear him. "That sorting stick you're holding in your hand isn't very useful unless you actually lift it up and do something with it."

Jake looked a little sheepish as he held the stick up and nodded. To my surprise, Gene continued talking, "One quick bop with that stick is enough to turn a heifer's mindset around. You need to show 'em you're not backing down. If they think they've got a chance to get by ya, they'll damn sure try you on. Believe me, bopping them with that stick is a lot easier on them and on you than it would be to run 'em up and down this alley all day."

Jake still didn't speak but I could see a new sense of determination in him as he trotted away from Gene and back to his starting point. This time, he gathered a little speed as he pushed the heifers down the alley. He was right on their tails. The heifers began to balk in the same place they had moments before. This time, Jake was right behind them and hollering as he used his stick to smack the heifers in their fleshy hind end. He pushed them forward so they never got a chance to turn around and he kept pushing forward in that same manner all the way up the alley. Jake was pushing on one side of the alley and Hank was on the other side of the alley. The two made a good team as they successfully made it all the way to the liner.

Gene looked up at me and nodded in satisfaction. I nodded in return and carried on walking to my office, knowing that Jake was in good hands. I began to smile and then almost laugh outright as I realized that Hank was nowhere to be found the first time Jake attempted to go up the alley. It was only the second attempt that Hank was beside Jake growling and working in his usual manner. Gene must've had that little cow working lesson planned right from the get go. He wanted Jake to fail just so he could properly teach him the best way.

Good old Gene.

When I got to my office, I happily plunked down into my chair and picked the phone up off the receiver. I was feeling more peaceful than I'd felt in a long time. And a peaceful man is always happy to be at work, going about his business. I knew I had a number of phone calls to make so I started right off, dialing most numbers by heart. I spent more time on the phone than I should have but it was hard not to engage in small talk when I was in such an easy-going mood.

It was only when I reached out to place the phone back on the receiver that I noticed my hand shaking. The tremble quickened until

I slammed the phone down, fumbling for a moment until it was in the proper position. I tried to pretend that I didn't know why I felt so unsteady. I attempted to push the thought from my mind that told me I deserved something that would make the rest of the day go by easily. I convinced myself that I was unaware of the fact that it had been 21 hours since my last drink.

I knew I had to consume myself with my work. It was the only way to keep moving forward. I knew I had to quit drinking for my own sake but that wasn't enough motivation. Instead, I decided to do it for Maggie and Jake. With that thought in mind, I took a few steadying breaths and looked down at my desk. I always took notes as I spoke on the phone. It wasn't so much an organizational thing. I just liked to keep my hands busy and I usually did so by jotting down words or phrases from the conversation. Something jumped out at me from my earlier conversations.

I had been speaking to Leonard Collins. He was an old boy from Duchess, Alberta. He'd had cows for years but never big numbers. His cows were more of a hobby for him than anything else. But the old boy decided to expand and was looking to get financed. He had explained that he wanted to leave a cow herd for his grandson to take over but he wanted to start building it up while he could still teach his grandson the ropes. It was a simple process because he didn't need much of a loan, he had the land and capital, and he was an easy approval. The only funny part was that he had mentioned again and again that he had never borrowed money to buy cows. He was proud of the fact that he had slowly built up his herd with no outside help. I even wrote down _Never Been Financed Through Us._

I came to The Stockyards in 1959 and, for whatever reason, I always used that year as a study guide when I first took this job over and I needed a reference or example. The finance program didn't give out near as many loans back then so it was easier for me to grasp how much money was going out and how much money was coming in. Something was tickling the back of my mind so I went into the next office where there were stacks of records kept in chronological order in filing cabinets. It didn't take me long to find the 1959 paperwork. I pulled out random pieces at a time until I found what I was looking for and brought it back to my desk.

I sat down and spread the paperwork across my desk. It was all there. A detailed record of the loan Leonard Collins had in 1959 for 20 cow/calf pairs. The top of the paperwork had Leonard Collins physical address and telephone number. Sure enough, it all matched the records I had for the Leonard Collins I had just spoken to from Duchess, Alberta who had claimed again and again that he'd never taken out a loan to buy cows.

Silly old pecker, I thought to myself. *Can't even remember back twenty years ago.* I would have simply left my clever findings to myself but the approval process was even more simple if someone was applying for a second time loan. I dialed Leonard's number to confirm with him before I started his paperwork. He picked up right away with a husky hello.

"Yah, hello, Leonard. It's Charlie Hyde from the Feeder Finance Program calling you back again," I said.

"Oh, hello, Charlie."

"I was just going through our records here, Leonard, and I see that you actually have had a loan with us before. In 1959." I paused, waiting for Leonard to say something but the other line was blank. "For 20 cow/calf pairs? That ring a bell?" I asked.

Leonard responded slowly. "Aghh… No. Sorry, Charlie. You have the wrong guy. Like I said, I've never had a loan through you guys. I promise ya that much."

I looked down at the paperwork and frowned. I didn't want to keep pressing. But the proof was right below me. "Hmm, my mistake, my mistake. Say, have you always lived in the same spot? Same address?"

"My wife and I were married in '48. Moved here in '51. Plan on staying here until I die, too."

I gave an obligatory chuckle and thanked Leonard for his time before assuring him his loan was all kosher and hanging up. I looked down at the paperwork again and rubbed my hand across my face. If it was any other day, I would probably let the whole thing go and carry on without worrying about it. There could be another Leonard Collins and the addresses got mixed up. Or Leonard Collins might have genuinely forgotten about this loan. There were numerous explanations.

But today, I desperately needed the distraction. My mind was fixating on something other than alcohol and I was going to allow my brain to pursue this trail for as long as I could. I pushed my chair back and marched back into the storage room and started rummaging through

174

the file cabinets again. I spent a little longer digging and scanning through everything, but eventually came across what I wasn't hoping to find. I walked back into my office, this time reluctant to lay the paperwork across my desk. I slowly made three separate piles on my desk to display the evidence. In 1958, Leonard Collins was given a loan for 15 cow/calf pairs. In 1959, he was given a loan for 20 cow/calf pairs; which I had already discovered. And in 1960, he was given a loan for 30 cow/calf pairs. Each pile of paperwork had the same name, same address, and same telephone number that Leonard Collins had just given me. The total amount added up to 25 thousand dollars. A lot of money back in those days. Too much money for a man to forget about.

I sat staring at the paperwork with a tightening knot in my stomach. I knew this wasn't my body's reaction to the first day without alcohol in months. This was something bigger and my gut was telling me so. The paperwork was meticulous. Perfectly filled out, easy to read, neat printing. There was a line through each number 7.

I felt numbed in place, as if my body was refusing to move. I didn't want to jump to a conclusion or make any rash judgments, so it felt safest to remain in place.

I didn't even hear the boots stomping towards my office so my head jolted up when Jake and Gene pushed through the door. They were in the middle of a conversation and barely looked at me as they plopped down into the chairs in front of my desk.

" – no telling what've happened then! Silly bugger," Jake grinned and Gene chuckled his low, deep laugh.

Gene's attention drifted towards me as he remarked, "Charlie, you look like you've seen a ghost."

I gave my head a little shake and quickly shuffled the papers together that I had spread across my desk. I gathered them abruptly and shoved them inside a desk drawer, slamming it shut a little too hard. "That's what happens to a man when he's stuck behind a desk all day. Should be doing more real work," I said. Gene nodded but I noticed his gaze drift down to the desk drawer I had just put the papers in. Nothing ever went unnoticed in Gene's presence. "Who is a silly bugger?" I asked Jake, changing the subject.

Jake was happy to ramble on about his day. He was oblivious to any tension or stress in the room as only a 15-year-old boy can be. He told his story about how a truck driver had gone in a liner to shut a divider but a latch had been broken. The driver had been fiddling with the latch and Gene and Jake had unknowingly loaded the next batch of heifers, right behind him. It normally wouldn't have been too big of an issue if they weren't Henderson heifers. I guess the truck driver was hollering his lungs out before they realized he was still in there. Jake got plenty of amusement out of the whole situation and he did an impression of the driver yelling *HEY!!! HEY!!! I'M IN HERE!!!*

I laughed at the story but mainly just because I got a kick out of seeing Jake so boisterous. I assumed Gene was probably laughing for the same reason. We chatted for a while longer before we collectively eased out of my office and towards our vehicles. I patted Hank on the head before we parted ways and my chest puffed up a little as Jake shook Gene's hand. He might still tell stories like a boy but he was becoming a man in many other ways.

When Jake and I pulled up to the house, I could see Maggie standing in the kitchen window. For some reason, I was reminded of my own mother. We always used to see her standing in the kitchen window. She would be working in there, cooking or cleaning, but sometimes she'd just watch us. My mother and Maggie were incredibly different. Maggie was frank, tough, and always trying to prove herself. My mother was softer, easier, and less ambitious. But the two of them had always gotten along beautifully. They both had a graceful edge in the way they lived and loved. I was grateful to have my own mother's presence hovering nearby as I grew up – whether I realized it at the time or not. And now I was grateful that Jake was growing up with the same strong maternal light always shining close by.

"What's Mom making for supper?" he asked when he noticed her face in the window. I had to laugh at the differences between his train of thought and my own.

"Leftover ribs."

"Ribs?! Our favorite! This day keeps getting better."

Jake and I walked up to the house and I slung an arm around his neck and squeezed a pretend chokehold. Jake wrestled away and dashed up to the door ahead of me.

We ate together that night as a family, laughing and visiting. It was the first time in a long time and it felt good. When the dishes were cleared, Jake suggested a game of Monopoly. He said it instinctively as Monopoly was always his reaction to the three of us having a good time together. But we all paused, thinking of the last time we had played and who would be missing from this game.

"Monopoly sounds good," I finally said. Relieved, Jake went to get the board. Maggie smiled softly at me but didn't say any words. This time, we didn't need to.

I think I even let them win. Again.

CHAPTER TWENTY-FIVE

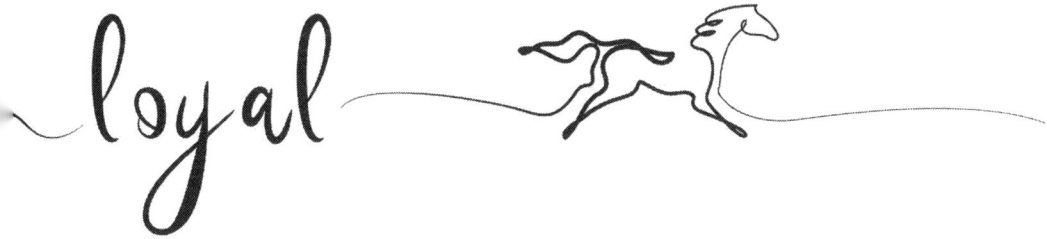

loyal

The next morning, I drove to work with a looming dread. I had successfully put my worries and concerns aside because I knew how important it was to have a night as a family. It was important to Maggie but it was also essential to our lives. We had been on the brink of completely cracking apart. Death, booze, stress, and fighting had somehow all managed to seep into our idyllic lifestyle. I was determined to push those demons away.

Last night was reassuring. Today, I was back in unchartered waters. I was going to phone Frank and ask him to come for a coffee in my office. Then I would simply show him the paperwork and ask him if he remembered it. Frank was a good man. He'd been a good man as long as I've known him. When I first started working at the Stockyards, Frank went out of his way to welcome me. He supported me when I was an outrider at my first Calgary Stampede. He helped make my brother's funeral memorable and impactful. He'd always been there for me throughout the times of my life that 'd needed him most. The least I could do was try to return the favor and give him the benefit of the doubt.

I actually needed to give Frank the benefit of the doubt. I wasn't sure I could handle coming to terms with anything else.

I sat down at my desk and busied myself with a few menial tasks. I knew I was putting off the phone call and with a sudden burst of motivation that stemmed from my desire to handle things like a man, I picked up the phone and dialed Frank's number by heart.

"Be there in twenty," he responded and hung up without saying goodbye when I asked him to come in. I was acutely aware of the papers still in my desk drawer but I didn't pull them out. I just sat silently, awaiting Frank's arrival.

When Frank poked his head in, something inside me told me to just drop the whole thing. I could just visit with him and carry on my day. Why bring up shit from twenty years ago?

But I knew myself well enough to know that it wouldn't work out like that. Something about the way I'd been raised meant that I had no choice but to discover the truth. Simply because it was part of doing my job in the best manner that I was capable of.

Frank and I chatted amicably and sipped on coffee when I lit a cigarette. I hunched over the smoke slightly, a habit from lighting so many cigarettes out in the wind and the elements. I inhaled slowly and breathed smoke out as I casually said, "Say, do you know a Leonard Collins? From Duchess?"

Frank stared at me. He didn't say a word. Our eyes met. He knew what I was asking. As the silence lingered on and Frank kept staring at me, I knew what he was saying by not saying anything at all.

I fought the urge to slap my hand down on my desk and demand answers. I knew this was no time to react abruptly. I was the first one to break eye contact. I looked down at my cigarette as I tapped it lightly over the ashtray on my desk. "I figured so," I said softly.

Frank still didn't say a word. His silence was beginning to really piss me off. But I refused to speak again. The ball was in his court now.

"When you took over this job, a part of me knew that somehow, someday, we'd sit here and have this discussion," he finally said. He popped his short-brimmed hat with his index finger, shoving it up and further back on his head. Then he threw his palms up in an exasperated shrug and said, "It's been a long time coming but I still don't know what to say."

"Why don't you start with why the fuck you did it," I snapped. My patience was wearing out but I knew I had to keep myself composed. Mainly because the look on Frank's face was as if I'd just stabbed a knife in his heart.

Frank stood up, slowly. "Let's go for a drive," he said as he walked towards my office door without ever looking at me. I wordlessly got up and followed him. He headed towards his pickup and I got in the passenger seat. I had no idea where we were going or what Frank was going to say. But I had such a burning pit of anger inside me that I didn't think it would matter. I couldn't see how I would ever forgive him.

Frank drove as we both remained silent. We were heading out into ranching country. Rolling hills and few trees. Not enough rain to make for fertile farmland but enough rain to graze cattle and keep them well fed. We drove for nearly 40 minutes before he shifted his truck down and pulled over on to the side of the road. We were on a dirt road and all I could see was barbed wire fences surrounding us.

"Pretty country, ain't it?" Frank asked.

I looked around but was uninterested in the land. "Yah," I obliged.

"I used to own this," Frank said as he pointed his finger out to the pasture on my right. Then he tapped the window on his side and pointed to the pasture on my left. "Owned that, too."

"I'm not exactly putting the pieces together here. I just want the facts, I didn't need to come on a Sunday drive," I said.

"And I'm trying to give you the facts!" Frank said with his voice escalating for the first time. He was beginning to tremble a little but he went on talking. "I owned these two quarters and more. I had a wife. A nice house. A good job. And I also had one hell of a gambling problem... So, I lost it all except the job."

He paused and let that sink in. For the first time in my relationship with Frank, I realized how little I knew about him. When I arrived at the Stockyards, I was a 17-year-old kid. He took me under his wing and I never had the decency to understand that I only talked about my life without ever asking him about his life. I figured it was my turn to be quiet so I said nothing.

"I never intended for any of it to happen, but that don't matter. I'm not making excuses. Not anymore, anyways." He paused again, then turned to me. "Fuck. You got another smoke?"

I couldn't help but laugh a little. I had rarely heard Frank cuss and had seen him smoke even less. The fact that he was resorting to both just to try to talk to me was enough for me to give him a little sympathy. I handed him my pack of smokes and the lighter from my front shirt pocket.

Frank took a few puffs before commenting, "Horrible habit." I let him gather himself as I awaited the rest of the story.

He started in, "Like I said, I owned this land. Had a good wife. The gambling started slowly. Looking back, I still don't know how it all spun so out of control," he shook his head slightly as he gazed out the window. "It was a different time. It started at casinos. Poker was my go to. My wife knew I was spending too much time and money playing poker. Lord knows that woman tried to stop me but I just wouldn't listen. The more she pushed, the more I pulled away. The Stockyards were different back then, too. More booze, fewer rules. More stupidity. It was in a poker game at the yards that I laid down my land title. I was drunk, arrogant, and out of control. Needless to say, I lost. The embarrassment wasn't nearly as crippling as the guilt when I had to tell my wife. She left me soon after. I couldn't blame her. Didn't figure I had any right to try to convince her to stay, either. I let her walk out and we never spoke again after the divorce was finalized."

My mind was reeling. Of course, I'd heard the rumors of past times when men gambled with land titles at the stockyard's poker games. Everyone knew that had happened. Most stories were about wealthy ranchers who owned 20 quarters of land and gambled away 1 or 2 quarters. I'd never heard Frank's story. I wasn't sure if people didn't speak of it out of respect for Frank or if they really didn't know. My guess was that the story had been discreetly hid from common knowledge. Because respect or not, people love to talk.

Frank continued, "I didn't have anything. I rented a little house in the city. I owed my wife a lot in the divorce settlement but I had no way of giving it to her. I still had my job at the stockyards and those weekly cheques saved my life. But it wasn't enough. And I wasn't quite finished with properly screwing up my life."

By this time, Frank had finished with his cigarette and he rolled down a window to drop it on to the dirt road. I grabbed the pack in the middle console and offered it in his direction, but he gestured no. I didn't know what else to do. I hesitated before asking, "How does Leonard Collins play into this?"

"After I lost everything, you'd think I'd have learnt my lesson. Maybe it's true that they say gambling really is an addiction. I don't know. I'm not looking for excuses or sympathy. Whatever the reason, I kept gambling. I found underground poker games in the city and I started attending those in the middle of the night. But when a man owes money that he doesn't have, that's when life really gets bad." Frank turned to me and looked me in the eye for the first time since he'd parked the truck. "The money from those loans never went to Leonard Collins. It went to me. I used it to pay back the thugs in Calgary who were starting to come after me looking to collect. I spread the loan out over three years and I used it to pay back the people I owed money to and settle up on my divorce. I also paid back every penny – with interest. I didn't pay it back when the books show I did, but I did pay it all eventually."

The blow of Frank's confession wasn't lessened by his attempt to do the right thing in the end. I felt like the wind had been knocked out of me. "Those are the exact words I was hoping I wouldn't hear you say," I muttered.

Frank closed his eyes and his head sank, just a little. "I know, Charlie. I know." Then he turned back straight ahead, started the truck, and shifted it into drive. I barely noticed the silence as we headed back to the city. I felt like I needed air. I cranked down my window and closed my eyes. The confusion washed over me as the cool air hit my face. Like my father before me and like most every other great man I'd ever met, I knew the difference between right and wrong. At least I thought I did. But this whole situation blurred the lines.

Just as we didn't speak on the drive out, we maintained the same silence on the way back to the Stockyards. Frank had been composing himself on the drive out and I was processing things on the drive back. Both silences carried a heavy weight. The air felt muddy.

When we were getting close to the parking lot, Frank cleared his throat and spoke up. "It was only through being a fool that I learned how to be a better man. And don't worry, that's exactly what I was – a. damn. fool. I know that. I think I had to stoop to my all-time low as a person before I could pick myself up and decide on what type of man I wanted to be. I know I've done a lot of wrong in my life but I've worked hard to right those wrongs and be a good man." Frank took a deep breath as he idled the truck close to my office. "Go on, now. I won't tell you what to do and I won't ask you to take pity on me. I told you my story and that's all I really wanted." Frank motioned me to step out of the truck.

I opened the door and stepped down on to the gravel. I peered at Frank. He looked like he'd aged five years since he first stepped into my office this morning. I didn't close the door and stood there a moment, facing him. "I thought this place meant more to you than to be able to steal from it," I said. Frank's whole life had always revolved around the Stockyards. I'd never known him to care about anything else.

Frank glanced out across the buildings and pens before he said, "My wife was a good woman and I loved her. But she left me and I still couldn't change my ways. Stealing money from here was the only wake-up call that made me realize what I'd become. I might not have always done the right thing but I've tried to make up for it by being loyal to the Stockyards until the day I die."

I stepped back and nodded before swinging the truck door shut. I turned towards my office building and walked towards the door without looking back at Frank.

CHAPTER TWENTY-SIX

disconnected

Maggie always could tell when something was bothering me. I didn't want to involve her in this and I didn't want to discuss it. But she pressed the issue again, "Charlie, we just got past blocking each other out. Let's not do it again. What's going on?"

That convinced me. I rolled on my side to face her as we laid in bed. It was dark but the moon was full and I could barely make out the outline of her face. I reached out and softly brushed a finger against her cheek. She had given me an odd look as soon as I stepped inside the house today and asked if something was wrong. I said everything was fine and she glanced over at Jake before deciding not to press the issue in front of him but she had been monitoring my mood for the entire evening.

"I found something at work. It's from a long time ago. But it's not good. I don't know what to do," I said softly.

"Okay…" Maggie said slowly. I didn't want her to worry. I wanted to protect her from this. But I was forgetting one thing – how strong she was. I gave in and started to pour the story out to her. It was only through telling the story and confiding in someone else that I realized how much weight I'd been carrying with me since I'd talked to Frank. I felt lighter instantly. I finished by explaining what Frank said before I'd went into my office.

Maggie rolled on to her back and looked up at the ceiling. She was processing everything just as I'd done earlier. It only took her a moment before she rolled back towards me and said, "I'm so sorry you have to deal with this. I know how much Frank has always meant to you."

When she spoke those words, in her own kind-hearted way, it took everything in me to keep myself from crying. I clenched my jaw and grimaced a little as I felt the knot move up my chest and into my throat. I took a few deep breaths and swallowed it down. Maggie understood the root of the problem. It wasn't so much the money or the stealing, no matter how much that fact had pissed me off. It was that Frank was supposed to be good. He was supposed to be someone I believed in. I didn't want to lose Philip and then lose Frank. The reasons might be different but the heartbreak would be just the same.

Maggie and I laid side by side and facing each other for a long time. We were wide awake but neither of us said much. Sometimes it's just the comfort of knowing you're not alone to get you through the night.

The next morning, Jake was out the door early to check the cows. He'd gotten into the habit of doing this without ever being asked. It made both of us smile as he headed out the door; clearly a man on a mission.

"So, what are you gonna do?" Maggie asked as soon as we were alone.

"Right now – nothing." I crunched on a piece of bacon. I needed time to think. I wanted to go to work and focus on my job and let this problem ruminate in the back of my mind. I also wanted to let Frank sweat it out for a few days.

Unfortunately, I didn't have the chance to do any of that. The phone rang and Maggie stepped up to answer it. She spoke for a minute before looking over at me, "It's for you," she said. As I walked towards the phone, she placed her palm over the speaker and whispered, "It's Arthur Langley's wife. She sounds upset."

I frowned a little. I couldn't remember the last time I'd spoken to

Arthur's wife. It probably would have been when I was still outriding for Arthur but he'd been retired from racing for years and I never really did get to know his wife, even back in the racing days.

"Hello, Mrs. Langley," I said. I couldn't remember her first name.

"Hello, Charlie." She sounded old and her voice was croaky and brittle. I couldn't imagine what she would be calling me about.

"How are ya doing?" I asked.

"Well… I'm not really doing very well. Arthur passed away yesterday. Heart attack."

She caught me completely off guard. Her voice sounded fragile but she spoke fairly casually. "Oh. I'm… so sorry." I temporarily forgot all social customs. "Is there anything I can do?" I asked her, happy to have latched on to something to say.

"Yes, there is. I'd like to see you before the funeral," she said.

"Of course. I can come right now," I obliged.

She thanked me and hung up. I slowly put the phone back on the receiver and explained the conversation to Maggie, who looked even more puzzled than me.

"What on earth would she want to see you for?" she asked.

"Guess I'll find out," I shrugged and headed out the door.

I was hit with a wave of nostalgia as I pulled up to Arthur's place. How strange to think of years ago when Rich and I had drove here for the first time. Arthur had never sold his land and moved into town the way plenty of older folks do. I imagined he was too stubborn to ever admit that he couldn't keep up with all the work of a rural life. It's probably what killed him.

I strode up to the front door. I'd never actually been inside Arthur's house. I'd spent a lot of time in my first couple years of racing out at his track and in his barn. But he'd never invited me in. We didn't have that kind of a relationship. I hesitated a moment before I knocked on the door, not knowing what to expect.

Mrs. Langley opened the door right away. She'd been anticipating my arrival. She looked older than I was expecting. I stepped inside and gave her a hug and told her I was sorry for her loss. She thanked me and patted my hand but there were no tears. *What a tough old doll*, I thought to myself. Mrs. Langley gestured me in to the kitchen and we sat down at the table. She wasted no time before explaining why she'd called me over.

"I wanted to show you this," she said as she slid a piece of paper towards me. It took me a moment to realize what I was reading. It was a copy of Arthur's will. She pointed down to a specific paragraph with her shaky, wrinkled hand. The words read:

For Charlie Hyde - My harnesses, wagons, bits, saddles, pads, and all other tack and horse related gear. My remaining horses – if I have any. My horse walker – if he wants it. My truck and trailer. All the hay and straw and feed in my possession. And my Calgary Stampede Championship bronze from 1959.

I read the paragraph over a few times as I tried to grasp the enormity of what Arthur was giving me. I focused in on the truck and trailer. I pointed to the page and shook my head a little as I looked up at Mrs. Langley, "These things can be sold for a decent amount of money. That should be going in your bank account."

Mrs. Langley didn't smile but she patted my hand again. "I'm well looked after, dear."

"Are you sure? It's no offense to me. I would be glad to help with an auction or – "

She cut me off and this time was a little firmer, "This is what he wanted *you* to have. Arthur and I did our wills up about ten years ago. I thought he would consider the whole thing a waste of time but he actually took it all quite seriously." She paused and added, "He was very fond of you. And always very proud of you, too."

I thought of all the times Arthur had called me a stupid farmer. He rarely ever treated me with respect. But then again, he never showed much respect to people or animals. I never even liked the man. And now he'd given me the remnants of his entire life's work. He'd passed on to me his most prized possessions – including the Calgary Stampede bronze that he had won the first year I was his outrider. It felt too sentimental to be true. I wasn't sure how to respond.

"Thank you." Then, looking at Mrs. Langley, I added, "This really means a lot to me." I said it for her sake more than anything else. She smiled for the first time since I'd arrived.

When she guided me back to the front door, she stopped and raised a finger. "There's one more thing. I would like you to give the eulogy at the funeral."

My eyes widened and every bone in my body was telling me that I did not want to do that job. I couldn't do that job. But what did I say?

"Of course," I nodded.

I climbed back into my pickup and stared at the house a moment before turning the key. "Shit," I muttered under my breath.

As I drove away, I was vaguely aware that I was leaving Mrs. Langley all alone. It was the day after her husband's death and she didn't have a single friend or family member close by to comfort her. Arthur had been an expert at keeping people at a distance for his entire life. He could be rude and insulting or dismissive and unapproachable. I couldn't tell you what Mrs. Langley's personality was like because I never got the chance to know her. I wasn't sure if that was her choice or Arthur's choice. But she seemed disconnected from most social gatherings in the community and the chuckwagon racing world. All I knew was that if I didn't stand up and do the eulogy, there wouldn't be anyone else to do it.

CHAPTER TWENTY-SEVEN

indiscretions

It felt like the blank piece of paper on the kitchen table was mocking me. I'd been sitting with a pen in hand, trying to come up with something to say about Arthur Langley. I tore the paper off the pad, crumpled it up, and threw it into the garbage can – even though I hadn't written a single word on it.

"Did you just - ?" Jake gave me a puzzled expression. He was standing behind me at the kitchen counter with a bowl of cereal held up close to his mouth and milk dripping off his spoon. He swallowed another mouthful without ever finishing his question.

"Oh hell, leave me alone."

Jake raised his eyebrows. "I don't see what the problem is. How many times have you told me the story about DS? Just talk about that." He pointed the spoon in my direction, "But maybe just omit a few parts of the story."

We both knew which parts would be omitted. Mainly the night DS took a lashing after a drunken Arthur stumbled into his box stall. But the rest of the story would be pretty suitable. After all, Arthur had given me DS. Never charged me a dime for him and it was the best horse I've ever owned. I was allowing my own personal feelings towards the man to block out the facts of the story.

"Good point," I said and put my pen to the paper for the first time.

Jake sauntered towards the living room and slunk down on to the couch as he pointed at his head and called, "It ain't just a hat rack!"

I chuckled and put my own head down and began to write. And when I was finished, I even surprised myself with what I had come up with.

On the day of the funeral, I walked in to the parlor with Maggie and Jake on either side of me. I wore a black felt cowboy hat and a grey suit jacket over top of my starched shirt and starched jeans. Maggie had shined mine and Jake's cowboy boots. I never fully understood why it was custom to get so dressed up for a funeral. Maggie wore a dress and Jake had the same suit jacket on that he had worn to Philip's funeral. Who were we dressing up for? Certainly not Arthur who never gave a damn about anyone's appearance. I was sure he never shined his boots to go anywhere.

The three of us slid into the front pew which had been reserved for us. I took stock of the people who had come. Plenty of old chuckwagon drivers and their families were scattered about. Arthur had won enough to make himself prominent amongst the old timers. There were also members of the agriculture community scattered about. Some people would have known Arthur pretty well. But there were others who simply didn't miss a funeral in the area because it was a social outing. Whatever someone's reason was for coming, I was just happy the seats were filled.

I waited patiently, going over my speech in my head until my name was called and I was asked to come forward.

I cleared my throat, shuffled the papers in front of me, and began.

"I met Arthur in 1957. I was 17 years old, naïve, and I'd never seen a chuckwagon race in my life. In the funny fate of the world, I landed a tryout with Arthur when he needed an outrider only a couple weeks out from the Calgary Stampede. When I showed up for that tryout, Arthur certainly had his doubts about me. He called me *Farmer* that day and carried on with that nickname the rest of his life. At the time, I thought Arthur was close minded about my potential. But looking back, I can see things differently. Now that I'm a professional chuckwagon driver myself, I can understand that a man needs to take his team seriously. Especially for the highest paying rodeo of the year. And Arthur certainly took his chuckwagon driving seriously. He was always in it to win. Many people here today can admire that competitive attitude he had.

When I showed up, Arthur wanted to test me and he put me on a flighty, sorrel gelding. That horse wasn't easy but he was something special – to me, anyways. After that day, Arthur decided to give me a chance and take me to Calgary. I'll forever be grateful for that. I may have never gotten into chuckwagon racing if it wasn't for Arthur Langley. That's the truth.

Arthur and I spent a lot of time together at the track at his house. We worked side by side for a couple years. I never did get used to the mosquitos out there but it didn't bother Arthur. I think he was too thick-skinned for bug bites. One thing I respected about Arthur was that every time I was out at the track working, he was also out at the track working. He put the time in and that's no doubt one of the reasons for the success he had as a driver.

If you knew Arthur, you know that he didn't exactly waste any time praising a job well-done. I don't think I ever heard a compliment from him. But he had a better way of showing me how he felt. After the first year I rode for him at Calgary, I told him I wanted to buy that flighty, sorrel gelding of his that I'd rode the first day. He laughed at me, told me I was an idiot, and then he gave me that horse. He never charged me anything. I grew up with horses but that was the first one I ever owned myself and he became the staple of my chuckwagon team. He was my lead horse for many years and he's currently living out his retirement in my pasture.

It never occurred to me until I sat down to write this speech just how big of an impact Arthur Langley had on my life. I'm sorry to admit that. I wish I could shake Arthur's hand right now and thank him for everything he's done for me. He'd probably scoff at me and tell me to get the hell outta here. But I'd like to do it, regardless.

Sometimes, for whatever reason, we just don't realize how much a person has given us."

I paused just a moment and scanned the crowd. I found an old man with a white, short-brimmed hat in his hands. He had a mournful look in his eye. I looked directly at him as I finished my speech.

"None of us in this life are perfect. We've got a little bit of good and a little bit of bad in all of us. Sometimes, we lose our way and stray off course. Sometimes Arthur strayed off course. I sure as hell know that I've frequently lost my way, too. And I bet every one of you sitting here in front of me today has lost your way, too. All we can ask for is that when it's our time to go, someone will stand up and remember the good things about us. Life's a lot easier on all of us when we just choose to see the good."

I didn't care if no one else in the room understood what I was talking about. I was still looking at Frank. A single tear rolled down his wrinkled cheek. I nodded my head at him before I returned to my seat. We both understood that I had made my decision.

I knew what it felt like to lose your way. I could've continued to push Maggie away and I could've spent the rest of my life drinking while pretending I wasn't an alcoholic. I thank the good Lord above that neither of those things happened. I also thank the good Lord that Frank was in my life as a non-judgmental friend who gently guided me back to the straight away.

I never knew if I made the right or wrong choice when I decided to never tell anyone about Frank's indiscretions. I just knew that I was choosing to see the good in a man I deeply cared for.

I figured someday, someone might have to do the same thing for me.

"Life's a lot easier on all of us when we just choose to see the good."

PART 3

2019

"Agriculture is key to solving the world's greatest problems. And it is not revered as it should be. How do we change that narrative?"

~ Keegan Kautzky

CHAPTER TWENTY-EIGHT

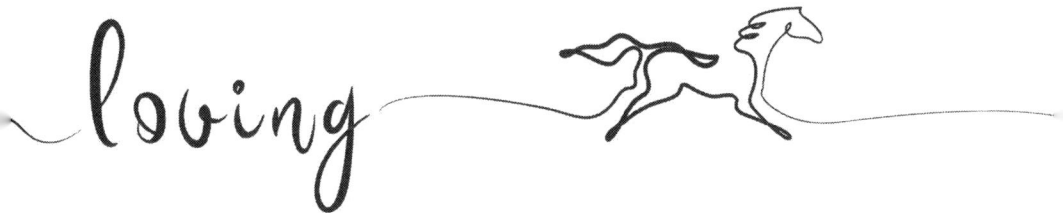

loving

I pushed my glasses up. They kept falling down my nose as I would peer over my left shoulder at the speedometer.

"Going a little fast, aren't we?" I asked.

My granddaughter kept two hands on the wheel and her eyes straight ahead as she laughed. She didn't take her foot off the pedal at all, just cruised along at the same speed. Sometimes I forgot how self-assured she was. She reminded me of her grandmother.

"Grandpa, do you not trust my driving?" she teased.

"Oh, I trust your driving fine. It's the speed at which you do it that bothers me."

She smiled again and this time eased off the gas. Just a little. I settled back into the passenger seat. How could she already be 23 years old? A young woman. To me, she'd always be the freckle faced little girl who would refuse to get off her pony. The wild child with a kind heart. The light of mine and Maggie's lives, along with her younger brother.

She reached over and pushed a button and the truck filled up with music. An awful racket, whatever it was.

"Don't you have anything good? Some Willie Nelson?" I asked.

"You and I have been listening to Willie Nelson my whole life! Don't you want to enjoy some new music? This is Thomas Rhett. He's pretty good. You might actually like some of his stuff, if you give it a chance!"

I gave a harrumph and didn't push the issue any further. The truth of the matter was that Kylie could play any music she wanted. I'd been letting her get away with whatever she wanted throughout her entire life; that probably wouldn't change now. I looked out the window and watched the fields passing by. I didn't bother listening to the music; I let the scenery control my thoughts. The sun was beating down and the field would soon be glistening from the irrigation that would spray throughout the night. It was going to be a good year for hay crops – farmers were already on their second cut. Good hay meant good cows which meant good prices. Everything in agriculture was always connected. I was retired from The Stockyards but I never stopped thinking about it.

We pulled up to the rodeo grounds and Kylie expertly swung the truck and trailer into place amongst the row of other rigs. There were about 20 trucks and trailers lined up along the side of the arena.

"Should be a small jackpot," I noted.

"Yup. We'll be in and out! Then we can listen to more Thomas Rhett on the way home," she winked at me.

I waved my hand at her and frowned, while secretly basking in every moment of her teasing. "You go ahead and get on your horse. I'll put your name down."

Kylie and I both knew what that meant. She was a professional barrel racer but I had hopped in with her to come to the little, local barrel racing jackpot. There would be about 40 or 50 runs made as local girls competed against one another and the whole thing wouldn't take more than an hour. But no matter how big or small the event, I never missed a chance to watch Kylie run barrels. She had a gift with horses. It had been passed down through the generations. I'd witnessed my own grandmother stand out as a horsewoman and now I was watching my granddaughter train horses in the same manner.

She also worked her butt off.

I walked up to the entry office and smiled at the lady writing down names. I handed her 40 dollars cash from my wallet and told her to put Kylie Hyde in. I always paid Kylie's entry fees when I tagged along with her. The woman chomped on her gum as she tapped her finger along the page and finally said, "There we go. She'll be number 32."

I thanked the secretary and had barely taken a few steps away from the entry table when a woman poked me in the ribs and said, "I see Kylie brought her personal bank machine with her!" I gave a small chuckle but there was no sincerity behind my laughter. I didn't find it funny. But then, the woman wasn't saying it just to be funny. I couldn't remember her name but I'd seen her around at plenty of jackpots. She couldn't ride a stick horse, let alone a high-powered barrel horse.

"Beautiful night out here, I wouldn't miss a chance to come watch my girl," I commented as I carried along without stopping to talk.

I was 77 years old and I still hadn't gotten comfortable with being a wealthy man. Of course, Maggie and I had more in our bank account than we knew what to do with. But it was nothing compared to what Jake had.

Our son seemed to have been born with a magic touch for making money. He started by earning a good profit on cows after we gave him his first herd when he was 15. That ignited a fire in him. He studied business at the University of Calgary but he never had the chance to graduate because he was already running his own company by his second year at school. He took after Maggie's father and started his own oil company. The first one was an oilfield construction company. At this point, I've lost track of how many companies Jake has started and sold. He's already multiplied any inheritance he would have gotten ten times over. But to this day, Jake still runs a few cows. He says it's the only thing that keeps him sane when he can saddle a horse up and go check his herd. I've urged him to slow down and do it more often. I don't know if he'll ever listen but, in the meantime, I'm happy to take over and spend as much time with his kids as they'll allow me.

I walked up to the side of the arena and perched a leg up on the bottom rail of the fence. I pulled a pen out of my front shirt pocket and wrote the number 32 on my hand so I wouldn't forget what number out Kylie was. I played with the pen and rolled it through my hands before bringing it up to my mouth and chewing on the end. An old habit after I'd quit smoking. Doctor's orders.

I watched all the women riding their horses around the arena as they warmed up and prepared for the jackpot to start. There was every level of rider and horses. I didn't really care about anyone else. I fixated on Kylie and watched her effortlessly long trot her horse along the fence. She didn't ride thoroughbreds, like I always had. She was on the back of a big, yellow quarter horse. She stood out from the rest of the girls. Her horse was better looking and she was a good rider. The fact that she came from money just gave everyone else an excuse when they looked for a reason as to why she always beat them.

The jackpot started and then moved in a slow, casual manner. No one got in too much of a hurry at these local deals. Finally, they announced number 30. I pulled my iPhone out and held it up. I held it a little further back from my face and then swiped the camera open, just as Maggie had shown me. The grandkids said they would happily teach Maggie how to operate her phone first and then she had to be the one who taught me. Whatever that meant. I waited patiently while number 31 made her run. Then they announced Kylie's name and I pointed my gnarled, leathered finger at the red dot. I heard a little *ding* when I made contact with the screen. I followed Kylie as she ran into the first, second, and third barrel. She made a beautiful run and picked up her over and under on the way home. Her horse was stretched out and gliding when she crossed the electrical eye that stopped her time.

And we have a new fast time, the woman over the microphone praised. I pulled out my pen again and wrote down Kylie's time on my palm. Then I walked back to the truck and got into the passenger seat. I'd seen all I came to see.

I waited patiently inside the truck with my window rolled down until Kylie collected her winnings, loaded her horse in the trailer, and joined me on the driver's side. She hopped in the truck with a light and airy disposition as she smiled at me. No matter how little the jackpot is, winning is always a good feeling.

I proudly handed my phone over to her and displayed the video I had taken. She hunched over the screen, eager to watch. After she watched herself round the third barrel and head home, she looked up at me with raised eyebrows, "This is actually a really good video!"

"Yah, well, I still hate that damned phone but I've gotten better."

Kylie smiled and then replayed the video over a couple times. She paused it and played it in slow motion, and I watched her as she silently critiqued herself and her horse. Finally, when she was satisfied, she set my phone down on the console and started the truck. "What do you think?" she asked.

"I thought it was a great run. He's firing on the way home more. He strided out really nice."

Kylie seemed to let this sink in. "I needed to ride harder on the way to the second barrel," she finally said. "But you're right. He's building up his air. It's made a big difference since I started sprinting him out in the field like you said."

It was always like this between me and Kylie. We could talk about horses endlessly. We were continuously working on improving things. There was never any judgment or criticism. We were a team and I knew I was going to watch her do great things. She already was.

The drive passed quickly with a constant chatter between us before we arrived home again. Kylie had moved back in with her parents when she completed university. Jake and his wife, Michelle, had built a house a mile and a half from the log house Maggie and I still lived in. It had been a blessing to be so close to our grandchildren and watch them grow up. It wasn't always perfect living in such close proximity to your son and your daughter-in-law. There were moments of tension and more than a few disagreements throughout the years. But I wouldn't change a thing about it.

Kylie unloaded her horse from the back of the trailer and led it over to the cement pad underneath a lean to. I followed behind her. She pulled the saddle off and effortlessly swung it on to a saddle rack. I brought out the hose and started cold hosing her horses' legs. He stood casually throughout the process; having been through it a hundred times before. When I was satisfied, Kylie was there to spray witch hazel on his legs. A lot had changed in the horse industry since my time as a professional chuckwagon driver. There were more supplements, lotions, and devices for a horses' health than I ever could have imagined. But witch hazel was a simple, useful routine that I had passed down to Kylie.

We parted ways after she kicked her horse out into the field. I hopped into my truck to drive the mile and a half home on the winding, dirt road that separated our houses. Kylie waved goodbye and mouthed the words *thank you* as I passed her. I held up a wrinkled hand in response.

I drove slowly as I fumbled my hand around, patting my body, until I found my cellphone. I latched on to it and pulled it out, opening up my recent phone calls, and hitting the last number. Rich's name popped up on the screen while I waited for the call to connect before holding the phone up to my ear.

"What's going on?" Rich asked, not bothering to say hello.

I told him I was just driving home and that Kylie had won the jackpot. We talked about the weather and the crops and the same things we talked about every day. Rich said he'd went in to the steak house for supper and he saw an old customer in there and he'd sat down and ate supper with him at the bar. We talked about everything and nothing as I pulled up to my house and remained seated in the truck until we hung up.

Rich and I talked to each other every single day. We saw each other often but we still touched base at least once a day. That was one of the beauties of cell phones. I'd made a point to reach out to Rich every day after Georgia died and the habit had stuck between us. Rich lived all alone now and he was soon going to need to move into a home. He was aging fast without Georgia there to cook for him and keep him active. It had always been just the two of them and it was understandably hard on him when she was diagnosed with ovarian cancer. She put up a strong fight but, in the end, she was just too tired and weak to keep it up. It was hard on Maggie and Jake, too. Georgia might not have been blood related but she was always family to us.

I stepped out of the truck, and walked over to Maggie who was on her knees in the dirt beside our sidewalk, pulling weeds out of the flower bed. She was 77 years old and still active. She'd kept her slim figure throughout her entire life and it was no doubt one of the testaments to how hard she worked. She seamlessly tugged up a few more tiny green pieces until she was satisfied and held a hand out to me. I grabbed her hand and pulled her up off the ground. She took a moment before properly getting her footing and standing up tall beside me. "Well, how'd she do?" she asked, brushing the dirt off her hands.

"Won it," I said with a wink.

"You get a video this time?"

"Sure did. Kylie even commented on how good it was. Practice pays off."

Maggie smiled at me and we walked hand in hand towards the front door. This was a day in my life as an old man. Killing time, watching my grandkids, talking to Rich.

And after 59 years of marriage, I was still loving on Maggie.

CHAPTER TWENTY-NINE

exhausted

I was rubbing my eyes awake and taking the first few sips of coffee when the house phone rang. Not very many people dialed our house number anymore. I walked stiffly over to the receiver, my body not yet loosening up and moving properly for the day. I couldn't see who was calling without my glasses on, but I picked up, my voice still hoarse and jagged. "Hello."

"Morning!"

I instantly softened when I heard Kylie's voice on the other line. "Oh, good mornin'. What's happening today?"

"I was going to ride through the replacement heifers. Thought I could saddle up Roanie for you, if you wanted to join me?"

The question hung in the air. I moved my body a little, testing out how I felt. Suddenly, I didn't seem quite so stiff. "Sure. I'd like that."

"Cool. Hey, Mom wants to talk to you."

I waited for another voice to come through the line. "Morning, Michelle," I greeted her politely.

She attempted small talk for a while before getting to her point. "Anyways, Sawyer is coming home for supper tonight! He's bringing a friend with him, actually. Would you and Maggie like to join us?"

Sawyer was my grandson who was currently finishing up his degree at the University of Calgary. He'd majored in engineering and was taking summer classes on a fast track to complete his studies. He never had much desire to partake in the rural lifestyle. He rode horses when he was younger but he only entered a few rodeos before we were unable to convince him to enter any more. Sawyer was bright and disciplined with his schooling. He was a good kid. Him and I just had less to talk about than Kylie and I did.

"That would be very nice, Michelle. Thank you," I responded before hanging up.

Maggie had been standing close enough to me to overhear the conversation. She raised an eyebrow at me and said, "What do you think she'll cook?"

"Lord only knows," I muttered as I padded back into our bedroom to change into my blue jeans.

Maggie and I sat together to finish our coffee. She snacked on some fruit and I had a bowl of cereal with a heaping spoonful of brown sugar poured over top. We had the radio turned on and listened to the news, commenting to each other on anything of interest. After clanging my bowl into the dishwasher, I pulled on my boots and an old straw cowboy hat and headed out the door, happy to have a purpose for the day.

I pulled up to see Roanie already tied to the fence and saddled. He was a trustworthy, old gelding that Sawyer had rode as a young boy. Roanie's days were numbered but him and I fit each other like a glove. I was becoming increasingly aware of the fact that one of these rides was going to be our last. I was stepping into the saddle less frequently all the time and I usually paid the price for a day afterwards. But right now, it was worth it. I still felt most at peace with the world when I was with a horse.

I stepped over to Roanie and tugged his lead shank loose from the wooden fence. "Hey, there, old boy," I said in a low, soft tone. Roanie just looked at me with tired eyes and I knew he was probably thinking the same thing about me. I patted him gently before slipping a bit into his mouth and tucking the headstall behind his ears. I clucked to him to lead him towards Kylie, who was finishing saddling her colt, a waspy little black 3-year-old.

"Ah, now I see," I said as I approached her. "You just want me and Roanie here to help you keep your colt calm out in the pasture."

"Grandpa, I just enjoy your company and I have absolutely no idea what you're talking about." Her voice was intentionally seeping with sarcasm.

I gave a snort which caused her colt to shy away a little, ears pointed straight ahead. My snort gradually changed to a grunt as I worked my foot up into the stirrup and grabbed a hold of the saddle horn to slowly pull myself up. Kylie's watchful eyes were on me but she said nothing. "All ready," I reassured her.

I thought of all the times I took for granted how easy it was to swing up into the saddle. Especially when I was working as an outrider. My mind shifted back to my first year at Calgary when DS had been rearing in the air and spooking so badly that I couldn't get on him. Now, Roanie stood like a soldier and barely even lifted his head while it took all of my effort to force my boot to make contact with the stirrup. All I had left to prove my worth as a horseman were memories and stories. I turned to Kylie to tell her about the year DS reared up and I ended up on the cover of the Calgary Sun.

Had I told her this before? Certainly. Did it stop me from retelling it? Almost never.

We walked over to the gate and I slowed Roanie up to allow Kylie to open it from the back of her colt. It was a good learning skill for a colt to stand patiently while you leaned over to undo a chain on a gate. The black gelding shied away a few times when Kylie leaned out. She never got after him, just firmly pressed a spur on his side and put him back where he was supposed to stand. Eventually, he relaxed enough to stay in one place and she pushed the gate open wide enough for us to enter the pasture. Roanie knew where we going and I barely ever touched the reins. He settled in to do his job for the day and walked a smooth pace. On my side, Kylie was pulling on the reins and trying to convince her little horse to do the same.

"He needs some miles," I said pointing at her horse. "Why don't you go on ahead and get him tired. Circle back to me. We'll be alright."

Kylie nodded and then was off at a lope. She had her hands full as I watched her go up and down the rolling hills. Sometimes she would break her horse into a small circle when he was pushing on the bit too hard. Other times she would squeeze him forward when he balked or spooked at something ahead of him. I watched until I couldn't see her anymore and then I pulled my hat down, kicking Roanie into a lope of his own. We only made it a few strides before my hips were begging me to stop. I figured it would go that way and I accepted the fact that I would only be walking today as I gently eased Roanie back down out of his lope. Just needed to test it out to be sure.

I walked along, listening to the grass crunching beneath the steady rhythm of Roanie's hooves. The leather on my saddle groaned with every movement of my horse. A breeze picked up and I watched it ripple through the grass before waving through Roanie's mane and eventually floating by me in a gentle whoosh. In a moment like that, it's hard to believe it could've been anything other than God blowing through and whispering in my ear. I like to believe that He was telling me I was exactly where I was meant to be – on a good horses' back with my granddaughter close by.

That good feeling stayed with me while I reached the small herd of heifers. Kylie trotted up beside me. Her colt looked like an entirely different horse by this point. His neck was lathered and sweating but now he walked along in stride with Roanie. No pushing at the bit and no spooking.

I always did find it miraculous how a little hard work could make such a difference in the character traits of a horse. A person, too, for that matter.

"They're settling in," I commented as we rode slowly through the heifers and surveyed each one. The first time we had gotten close to them on horseback, they'd headed for the hills and didn't want no part of us. Now they swished their tails and chomped on grass, barely noticing our presence.

"I've been riding through them every day," Kylie said.

"Good girl," I nodded.

We killed another hour walking through them before we returned home. Getting out of the saddle wasn't much easier than getting in it. I took off Roanie's headstall and started undoing the cinches. Kylie stepped up in a surreptitious manner when it was time to pull the saddle off and throw it on a rack. I never protested.

I walked Roanie back to his pen and turned him loose, hanging the halter on the gate. I gently slapped my hand on his hind end when he walked by me. "Thanks for looking after me, old boy."

"What are you gonna do until supper time??" Kylie called as I headed back for my truck.

"Nap!" I said raising a hand in a half wave goodbye, barely looking back at her.

She giggled as she turned and headed towards the barn.

When I returned later that evening, Maggie was in the passenger seat beside me. She had a plastic tub full of homemade oatmeal chocolate chip cookies riding on her lap. I reached over to the tub and she lightly slapped my hand away, just as I knew she would.

Michelle greeted us on the porch as we walked up. "Come on in, Sawyer and his friend are already inside, they just got here," she smiled. We headed into the house and heard her tone change just as we were pulling the door shut and she yelled, "*Kyyylieee, come in here!!!*" towards the barn.

Maggie and I exchanged a smiling glace. That was our girl; still outside working with her horses. Michelle was a nice person and her and Jake always seemed to have a good marriage. But she was a born and raised city girl. She was just different than us. Throughout the years, it had been hard to find common ground. Her and Jake had met during his short stint at university and they had married a year later. Michelle had never worked, which was fine by me. But she also hired someone to clean her house, she rarely ever made a home cooked meal, and she seemed to spend most of her time shopping for new home décor or getting her nails done. She was materialistic in a way that Maggie and I had never been, no matter how much money we had.

Sawyer came up to us immediately upon hearing our arrival. He hugged Maggie and kissed her cheek. "Grandma, my favorite!" he said, commenting on the cookies she handed him. She beamed at him and affectionately patted his cheek.

Sawyer turned to me and shook my hand, "Grandpa, good to see ya!"

"Missed you, bud," I said squeezing his shoulder.

The three of us entered the kitchen together and I had to stop myself from staring at the young girl sitting on a stool pulled up to the island. She was very pretty, no denying that. But she was… rather scantily clad. She had one of those shirts that rides up to a person's midriff and blue jean shorts that were comprised of so little denim it would be hard to classify them as shorts, at all. It was an interesting choice of an outfit to meet your boyfriend's parents and grandparents in.

"This is Tenille," Sawyer announced. She didn't stand up or come over to shake our hands. She remained seated on her stool and gave us a little wave before ignoring us all together and blatantly staring at Sawyer.

She was clearly infatuated.

I glanced over at Sawyer. I could see why. He was a handsome young man. Good genes, I thought to myself with a touch of pride.

Maggie, always the one to be gracious, approached the young girl and gently patted her hand. "Nice to meet you, dear," she crooned.

The girl lit up with a happy smile, "Awww, you tooooo."

We were joined by Kylie and Michelle. Kylie darted straight towards her brother. They grinned affectionately at each other, bumped knuckles, and instantly fell into a banter about who Grandma truly did bake the cookies for as Kylie dug into the plastic container.

Kylie bit into a cookie as she seemed to notice Tenille for the first time. She paused just a moment too long before cheerily saying, "Hey! How's it going? I'm Kylie."

"Oh, girl, I've heard all about you! You're, like, a real cowgirl, right?" Tenille asked.

Kylie laughed a little and glanced at Sawyer, "Yup, I guess you could say that." She turned to face me, her back at Tenille. She looked right at me with wide eyes and a face that said exactly what I had been thinking. I carefully kept my expression neutral.

Michelle chimed in, "She definitely is our cowgirl," and added, "For that reason, Tenille, honey, you'll have to excuse her for not cleaning up before dinner," Michelle said as she tossed a dish rag at Kylie's head.

Kylie ducked and feigned innocence, checking out her shirt and pretending to sniff it, "What do you mean?" she mumbled with a mouthful of cookie.

Jake came striding into the kitchen, greeting everyone while apologizing for holding up dinner. He said he was leaving his cell phone in his office and wouldn't be working for the rest of the night. I trusted that he would spend some quality time with his family but I wasn't so sure he wouldn't be back at his computer or on his work phone before the night was over.

We all seated ourselves at the expansive kitchen table with plush, cozy dining chairs. Michelle moved in a flurry as she set all the food on to the table. She had cooked a ham. *Good for her*, I thought. And then she placed the potato salad on the table. It was in a plastic tub. Store bought.

The conversation circled with people talking over one another in the way that only close families can do without anyone getting offended. We passed the dishes around and scooped food onto our plates. I felt the familiar wave of gratitude wash over me that I always experienced when I had my whole family together.

In the midst of the swarming food, Michelle reached the plate of thickly sliced ham over to Tenille, offering to drop a piece on to her plate that was already stuck on the serving fork.

"Oh, no thank you," Tenille shook her head. "I'm vegan."

For a moment, the clang of silverware on dishes and the scraping of food came to a complete halt. No one responded. Tenille looked to Sawyer as she visibly shrank back in her seat. Michelle, regaining her composure, simply passed the ham across from Tenille and on to the next person. Everyone started back up, slowly at first and then back to normal.

I cleared my throat. "So, what's your reason for that, then?" I directed the question at Tenille. My tone was flat.

"I just… don't exactly have the stomach for it."

She was clearly uncomfortable. I hadn't necessarily meant to call her out but I also couldn't let the topic go by undiscussed. My whole life had been built around the premise of people eating meat. To me, the idea of not eating meat, was ridiculous and foreign. A vegetarian casually coming to visit my own ranch made me feel strangely disconnected from the outside world.

Maggie, very gently and very subtly, laid a hand on my knee under the table. I knew what that meant. She was telling me to retreat. This was not the place and the girl was surrounded by people who would never understand her viewpoint.

"And where are you from?" I asked her. I would never offer any approval or understanding on the topic of being a vegetarian. But I could change the subject.

"California!" she bounced back upright.

I simply nodded. Figured.

I half way listened as she explained how her mom had been Canadian and she'd always wanted to move up here. I stopped caring altogether as Maggie, Jake, Kylie, and I began to discuss the replacement heifers, our ride through them earlier that day, and Kylie's young horse. I was back on familiar footing, discussing how the heifers looked fatter every time I saw them and how the grass was going to last us longer into the fall than usual.

I was so immersed in our conversation that I had almost forgotten Tenille's presence until she asked Kylie, "So, do you, like, get to ride in the Calgary Stampede?"

Kylie pulled away from our conversation to talk to Tenille. "Yah, actually. I qualified last year. This will be my first time ever competing there."

"So I'll get to watch you there!!" Tenille gushed. The girl couldn't fathom how hard Kylie had worked to qualify for Calgary. In our world, this was a very big deal. Competing at Calgary was a badge of honor signifying that you had reached the highest level in your respective event. With my own weaving history of Calgary Stampede accomplishments, it had become a sacred event amongst our family.

The supper passed by quickly and soon everyone was standing to clear away dinner plates and wrap the food in saran wrap. The lid went back on the potato salad and I placed it back in the fridge.

Michelle caught sight of my face and said, "I hope you didn't mind the ham, Charlie." We always butchered our own beef and we kept deep freezes full of home raised meat. It wasn't very often that I ever ate anything other than beef.

"Sometimes a change of pace is nice," I assured her softly. "Damn fine meal." The relief that washed over her face told me that I needed to give the woman a few more compliments.

When the kitchen was cleaned, Kylie offered to take Tenille out to the barn to show her the horses. Maggie and Michelle both tagged along. As the women all wandered down the path towards the barn, Jake, Sawyer and I settled into chairs on the front porch and watched them walk. Jake and Sawyer both had beers in their hand and I cracked open a coke. I'd quit drinking a long time ago. Never did begrudge anyone who wanted to have a drink or anyone who wanted to have a party, but I'd closed off any desire to let alcohol back into my life after I'd worked so hard to let it go.

We all sat quietly, listening to the chatting voices of the women slowly fade away and be replaced by the crickets chirping around us. I was the first to speak. "Cooling off out here. That girl might catch a cold if you don't offer her some more clothes, Sawyer."

Jake stifled a laugh, "I was waiting for it," he said to Sawyer.

"So was I," Sawyer shook his head and sighed. "She's from California! It's normal to dress like that down there."

I ignored their remarks and continued, "Lord knows she can't afford to get sick. She'll never have the strength to fight anything off if she won't eat any meat."

Now Jake was laughing out loud, "And there it is."

Sawyer smiled, too, as he continued to shake his head. "She's a nice person, Grandpa."

"If you're hanging about with her, then I have no doubt that she is," I nodded. "But if she comes back and we cook her up a good, homegrown steak, I will be deeply offended if she doesn't at least try it."

To me, coming to a ranch and refusing to eat meat was like going to Disneyland and refusing to get on a ride. Or visiting the ocean and not putting your toes in the sand. You were missing the whole point of being there. Sawyer agreed – mostly to please me, I think – and we let the conversation die. Instead, we chatted about baseball and Sawyer's schooling. Jake and Sawyer showed each other videos and pictures on their phones that would make them both laugh. When I'd ask what they were looking at, they'd hold the screen up to my face and then pull it away so quickly that I barely had time to focus on what they were showing me, let alone register it. I would nod along as if I understood what the hell was so funny.

When the girls all returned from the barn, Tenille sidled up beside Sawyer on the chair he was sitting on. She put a hand on his knee as she recounted each horse she'd had the chance to pet. Sawyer listened intently and I wondered how he could act so interested in these stories. Petting a horse on the head is hardly a tantalizing experience for a person who has been doing so since the time they could walk.

Kylie came and sat on the porch step close to my chair and said quietly to me, "She tried to pet my little black colt. She marched right up to it – hand stuck out for its head. He about crawled out of his skin trying to get away from her," she giggled softly. I chuckled along with her. Horse sense is only common sense for people who have been around them.

Tenille piped up, pulling our attention back towards her, "AND I got to meet the pretty, yellow one. So, now I know the horse that Kylie will be riding at the Calgary Stampede and I can cheer EXTRA loud for her and…and…" she trailed off, as she tried to remember the name of Kylie's good horse.

"Deuce," Kylie filled in for her.

"Right!" She clapped her hands together. "Kylie and Deuce."

Michelle piped up, "Tenille has never been to a rodeo before. I told her Calgary Stampede is actually the first rodeo I ever watched, too. Might as well start with the very best, right?"

"Oh, I can't wait," Tenille smiled. "Although, I'm not sure if I want to stay for the… what do you call it… wagon racing? I've seen some really horrific articles about that -"

I instantly bristled and took a sharp intake of breath, ready to inform her, in the politest way possible, about everything good in the chuckwagon racing industry and how any article she might have read didn't even come close to telling the truth from anyone's perspective who actually knew a damn thing about it.

I never got the chance. Before she had barely gotten the words out of her mouth, Sawyer cut her off, squeezing her shoulder and lifting her up on to her feet abruptly, "It's getting late and we need to head back into the city," he said.

"Good idea!" Michelle was guiding them towards their vehicle and practically shooing the girl away from me. "Err, just, I mean, you're right, it is getting late," she gave a nervous laugh.

The whole thing happened so quickly that they were waving and driving away before I even settled down enough to realize I never got a chance to say goodbye to Sawyer. I felt drained and exhausted. "Let's go home," I said softly to Maggie.

In the truck, I tried to keep myself composed. I drove silently, focusing on the road before me until I couldn't hold it in any longer. "Why the hell are the men in this family so drawn to these damn city girls?" I burst out.

Maggie smiled and took a deep breath. She seemed to be considering what to say. Finally, she reached over and rubbed my shoulder. "I'm just glad you weren't," she said.

The tension released from my shoulders and then from the rest of my body. I shook my head and returned the smile. "No," I agreed. "I sure wasn't."

excitement

"Your turn," Rich urged me. There was a crib board placed between us and we were in the middle of a game.

"Oh. Sorry." I glanced down at the cards in my hand before laying one down.

Rich studied me. "Where the hell's your head at today, old timer?"

I'd been distracted the whole game. Usually a crib game between Rich and I played out quickly but I kept forgetting when it was my turn and taking too long to think about which card to play. I grumbled as I threw the rest of the cards in my hand down on to the table, completely forfeiting the game. "Oh, it's this girl that Sawyer brought out to the ranch last night."

Rich waited patiently for me to continue.

"She's a… vegan. And probably one of them animal activists, too, because she almost went off about chuckwagon racing before Sawyer stopped her." I shook my head and pushed my chair back from the table. "The whole damn world is going crazy."

Rich picked my cards off the table and shuffled the deck back together. He stood up to carry the crib board back to the cupboard he had brought it out from. "There's gettin' to be more and more of them vegans," he called over his shoulder. "I read an article about 'em. They seem to think they're saving the planet by not eating meat. Personally, I have a hard time seeing the correlation between the two."

It felt good to vent with Rich. I loved my family but sometimes you have to say nothing just to keep the peace. Here with Rich, I could say whatever I pleased. We had been friends long enough that no discussion was ever off the table. And the older we got, the less filtered we were.

"She said *she just didn't have the stomach* for eating meat. What the hell does that mean?"

"Doesn't have the stomach for it? I'll be damned if I know. There's all these people that won't eat dairy or wheat now, too. She one of them?"

"Hell, probably," I threw my hands up. "Aghhh they probably won't be together much longer, anyways. Good looking boy like Sawyer? He'll find something better."

"'Course he will," Rich agreed.

And with that, we shifted from discussing what's wrong with the changing ways of the world to reminiscing on our own days as young men. Somehow, through the retelling, we convinced each other that we'd been out with a lot more girls before settling down with Maggie and Georgia. The facts of the past weren't near as important as the laughs we got from telling stories.

Time always passed by quickly with Rich. I pulled my phone out and pressed on the screen and was startled to find it was nearly supper time. Maggie would be waiting for me. I got up to leave and walked to the door. As I was heading out, Rich was heading to the easy boy chair in his living room. I suspected he would stay there for the rest of the day.

Maggie was just starting to cook supper when I got home. "I was going to call you and see when you'd be home. How's Rich?" she asked as I walked in to the kitchen.

"He's looking old. I think we should have him out for supper tomorrow night. I don't know if he's eating."

Maggie nodded. I could see the sadness in her eyes. I knew it broke her heart to think of Georgia being gone. She always did everything she could to help Rich. This was one of the bitter truths of getting old: you start to watch your friends around you die. Somehow, we simply accept it and everyone knows that their turn will come in due time. Maggie and I had an early experience with watching someone we love die on us. For me, it seemed to make the others easier.

Our grandchildren kept Maggie and I active. But it was also our lifestyle. Rich lived in town and now he paid someone to mow his grass and shovel his sidewalk. He was slowly letting his body degenerate by no longer choosing to remain active. It was less of a choice for Maggie and I. If we were going to continue to live out here, we had to continue to move our bodies and do the work that was required. We both knew that we'd be here until we were physically incapable of it. Personally, I hoped to die out here. Because I'd sooner be dead than be trapped in an old folks' home.

I wanted to go the way my old buddy Gene had. He was working right up until his last day. Then he just died in his sleep. It'd gotten so that it was awfully hard on him to walk down the cement alley but he always pushed through. By the end, he started spending more and more time in my office. We had long visits and sometimes we just sat in silence while he patted his dog's head and I worked. Both were a great source of comfort to me.

During one of the last conversations we had, he'd completely shocked me with a revelation. We'd been casually discussing one of the yard workers stealing a couple square bales of hay. The worker had been caught and reprimanded. Gene looked right at me and said, "Ya know, I know all about Frank."

We'd been on the topic of stealing but I still wasn't sure if Gene and I were talking about the same thing. My eyes widened. I was sure that no one knew about that except for me and Maggie. "Oh?" was all I managed.

"Aw shit, don't look so surprised. I see everything that goes on around here."

I felt the corners of my mouth turn up just a little. This was true. My mind was reeling with questions. I wanted to ask him how he knew. But more importantly, I wanted to ask him why he hadn't told anyone. Instead, I remained quiet. I'd come to learn that Gene always said everything he needed to say. It just took him a little longer than it took most people.

He thoughtfully stroked his dog's head a few more times before he began. "Were you here during that one poker game… Can't remember what year it was. I know Rich was here. But that skinny American came in and Frank accused him of cheating and then the whole bunch of men turned on that American. That big steer wrestler ended up pinning him down and tickling the poor son of a bitch."

We both chuckled at the memory. "Yah, I remember that. I was there," I said.

"Yah… Well… That night it was just the American, me, and Frank left at the poker table. Frank set that American up to look like he was cheating. Then when everyone's attention was properly shifted to other things, Frank gathered up the money in the pot, real discreet like, and he headed out of there. I never said a thing – just watched it all play out. But the next day, I went into Frank's office. I charged in there mad as hell. Picked him up by the scruff of the neck and held him up against a wall. I told him I didn't hang around liars or cheats. Well, Frank, he just turned into a blubbering mess, right in my hands. He told me the whole story and admitted to everything he'd done. I think he was so guilty about it all that he was almost relieved to be caught. I think he wanted someone to hand out a punishment." Gene softly shook his head at the memory. "He owed a lot of money to some bad people. Really bad people. His life was on the line. I know it was his own damn fault that he was in that situation in the first place. I ruminated on the whole thing for about a week. Finally, I decided that there's a right and there's a wrong. I was heading up to tell Frank that I was going to turn him in. And on the walk to his office, something inside me just shifted. I realized that I haven't got very many friends. Lots of acquaintances – very few friends. I didn't want to lose the one friend I had just because he'd been a dumb motherfucker. So, I wrote Frank a cheque. Can't remember how much it was for. But he needed every dime he could to appease those thugs he owed money to. Frank paid me back and he showed me how he'd rigged the books and showed me when he paid back The Stockyards, too." Gene ended his story with a little shrug, as if the whole thing wasn't really that big of a deal.

I was in disbelief. I'd had a hard time coming to terms with the fact that I would forgive Frank and let him off the hook for his serious transgressions. I felt that if I allowed Frank to do what he did, it meant that I would do the same or that I was condoning it. I never would have believed that Gene could come to terms with Frank's actions. Straight and narrow, black and white, solid ol' Gene.

Talking about Frank with someone else turned out to be highly therapeutic for me. Although Frank and I never quite were on the same terms. We continued to see each other – always carefully evading certain subjects – but the energy was off. I'd had Frank on a pedestal and he was no longer there. When it got too hard for me to be around him, I reminded myself of the good things Frank had done. I remembered that it was only through his recommendation and his training that I had the job I had. I thought of Frank at the front of Philip's herd after the funeral.

When Frank passed away, he left his life savings to The Stockyard's. There wasn't much there. But it caused a great stir amongst the community. For a man to devote his entire life to an auction mart, work day in and day out, and then give back everything that he'd been given was an unprecedent act.

Only Gene and I knew the truth behind the gesture.

We never said anything about it to a single soul.

Maggie lightly shook my shoulders and I was jerked back to reality. She was standing above me in my easy boy chair. "You fell asleep," she said softly. "Supper's ready."

I groaned and stretched and patted my stomach. "Guess I was dreaming," I got up and moved to the kitchen table.

We flicked the radio on and sat down to our food. Another day passed – similar to the ones before it and probably similar to the ones to come. When we crawled into bed that night, I said, "I'm glad the Stampede is coming up. I could use a little excitement in my life," as I flicked the lamp off on my bedside table.

"I can't hardly believe that we'll be watching Kylie run there this year," Maggie agreed. "Although, of course it's been a long time coming." She laughed a little, "Remember how she used to sit on the edge of her seat when we took her there when she was little? She wouldn't speak a word the whole time. Everyone around us would say *my, what a well-behaved little girl* but she was just completely enthralled with the rodeo."

"Yah and Sawyer would be chatting everyone around us, in and out of his seat, looking at the clown, eating popcorn, doing anything except watching the rodeo," I said fondly.

"Well, they're both doing exactly what they're meant to be doing now."

With that statement, we both drifted off to sleep together. I had no idea just what kind of excitement I was about to make for myself.

Hell, no one could've guessed what we were about to be in for.

CHAPTER THIRTY-ONE

composure

The July sun beat down with an unrelenting heat. I could feel little droplets of sweat gathering on the side of my forehead. I took my straw cowboy hat off, wiped my long sleeve cowboy shirt across my brow, and then firmly planted the hat back on my head, sucking it down just a little.

"You doing okay there, Grandpa?" Maggie asked me. It felt like we had been walking for miles.

"Better than the old bastard beside me," I jerked a thumb towards Rich. I was making fun of him but he actually was having a hard time. We had continually walked slower and slower as we went. Rich seemed to be fading as he took short, gulping breaths.

"Just get me inside and get me an ice-cold beer and I'll be ready to go," he said.

We were walking in to the Calgary Stampede grounds. For some reason, it seemed like it was more expansive than I remembered. Had there always been this much walking? I was beginning to regret not taking Jake up on his offer to drop us off closer to the entrance before he parked the truck. Maggie, Rich, and I had hopped in with Jake and Michelle. Today was the first day of the rodeo and Kylie drew up amongst the first set of contestants so she would be racing today. She had come in the night before to ride her horse in the arena. Sawyer and Tenille (evidently, they were still together) were going to meet us here.

I had spoken to Kylie on the phone that morning. Maggie and I called her and put her on speaker phone to wish her luck. We had both sat at the kitchen table, hunched over my cell phone, speaking loudly into it, when Kylie laughed and said, "You guys know that you don't have to talk louder just because it's on speaker phone, right?" She was in a fit of giggles by the time she hung up, telling us she loved us both. I had admired the way she handled herself. This was one of the biggest days of Kylie's career as a professional barrel racer and she was taking on the day in her same happy-go-lucky manner that she greeted every day with.

When we finally approached the gates, Michelle pulled out everyone's tickets and passed them out to us. A lady wearing a white cowboy hat and a red handkerchief around her neck used her handheld machine to scan each ticket before allowing us through. She said a cheery, "*Welcome to the Stampede*," each time her little machine beeped its approval. I walked along, reveling in the atmosphere. The excitement was palpable in the thick, muggy air. There were signs everywhere reading WELCOME TO THE GREATEST OUTDOOR SHOW ON EARTH. Every time I came to Calgary, a part of the old adrenaline kicked in. I'd won thousands upon thousands of dollars here. I kissed the love of my life for the first time at this rodeo grounds. I rode great horses here and raced teams that any chuckwagon driver would be forever blessed to call his own. The sanctity of these rodeo grounds was deep rooted into my entire being. It represented everything good and pure that I had accomplished in my life.

Our little group moved together through the crowds. The amusement aspect of the stampede had continued to explode throughout the years. Food trucks, trade shows, games, rollercoasters, performers, and everything else you could ever imagine. Many people came to the rodeo who weren't interested in the rodeo, at all. There were social aspects built in to the Stampede for young people looking for a party, families wanting a wholesome day out, or older folks looking to get out and see the sights.

I enjoyed seeing all the cowboy hats in the crowds of people. Most of the folks wearing them only put a cowboy hat on once a year when they came out to the rodeo. The hats were bent out of shape, ill fitting, and discolored. I saw plenty of people who unknowingly had their hats on backwards. Some western folks liked to make fun of the way city people put a cowboy hat on to come to the rodeo. I never did approve of that. I figured anyone who respects the lifestyle enough to try and put the hat on was okay in my books.

We ambled along when a little girl bumped into my leg. She must've been about 4 or 5 years old. I shifted out of her way and she tumbled on to her side, losing balance.

"Whoops!" I crouched down to pick her back up on to her feet. She was blonde with blue eyes and about as cute as they come. "Sorry, little girl," I said, remaining down on her eye level. She peered shyly at me.

Her parents were right beside her. "You're alright!" her Mom said cheerily while she gently stroked the little blonde head. "Tell him you're alright!"

The girl eyed me up and then burst through in her happy, upbeat little voice. "I'm alright!!"

Her Dad smiled down at her, "That's a girl." Everyone stood for a moment, unsure of whether to carry on or keep talking. The Dad seemed to take note of my hat, buckle, and cowboy boots. "It's our first time coming to a rodeo." He gestured down at the little girl, "She's been excited for weeks. She loves horses."

"Well, I love horses, too" I said to her. "Now, can you do me a favor?" She looked up at me with wide eyes. "When you watch the barrel racing, can you cheer extra loud for Kylie Hyde? That's my granddaughter. She's going to be on a big, yellow horse. And, I tell you what, if you give her some really good cheers, your Mom and Dad can meet me down on the tarmac after the rodeo and I can let you pet her horse." I spoke in the soft, kind tone that we all seem to reserve specifically for little kids. "If it's okay with your mom and dad," I said looking up at the two of them, reverting back to my normal voice.

The little girl took a deep breath in and practically squealed in delight. "Can I?!" she pleaded.

"Wow, oh my gosh, that is so, so nice of you," the mother smiled.

We made plans to meet after the bull riding and parted ways. We continued to amble through the crowd, never making it very far without seeing a familiar face. Rich was in high spirits, laughing with everyone and visiting people we only got the chance to see once a year. Somewhere along the way, he'd found a beer stand and the silver can of Coors Light was dripping beads of condensation down onto his hand. He'd mutter *ohhh, that's good* and smack his lips together appreciatively after each sip. Everyone who knew us told us they would be cheering for Kylie. Maggie always held her hands up, crossing her fingers, and smiling broadly. When we decided to go find our seats, a man Jake's age called out at him. "Thought a high roller like you would have shelled out for a box!" Jake gave the obligatory chuckle that we all used when someone commented on our money. There was never anything else to do or say. "Better view to watch Kylie from down here!" Michelle called back to the man. I smiled approvingly at her.

When we got to our seats, Sawyer and Tenille were already there, sharing a bag of popcorn. Sawyer reached over and shook my hand with his easy-going, "Hey, Grandpa." When he spotted Rich, he broke into a wide grin and the two chatted away, happy to be catching up with one another. Tenille sat silently the whole time. She was in a similar outfit to the first time I had seen her except now she had on chunky, thick jewelry and a pair of cowboy boots to go with it. To be honest, I was so hot in my blue jeans and long-sleeved shirt that I held more understanding for the amount of skin she was showing.

When we settled into our seats, Maggie was on one side of me and Rich was on the other. Rich leaned over and said quietly in my ear, "That the vegan?" He was referring to Tenille.

"Yah."

"Well… I see why the boy likes her."

We laughed out loud, conspiring with our heads together and then shifted apart and settled in to our seats. It wasn't long before fireworks banged, smoke filled the arena, and the announcer's booming voice rose above the blasting music. Natives were dancing down below, an intricate, beating rhythm. A jet flew above us, doing a low swoop. Action and excitement were everywhere you looked… I guess they don't call it The Greatest Outdoor Show on Earth for nothin'.

We watched horses buck and cowboys throw their hats in the air and ropes swing crisply. There was barely time in between each contestant to comment on how they did.

When a shiny Dodge pickup truck pulled into the arena with three barrels on the back, a silence settled amongst our row. The barrels were being placed on their markers in the arena and the electric eyes were being set up. Kylie was number 8 in the draw. I sat calm and collected. There wasn't a need for me to be nervous. First of all, I knew she was ready. She had done everything in her power to prepare for this moment and her horse was working outstanding. Second of all, it really didn't matter how she did. Of course, I was cheering for her to win. But I wouldn't be any more or any less proud of her based on her performance. I knew the whole family felt the same way.

The first set of barrel racers were a tough group of women. Plenty of big names from the states were up today. We all watched intently as they made their runs. Some were fast, some were slow. Some knocked barrels, adding a 5 second penalty on to their time. When it was Kylie's turn, the announcer hollered, "Now, ladies and gentleman, how about we give it up for a HOMETOWN COWGIRL.... That's right, you heard me, this is Kylie Hyde and she's from just down the road, Strathmore, Alberta!!!!"

Kylie walked her horse down the alley. He was prancing and ready to run. She kept him in her hands all the way up to the gate before pushing the reins up and towards his ears. He skyrocketed forward in his explosive way. My instinct quietly kicked in. I'd watched Kylie enough times to know this was going to be a good run. I could tell by the way she was riding into the first barrel. "*She's going for it,*" I said under my breath, not sure if anyone could even hear me. Kylie pushed forward and kicked to the second barrel and Rich said back, just as quietly, "*She damn sure is.*"

When Kylie was running home from the third barrel, her over and under whip in hand, Maggie nearly jumped out of her seat. She was bouncing up and down, cheering, "Yes, yes, go, go!!!!!" with her hands in tight fists.

We all knew it was going to be fast before we saw the time on the big screen. Then we erupted. "NEWWWW LEEEEADER," the announcer droned.

I put an arm around Maggie and squeezed tightly. She looked up into my eyes. We never said a word to each other; there was no need.

We both felt the same way. I knew that when we were lying in bed together that night we would go into great detail about Kylie's run. We would praise her and say she was the best rider there; say she had a way with horses like nothing we had ever seen. But right now, with all of the surrounding eyes on us, and the claps on the back from friends and family, we simply looked at each other and smiled.

"Pretty damn good," I humbly repeated over and over while surrounding people congratulated us. We watched patiently as the remaining girls in the performance made their runs. Kylie was knocked into second place by a couple one thousandths of a second. It wouldn't have mattered if she was first, second, or last. We were so proud.

I shifted impatiently in my seat throughout the Bull Riding, eager to get down to Kylie. I could see her on the track below. She was taking the protective boots off her horse, putting a halter on him, and walking him out to cool down while constantly reaching up and patting his neck. When the last bull bucked, I made a beeline for the place on the tarmac that I had promised to meet the little girl from earlier. She was already waiting with her parents – all three of them looking eager and searching for me. I greeted them briefly and directed them to follow me. We met Kylie and I gave her a wink before introducing the little family tagging along behind me. Just as I knew she would, Kylie was kind and patient with the little girl. She picked her up and let her pet her horses' neck. The mom stood a short distance away, documenting the whole thing with her cell phone held up in front of her face to take pictures and videos. The dad asked Kylie questions and repeatedly thanked her for her time. The whole meeting took only a couple minutes and ended with Kylie signing an autograph. She wrote:

Being a cowgirl is a condition of the heart.

Kylie Hyde

We waved goodbye to the family knowing we would likely never see them again but that a little girl's day had been made. Then Kylie and I walked toward the horse barns, side by side, with her big yellow horse trailing behind us and now completely calm after the adrenaline rush of being asked to give his very best effort earlier in the afternoon. Kylie kept reaching back and gently stroking his head while we walked. Their bond was stronger than ever. When we got back to the barns, I took the lead shank and held her horse while she unsaddled and brushed him down. Then she led him over to the nearest hose to wash him off and I pulled out a bucket, flipped it over and pushed it up against the wood of the stall. I groaned as I lowered my body onto the bucket and laid my head back against the stall. The heat was still unrelenting and the shade of the barns felt good. I relaxed, savoring the quiet after all the excitement of the day. People and horses walked past me in the alley of the barn but most everyone just smiled briefly at me and carried on their business. I was just beginning to fall back into memories of looking after my own horses in these barns, when a face from the past was suddenly looking down at me. It was Cody Lockett – one of my old outriders. Cody and Kyle were brothers that had rode for me for years. They were great men, salt of the earth people. I remembered how thoughtful they'd been after Philip's death and the accident with Hubba Bubba breaking his leg. I rarely saw the brothers anymore but Cody had a son who was a Tie Down Roper and was here competing.

Cody stopped midstride and recognition lit up his face. "Well, son of a bitch, I was wondering who this tired, old man was sitting on a bucket," he grinned.

I laughed as I worked my way upright and shook his hand. "How the hell are ya, young feller?"

"Not too many people call me young anymore, Charlie."

We fell into a light banter, just like old times. We discussed the day's performance as he praised Kylie and I praised his son. That's the way it always was in the rodeo world. Congratulating other people only to have them humbly brush it off. We were discussing how far the rodeo world had come since our own day and how the horses just kept getting better and better when Kyle said, "I tell you what else has changed is these damn animal activists. They're getting worse. They were out parading and holding signs when I drove up today."

"Ah, let 'em make signs. They don't know what they're even saying. Haven't got a clue what it's really like around here," I said as I gestured about at all the people currently working hard to look after their horses.

"Maybe someone oughta tell 'em," Cody said.

I nodded and agreed. Cody was just making light conversation. But for some reason, his words resonated with me. Someone should tell them.

We were still standing in the same place when Kylie came back and led her horse into the box stall that was piled high with clean shavings and already filled with water buckets and hay nets. She was trailed by a young man in starched jeans and a starched shirt with sponsorship patches sewn on to the front. He was holding a rope in his hand and casually twirling a loop around so naturally that it was evident he probably had that rope in his hand more often than not. I vaguely recognized him until Cody piped up.

"Charlie, you remember my son? Probably haven't seen him in years, hey?"

"Ah – Tyler!" I shook his hand. I hadn't seen him since he was a boy but he was a grown man now.

"Well, Kylie, the rest of the family will be waiting for us. We should go get something to eat," I finally said after making small talk.

Kylie faltered a moment. "Um, actually, Grandpa. I might just go eat with Tyler." Her cheeks flushed slightly and Tyler smiled at her, carefully avoiding my gaze.

I gathered my composure. "No worries, I'll call you later, then." Cody and I walked away together and simply raised our eyebrows at each other, with me wanting to avoid the subject and Cody knowing better than to comment.

CHAPTER THIRTY-TWO

better

Day two of the stampede began similar to the first. Maggie and I called Kylie in the morning at the kitchen table. We were more conscious of the volume of our voices but we remained hunched over my cellphone together. We told her how proud we were and said we knew she would do the same thing today. Then Maggie interrupted me when I was discussing the weather forecast for the week. "Oh, Grandpa, nobody cares about that," she softly swatted my shoulder and then leaned back over the phone. "Honey, I want to know about the date!"

Kylie burst out laughing. "The date was good. He's… really nice."

"I looked him up in the souvenir program I bought yesterday because there's a head shot of each contestant. That boy is _cute_."

That got Kylie talking and the two of them gushed over the phone as I excused myself to refill my coffee cup. I remained standing in the kitchen until Kylie said she had to go. Then I hollered out, "You just get ready for today and focus on another good run!"

"Don't gotta get ready when you stay ready, Grandpa," Kylie teased back and hung up.

Maggie got up and puttered down the hallway to our bedroom to get herself ready for the day. She looked back over her shoulder and casually said, "You know, it's about time she found a young man to hang out with instead of spending all her free time with you," as she walked.

I gave a grunt loud enough for her to hear and then sat back down at the table, smiling softly to myself. My little girl was growing up and I'd be damned if I was ever going to hold her back from finding happiness.

Once again, Maggie and I caught a ride with Jake and Michelle. We picked Rich up in town on our way through. The five of us piled into Jake's truck. I was happy to be getting Rich out of the house every day and enjoyed his company immensely. The two of us would get lost in our own conversation as Jake took numerous phone calls about business and Michelle and Maggie quietly chatted to one another.

When we arrived and were making the same walk into the rodeo grounds that we had the previous day, we were bombarded by chanting and protesting. People were complaining about the rodeo and saying it was animal cruelty. Some of the western folk would yell back telling them to get a job or do something better with their time. Our small group simply carried on, choosing to ignore the whole scene and stare straight ahead. I walked with my head held high but when we were past them, I shuddered. "Sure am glad I never had to deal with that shit when I was racing," I said.

Jake just shrugged, clearly unphased. "We get them sometimes at our downtown office. Oilfield protestors. They're probably the same damn people that are here," he jerked his thumb back towards the crowd we had just passed. "Lots of them are paid protestors. They don't even care what the cause is. They just want the money to stand there and hold the sign."

I shook my head, confused. Things had changed so much that I couldn't even try to keep up with what was happening in the world. I did know that everyone these days appeared to have a cause they were fighting for. It seemed to give people a sense of purpose.

The protestors were easily forgotten once we were through the gates. We spotted more old friends and talked to everyone. We slowly worked our way to our seats and waited for the time to pass until Kylie was up.

She didn't place in the performance. Another good run with a slight bobble on her second barrel that was enough to put her out of the money. Her time didn't matter, our row cheered just as loud for her as we had the previous day. When the performance was over, I didn't rush over to her. I stayed with Maggie and we continued to visit with people as the stands cleared out. I was aware of Maggie's earlier statement about Kylie spending less time with her Grandpa and I decided to give her a little space. But I still kept an eye on her and I gave Maggie a little shove and pointed towards her when I saw her walking back to the horse barns with Tyler Lockett as they each led their horses behind them. Maggie gave a small whistle under her breath and we smiled at each other.

"Wasn't so long ago that it was you and I falling for each other at this very same place," Maggie said quietly to me.

I chuckled softly. "It was actually very long ago," and I squeezed her hand.

Maggie sighed deeply. "Feels like yesterday to me."

Our small group began to assemble and we were going to start making our way back to the truck with another rodeo performance behind us. Jake and Michelle were making supper plans and arrangements for us. We were going to meet up with some old friends and then come back later for the chuckwagon races. When Kylie started barrel racing, I became more immersed in the rodeo performances and gradually fell away from the chuckwagon community. But I was looking forward to being back in the atmosphere and watching the horses run tonight.

We were all shuffling along slowly, the way that groups do when three of the members are over 75, when a growing crowd of people appeared to be causing a ruckus by the race track. I stopped, peering over at the group. A news van was setting up and policemen were forming a small circle. Without really noticing what I was doing, I headed towards the scene. I was mainly just curious. When I got closer, I saw a young man had handcuffed himself to the inside rail of the racetrack. He was sitting in the dirt with his hands raised above his head and the steel chain of the handcuffs was over top of the metal pole. His expression was completely blank. I kept looking at his face as I got closer, trying to get a read on him. He had long hair that was swept up on top of his head in a bun; the same way Kylie often wore her hair. He had stubble on his cheeks and chin and the muscles on his shoulders were defined as he held his arms up. He didn't look upset, defiant, happy, or attention-seeking. He simply sat without saying a word.

"What have we got happening here?" I asked a young man standing close by in a cowboy hat.

He shook his head, letting his disgust show. "Tree huggers," he muttered as if that explained everything and no other words were needed.

I pushed my way forward. I wanted to talk to the young man in the handcuffs. I was almost all the way up to him when I crouched down, getting to his eye level. "How's it going?" I asked. I wasn't sure what to say to him under the unusual circumstances but I ultimately decided to just start a conversation in the same way I'd start any other conversation.

He looked directly at me. The surprise was evident on his face. It was the first time he had broken free from his carefully placid disposition. But he remained silent.

I felt a gentle tapping on my shoulder and looked up to see an RCMP officer in his red and black uniform. "I'm sorry, sir, I'm gonna have to ask you to stand back," he said.

I nodded and stood back upright, backing away without having the chance to speak to the young man. I kept my eyes on him, wondering if he would look at me again, but he was already staring straight ahead, clearly uninterested in who I was. I watched as a reporter fixed her shirt and smoothed her hair. She was standing right in front of the young man and holding a microphone in her hand. She was busy pointing and giving orders to the people behind the cameras and I heard her sharply say, "We need to get this shot *now* before he's removed from the track." My head was swirling and my heart was pounding as I realized what was about to unfold.

Soon she had the microphone held up to her mouth and she was looking directly into the camera. "I'm Kate Linderman and I'm reporting for CTV NEWS Calgary on the scene at the Calgary Stampede racetrack where a young man has taken a stand against tonight's chuckwagon races." She gestured behind her to show the man sitting in the dirt with the handcuffs above his head. "Tensions are rising as animal activists are coming to a head with rodeo fans and competitors."

When she finished saying that, the young man lifted his head up and called out loudly, looking right at the camera. "THE EXPLOITATION OF THESE BEAUTIFUL ANIMALS HAS GOT TO END NOW. NOW IS THE

TIME FOR ACTION. WE CAN NO LONGER SIT ON THE SIDELINES AND ALLOW THESE ANIMALS TO BE TORTURED FOR AMUSEMENT."

I smirked. The son of a bitch certainly had no problem talking once the cameras were rolling. I stepped forward. I wasn't going to back down from this. I got as close to the man and the cameras as I could without raising concern from the Mounties. "Well, son," I started, loud enough to get his attention and the reporters', "You and I can agree on one thing from what you just said. They certainly are beautiful animals. I'm going to have to disagree with you on the whole torture subject, though."

The reporter sized me up. She seemed to be assessing whether or not I was worth paying attention to. I knew what she was thinking because all the previous indicators said that she was a woman who got straight to business. She was wondering if I would make the story better or worse.

"I'm a retired professional chuckwagon driver and former Calgary Stampede champion, if that helps," I said to her.

She raised her eyebrows. "Get him a mic," she said to someone who quickly scrambled to the van. They put the mic in my hand and placed me beside the woman before I even had time to realize what was happening.

She held her hand out to me. "Kate Linderman."

I took her hand. "Charlie Hyde."

Her handshake was quick and aggressive – seemingly just like her.

I instantly liked her.

"I'm joined by former professional chuckwagon driver and Calgary Stampede Champion – Charlie Hyde." I gave a little nod to the camera, hoping that I didn't look like a deer in the headlights. Kate squared her shoulders toward me and titled her head to the side. "Charlie, tell me how you feel about this scene behind us. What's running through your mind right now?"

It was a good question and it allowed me to gather my wits a little. I took a breath. "Well, I'd just like to have a conversation with some of these people who hold such differing viewpoints. It's hard for me to understand where they're coming from when I've been working with horses my whole life. I can't see what they're even protesting."

The man behind us hollered out again, "HORSES DIE DURING CHUCKWAGON RACES. I'M FIGHTING FOR THEM."

Kate cleared her throat and raised her voice, trying to regain control of the interview. "There have been recorded fatalities of horses in the chuckwagon races in the past. What do you have to stay about that issue?"

"They're getting better and better at applying safety regulations. It's changed a lot since my day, most of it for the better. But, yes, there have been fatalities in the past. This is always tragic. My heart goes out to anyone who has ever lost a horse. My heart also goes out to anyone who has lost a family member in a vehicular accident... or a friend in a helicopter crash... or a pet from an illness. There are accidents in all aspects of life. Most of 'em are out of our control no matter how many safety regulations are put into place. Accidents can't stop us from livin'..."

I trailed off and the man in handcuffs piped up again. "CHUCKWAGON DRIVERS ARE HORSE ABUSERS."

I wasn't sure if he had heard me earlier or not. I had nothing to say so I waited for Kate to speak again. She seemed unsure which direction to take next. She glanced quickly behind her and then said, "As a former Calgary Stampede Champion, I can assume you've won hundreds of thousands of dollars as a chuckwagon driver?"

I gave a brief, small nod.

"With that being the case, what would you say to people who feel you are too economically invested to see the cruelness of it all?"

Whew. It was a hell of a question. I gave up on looking at the camera. Instead, I looked right at Kate. "I would say that those people are too far removed to see the kindness of it all."

A brief look flashed through Kate's eyes. Understanding. I turned back to the camera with my chest poked out a little further than when I had first stepped into place. *Guess it was a hell of an answer, too,* I thought to myself.

Kate wrapped up the interview. I glanced around and saw Jake, Michelle, Maggie, and Rich standing in a group close by. Michelle's jaw was open and she looked like she was in a state of shock. Rich was beaming and smiling and nodding his head. Jake and Maggie stood next to one another with neutral expressions.

I walked over to them while people shouted things out to me.

"'Bout time someone from our side spoke up!"

"Heck of an interview, old timer!"

I smiled politely and nodded but carried on to my family. Michelle was the first one to talk when I reached them. "Charlie! We were just walking along and suddenly you disappeared and no one could find you through the crowds. How the heck did you end up doing that interview?"

I shrugged. "Someone said yesterday we oughta tell 'em what really goes on around here. So that's what I tried to do."

Michelle, shook her head, seemingly in disbelief. Rich was still smiling when he thumped me on the back, "Took me a lot of years and hard work but I'm glad you managed to pick up a few things from me. You were a smooth-talking fool just now. Cool as a cucumber, too. Couldn't have done it better myself!"

Then we all carried on and started walking to the truck, as if nothing had happened. I glanced over my shoulder. A welding truck had backed up on the track to where the young man was. They were going to cut the handcuffs. The mounties had backed everyone farther away and they were surrounding the young man. I briefly wondered what would happen to him once the handcuffs were cut, before turning around and walking out of sight.

Jake had made reservations at a sports bar. We were late and our friends were already waiting for us. I sat down, feeling hungry and eager to eat some food. The main topic of conversation was my interview on the racetrack. I mostly stayed silent and listened to everyone else discuss the goings on. Maggie would occasionally reach under the table and pat my knee. I knew that I would have plenty more to say about the incident when it was just her and I lying in bed.

Just as I was taking one of the last bites of my burger, someone pointed at one of the big, flat screen TVs in the corner. I looked over at it and saw my own face, right beside Kate Linderman. They had my name on the bottom banner above *Former Professional Chuckwagon Driver.* There was no sound from the interview, only loud music playing throughout the bar. But we all watched the whole thing intently. I knew what was being said and I hoped to God it was good enough to make people stop and think.

When the news cycle switched to a different story and my face was no longer on the screen, everyone looked at me. I knew they were waiting for me to comment. I chewed thoughtfully and looked down at the last bite of hamburger in my hands. "This better damn well be Alberta beef," I said casually.

Everyone laughed, including Maggie. Then she piped up and talked about the time my picture had ended up on the cover of the Calgary Herlald. Jake, Rich, and Michelle knew the story well. But our friends all listened with baited breath. Maggie had a flourish for story-telling. She kept them laughing throughout and ended by saying, "I guess Charlie just has a knack for publicity when it comes to this Stampede."

I had to agree with her. So often throughout situations in my life, I chose to be quiet. I never was a fan of small talk. I believed actions were louder than words. And my best friend had always been the storyteller so I was content to stand by and let him take the spotlight. But something about the Calgary Stampede seemed to always bring out the hidden grandeur of my personality. I figure it was probably because the stampede was the closest thing I had to a celebration of my life. It represented most everything I believed in.

We all finished eating and headed out. Jake paid the bill for the entire lot. "I can write it off," he winked at me as the two of us trailed out behind.

When we arrived back at the stampede grounds, Sawyer and Tenille were waiting in their seats. Sawyer was already talking excitedly to me before I was even close enough to hear him. I caught the tail end as he said, " – and it's blowing up on Twitter! Everyone is hashtagging The Kindness Of It All."

I stared at him blankly. He may as well have been speaking another language.

We all sat down in our seats and Sawyer laughed, realizing I didn't know what he was talking about. "Anyways, Grandpa, it was an awesome interview. I can't believe you did it."

"I know!!" Michelle piped up as she slapped her hands on her knees. "That's the thing that I just can't get over. You, Charlie, of all people. I just did not expect you to have a conversation with a protestor or try to explain your point of view to a reporter. You barely even have the time for someone who doesn't understand the difference between a quarter horse and a thoroughbred. Let alone those people."

I felt a twinge of guilt as I realized Michelle was probably referring to herself as the person who didn't understand the difference between a quarter horse and a thoroughbred. "Even an old man can acknowledge when he needs to do better," I said.

We all placed bets with each other on the chuckwagon heats. I won the most, gathering loonies in my pocket and bragging each time. It was a beautiful night, surrounded by my favorite people, watching fast horses work.

There were no fatalities.

CHAPTER THIRTY-THREE

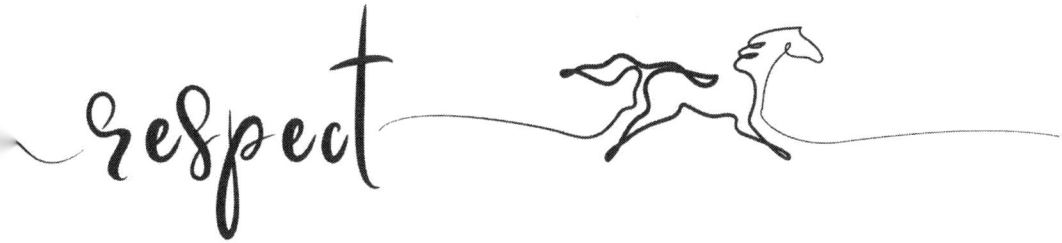

respect

The next morning, Maggie and I groggily made our way to the kitchen. We both sat at the table, sipping our coffee, reluctant to do anything else. It was only Day 3 of the Stampede and we were already wearing down.

"I used to wake up feeling like this during the Stampede when I'd been drinking all night and only got an hour or two of sleep. Any chance you spiked my waters last night?" I muttered to her with an eyebrow raised.

She smiled softly as she rubbed her eyes and yawned. "I wonder how Rich is doing."

Rich had steadily sipped on beers all day yesterday. He would swallow a little bit down and then nod in appreciation, often commenting on how good it tasted. I chuckled at the thought of him smacking his lips each time he cracked a beer open. "We've got a lot of days of rodeo left," I commented.

Maggie nodded. Then she lightly smacked her hand down on the table and perked herself upright, summoning up some energy. "Well! Let's call our girl!" She tossed my cell phone towards me and I called Kylie who was already up and at it. She'd fed her horse and walked him out and ate at the complimentary breakfast for contestants.

"Grandpa, you really started something!" she said. "Everyone is talking about your interview. Did you hear what Mark Anderson said last night?"

Mark Anderson was a big name in the chuckwagon racing world. He was currently at the top of the game and he'd had the fastest time of all the heats last night. I had no clue what Kylie was talking about but she explained.

"When they interviewed him, he said he wanted to send a special shout out to his old friend Charlie Hyde. He said he wanted to dedicate his race last night to everyone who understood the kindness of it all. I watched the video this morning, I'll send you the link."

Maggie and I exchanged glances. This certainly was gaining a lot of momentum. "Isn't that something..." I said to Kylie.

She laughed. "You know, other people might be surprised by your interview with that lady but I'm not. You've been spouting off wisdom like that to me every day of my life."

"Oh, honey," Maggie shook her head. "Don't let your grandpa's head get too big, now."

Kylie laughed again and told us goodbye. I felt rejuvenated by our conversation. Kylie had that affect. She was always so light and happy, a beacon of energy. I had no doubt that she was keeping me young. I took off to the bedroom to get dressed for the day, eager to watch her make another run.

When we all entered the stampede grounds, the animal activists were still holding up signs and protesting. No more and no fewer than there'd been yesterday. It was a good reminder to myself that I could spout off a few words but not much had changed in the big scheme of things.

When we got to our seats, Michelle said she was going to grab herself an iced coffee. Rich surprised everyone when he piped up and said he wouldn't mind trying one of those. When Michelle returned with two iced coffees and handed one over to Rich, we all watched as he took the first sip. He immediately scrunched up his face. "Tastes like shit," he said and then immediately put the straw in his mouth and tried it again. "But it grows on ya."

When it was time for the barrel racing, I had to nudge Rich with my elbow. His chin had fallen down onto his chest and he was sleeping soundly in his seat. "Hey, old timer. You not quite feeling up to snuff today?" I asked him with a sly smile, already knowing the answer.

Rich cleared his throat and readjusted his cowboy hat. "I'm fine. Perfectly fine. Just don't know why the hell I'm so damn parched when I drank so much yesterday."

We all laughed before quieting down to watch Kylie. She had another great run, finishing second for the day again. The announcers had continually talked her up as a hometown cowgirl and she was becoming a fan favorite. The whole crowd would cheer loudly, stomping their feet, clapping their hands, whooping, hollering, whistling. Kylie and her horse both seemed to thrive under the circumstances. They were going for it every time. I was so proud of her confidence. She believed in her horse and it allowed her horse to give his best every time. It was something special to watch.

The days seemed to blur together after that point. More visiting, more suppers, more rodeos and chuckwagons. Every night we would go back to our own homes which was only a half hour drive out of the city. I drove us home a couple times when Michelle and Jake wanted to have a few drinks. Maggie and I snuck in a few naps when we got wore out but nothing would have ever kept us away from watching Kylie each day. Rich stayed with us every day although he was walking slower and slower as time went on. He always seemed to find a second wind with a cold beer and a conversation with an old customer or friend.

Kylie ended up placing in three rounds and qualifying for the Sunday championship. It was a dream come true for her to even make it to that round. But she wasn't slowing up at all. She was going for the win.

My interview momentum carried through the entire rodeo. All of our old friends brought it up. A few old timers mentioned that the fellow in handcuffs should've just been left there while the races took place. I always laughed and usually agreed with them but something inside me said that we were never going to accomplish anything with that attitude. The agriculture and western communities had been making jokes amongst ourselves and turning our noses up at those who didn't understand us for as long as I could remember. I knew it wasn't doing anything to help the divide between us.

Sawyer and Tenille came to every performance to watch Kylie run. I had some great conversations with Sawyer. He was becoming a young man that could hold his own in terms of smarts and humor. I liked to listen to him talk about his schooling even though I didn't usually understand it all. Once he was on a subject and no one interrupted him, he would become more animated. It would light up his whole face. I knew that he didn't want to be involved with horses or the agriculture community but he still had the same passion that ran through our family. He simply pointed that passion in a different direction.

When Showdown Sunday finally rolled around, I began to feel a ball of nerves in my stomach. It was the first time I'd actually been nervous for Kylie. The truth of the matter was that the winner was going to take home a hundred thousand dollars and that was a lot of money. The atmosphere of the stampede combined with the looming prospect of the payout had me on edge. I could feel my stomach going around the way it used to before a big race of my own when I was still a chuckwagon driver. The difference was that back then, I would take action to calm myself. I could check my horses, running a hand down their powerful hind end, reassuring them and myself. I could go over all the equipment. I could check the ground and the conditions of the racetrack. All the little rituals that brought me peace of mind. But now there was nothing to do except sit and wait and I found that task a lot more daunting.

Kylie was going to be racing against the toughest women in the world. To qualify for Showdown Sunday, contestants either had to make it through their set like Kylie did or slip in on the last day during Wildcard Saturday. No matter how they got there, it was going to be a tough race. The sun was beating down and the arena dirt was perfect which always made for faster times.

The afternoon performance had 10 contestants and then 4 from that set would move on to the last round – where they gave away the $100,000 prize money in a sudden death show down.

Kylie blasted them in the afternoon. She won the performance. She was moving on to the final four and the crowd went completely wild for her. As the majority of our row cheered and screamed along with the rest of the grandstand, I simply clapped a few times and smiled at Maggie. That was as good of a run as I'd ever seen her make. I let out a shaky sigh and then gathered myself together to watch the bull riding.

We all went to see Kylie at the horse barns as we waited for the Final Four to start. By the time we got there, her horse was unsaddled, brushed, walked out, and now happily standing in front of a water bucket and a pail of grain combined with some supplements. It was hard to believe that he was the same horse that had just fired so hard that he outran the top horses of the world. Now he stood lazily swishing his tail, his head lowered and a relaxed look in his eye.

Kylie was overjoyed. She beamed at all of us as we remarked on how good of a run it was. She watched her video over and over. It was one of the few times that she never offered a self-critique for something she should have done better. She was simply soaking it all in and enjoying the moment. We all rotated around and took turns sitting beside her and wrapping an arm around her. It was just our family along with Rich and Tenille and I was glad there were no more people around us. No one had to watch what they said or be mindful of staying humble. We could all praise Kylie and her horse openly.

Tenille was accepted by everyone; admittedly most everyone was more welcoming than me. Maggie always made a point to talk to her and ask her questions. But the entire time we were at the horse barns, she was on her phone. Just as she had been the entire time we sat in the stands during the rodeo performances. Her phone was either in her lap with her head bent down looking at it or she held it up, almost right in front of her face. She'd tap like crazy on the screen for one minute and then flick her thumb and scroll the next minute. I had no idea what she was always doing on it that kept her so focused. But I found it hard to engage with her when she was always so clearly engaged with the device in her hands.

Eventually a reporter meandered over to our little group by the horse barns. She was a well-known rodeo reporter who had met Kylie the year before during her qualification at the Canadian Finals Rodeo. The reporter stole Kylie away and they chatted privately for a while. It felt like time passed quickly and soon we were all heading back to the grandstand to take our seats and watch the final showdown.

As always, the Calgary Stampede committee put on a grand show before the final four. There were firecrackers popping loud enough to make my ears ring and my chest thump. I vaguely wondered what was going through Kylie's mind, wishing I would have given her more of a pep talk before I left. I had chosen to walk away with a wink and a smile as everyone said good luck to her. As everyone peered into the arena at the elaborate opening ceremonies, I pulled out my cell phone from my shirt pocket and began slowly hitting the keys to type out a text to Kylie.

Go for it, I wrote.

My phone pinged almost instantly with her reply. *You know I will.* Then she sent two little icons, the yellow heart and the strong arm. Satisfied, I tucked my phone back into my pocket and focused on the rodeo.

When the barrel racing began, we all held our breath. Kylie was going to be the last girl to run. We watched as the first, second, and third girls all made their runs. No one ran faster than Kylie's time earlier that afternoon. That was a good sign. We already knew that she could win it if she just did what she'd already done.

As Kylie walked up the alley, her horse prancing, the announcers asked for everyone to start cheering. The fans obliged and the roar that came from the grandstand was enough to rattle your insides. The announcer boomed into the mic, "Her granddaddy was a Calgary Stampede champion, this rodeo is in her BLOOD, now, let's show her some support!!"

Kylie dropped her hands as soon as the crowd started making noise and she pushed her horse forward. He exploded with his same power that we had been watching all week. She rode him hard all the way into the first barrel and he wrapped the barrel as tight as he could.

Too tight.

As she left the first barrel and was riding to the second, the first barrel slowly tipped over and hit the ground. She'd knocked it coming out of it. A knocked barrel was a 5 second penalty. It was over; she was out of it. The crowd gave an audible sigh. As Kylie rounded the second barrel, she could see the first barrel laying on its side. She quit kicking and pushing her horse but he continued to run. She rounded the third barrel easily. She didn't kick or whip on the way home, she knew her time no longer mattered. Instead, she reached down and patted her horses' neck as he stretched out and flew as fast as he could without any encouragement from her to do so.

I wasn't disheartened. I wasn't upset. But a single tear slid down my weathered cheek as I watched her petting her horses' neck and then saw her reach behind and pat his butt as she slowed him up. She had just lost her chance to win a hundred thousand dollars, to accomplish a life-long dream, and to gain notoriety and respect within the rodeo world. But her first reaction was to thank her horse, through those simple little gestures. I reached up and wiped the tear away and thought to myself, *that's what the kindness of it all really is.*

CHAPTER THIRTY-FOUR

reassurance

Life returned back to normal after the stampede was over. Kylie was out riding her colts the very next day because, well, life carries on. She never complained about the knocked barrel. I was amazed by her resilience. "Far stronger than I was at her age," I mentioned to Maggie who just looked at me in her loving way and replied, "Sometimes you sell yourself short." Throughout a lifetime of marriage, that was still one of my favorite things about Maggie. She could always surprise me. Sometimes she was sweet and soft, sometimes she was spunky and teasing. And she had the ability to always know which one I needed the most at any given time.

It was four days after the stampede ended that Maggie came to me with a pale face and an expression I had never seen on her face before. At first, I thought she was ill. She had just been out for a walk, all the way down our winding driveway and to the road.

"What's wrong?" I asked as soon as I saw her.

She didn't say a word. Just shook her head and laid a piece of paper down on the table in front of me. I was reluctant to tear my focus away from her. There was something in her eyes that I had never seen before. Fear.

When I looked down at the paper, I saw bold print, all capitals that filled the page.

CHARLIE HYDE

KILLS HORSES

Something built in my chest and rose to my throat. I made a sound that didn't form any words, it was more just a low growl. I wasn't scared or embarrassed or shameful – if that's what the intention of this was.

I was fucking livid. I couldn't even remember the last time I had felt an anger like that course through my body. I suddenly had a flashback from my youth: when I was a youngster sitting in church. The pastor gave a sermon on anger. He stood up there and told us that anger isn't the enemy. It had surprised me because I thought religion was supposed to be all love and good feelings. But the pastor explained that anger is an old friend. Not a nice or gentle friend. But a friend that tells us when we have been betrayed. He said that anger was meant to be tapped into and it can remind us to start acting in our own best interests. When we left church that day, my dad said it was the best sermon he'd ever heard. I never understood it until now.

I marched over to the phone and dialed Jake's number. I told him what his mother had found on her walk.

"I'm in the city but I'm coming home right now," he said and I was about to hang up but then I heard his voice call out again. "Hey, Dad."

"Yah?"

"Don't do anything until I get there."

I grunted a reply and slammed the receiver down. Maggie and I waited for Jake to show up. She would periodically ask a few questions.

"Who would do this?"

"What does it even mean?"

"Were there people trespassing on our property?"

I never replied to her. I patted her hand a few times and shook my head but I remained silent. She never pressed me and eventually got up and busied herself making a pot of tea. It was ready when we heard Jake's truck pulling up to the house. The time it had taken him to drive out had done me some good. I no longer felt the hot rage from earlier. I was still pissed off but I never did have it in me to stay mad for very long. I could feel myself beginning to relax a little.

I was surprised to hear two doors slam shut. I peered out the window and saw Sawyer walking around from the passenger side.

"Sawyer's with him," I said to Maggie and she immediately dug into the freezer to pull out a batch of cookies she always kept on standby for the grandkids.

Jake and Sawyer stomped their feet on the rug on the porch and then stepped inside, pulling off their shoes. My heart sank a little when I saw Jake's hand clutching a handful of papers. I took them from him and flipped through them quickly. They all said the same thing. I walked straight to the garbage can and dumped them in, just to make myself feel better.

"They were stapled to the telephone poles. The one in the driveway probably just blew off and ended up there. I don't think they would be stupid enough to trespass," Jake said. He seemed relatively calm and collected.

"I was just stopping in to see Dad at the office when you called him," Sawyer piped up.

Maggie swooped in behind him with the plate of cookies she had just taken out of the microwave and wrapped him in a hug after she set the plate in front of him. "Well, my day is better already now that I get to see you," she said warmly.

Sawyer smiled. Then he glanced at Jake, as if he was silently asking him something.

"Go on, tell him," Jake said.

Sawyer nodded. "Grandpa, it didn't take me long to find some stuff on the internet that explains all of this. I guess you… had some people look in to your past. I found an animal rights website that seems to focus mainly on horses. They're trying to get horse slaughter houses shut down and all that. But they're also trying to stop chuckwagon racing. They have a tab on their webpage that keeps track of every horse that's ever been hurt or killed at a professional chuckwagon race. Your name is on there from a race that happened in 1981?"

He paused and looked at me questioningly. He would have never heard about that race up north when Hubba Bubba died after another wagon wheel popped off and broke his leg. I wasn't sure how to go about telling him for the first time now. How do you explain your brother dying and a wagon wreck happening within a matter of weeks? How do tell your grandson that it was the lowest point of your entire life? Is it relevant that you couldn't stay sober or look at your wife for months and months afterwards? The story seemed too big and too vast to ever try to explain. So, I simply nodded.

Sawyer continued. "Well, they're trying to call you out after the interview you did at the Stampede this year. They have a decent sized following on social media and they've cast you as a… hypocrite. I won't read all the comments to you but – "

I cut him off. "I'd like to read the comments."

Sawyer had a panic-stricken look in his eye. He shook his head. "No, you really don't need to, social media isn't like real life. People say things they would never say to your face."

I looked at him, thinking about what he was implying. Then I thought about Hubba Bubba. "I need to see what people are saying," I said softly but sternly.

He pulled out his phone and tapped on it a few times. "This is Twitter. This is the profile of the animal rights group that is targeting you. This is their tweet about you here." He clicked on something and it expanded. Then he scrolled down quickly with his thumb. "And here are the replies."

I had no idea what he was talking about when he used his social media lingo. And the screen confused me. I stared intently before I could even understand where the comments were. When I finally started to read them, I understood why Sawyer had tried to stop me.

Rot in hell, you sick bastard.

Breaks my heart what happens to these beautiful creatures!

Looks like Charlie Hyde is exploiting animals just like every other person who partakes in rodeos and stampedes. #Shocker

I hope Charlie Hyde dies from a broken leg!!!!!!

Is this guy from Strathmore? Anyone know where exactly????

At that, I quit reading and handed Sawyer his phone back. Maggie looked at me and I gave her a slight shake of my head. I saw the affect that the paper she'd found had on her. I didn't want her reading those comments. Besides, I was the one that had gotten us into this mess. It was going to be up to me to figure out how to stop it.

The problem was that I had no idea where to even begin. They were fighting this battle on a war grounds that I couldn't even access. With a lot of work and patience, I had learnt how to text and take videos and pictures. But the internet and social media were still foreign concepts to me.

Jake waved his hand back and forth, dismissing the whole thing. "Look, we don't need to worry ourselves. This is going to blow over and be done within a week. These people have short attention spans."

I nodded, but I wasn't so sure. Sitting around doing nothing wasn't exactly my style. I didn't want to hide. I knew that I had spoken my truth when I did that interview. But I didn't know how to explain my story or who to explain it to. I was being told to rot in hell by strangers who had never met me and I couldn't even respond. Maybe that was the point. Maybe they weren't interested in my response.

Jake and Sawyer began talking about other things with Maggie but I wasn't able to listen or concentrate. I was lost in my own world of thoughts. I cleared my throat and pushed away from the table. I didn't know where I was going but I knew I had to get out of that house. I needed air and space. I walked toward the door and I heard Sawyer call out, "What are you gonna go do?"

I thought for a moment. "Gonna drive through the yearlings."

"Mind if I come along?" he asked.

I noticed the surprised look that flashed across Jake's face before he quickly returned to a neutral expression. I waved my hand at Sawyer to come with me. "Get your hat on, then," I said.

He grabbed two more cookies off the plate in front of him and hustled out the door.

We got into my farm truck and he silently handed one of the cookies to me. We chewed away as we drove out to the pasture and Sawyer quickly hopped out and got the gate when I pulled up to it. We rolled our windows down and I eased along slowly. You could hear the grass swishing against the tires as we moved through the pasture. Grasshoppers were jumping up as we drove. I kept my eyes peeled and finally spotted a herd standing together. I headed that way and got fairly close before parking the truck and turning the keys off. I reached into the back of the truck, feeling in the pockets of the back seat, my hands fumbling until I grasped on to what I was looking for. I pulled out a cigar and a lighter. I breathed in the scent of the cigar before putting it between my lips and lighting it.

Sawyer was watching me with amusement. "Thought you didn't smoke anymore, Grandpa."

"Doctor said I had to quit smoking cigarettes. He never said anything about cigars," I said, taking the first puff. Then I looked over at him. "Don't tell your Grandma."

He laughed and raised his hands in innocence, "I didn't see a thing."

We were parked there, both looking out at the heifers that were perfectly content and happy. Some of them were eating grass, others were laying down.

"Are you friends with lots of those… uh… vegetarians or vegans or whatever they call themselves?" I asked Sawyer suddenly.

Sawyer answered easily. "I know quite a few vegetarians and vegans. There are pretty much vegan options at every restaurant you go to in Calgary now. It's more mainstream. Lots of people who aren't even vegetarians are still trying to eat less meat."

"Well, what's their reasoning?"

"I think it's different for lots of people. Some people say it's helping the environment to eat less meat. Others won't eat meat because they say it's unethical. Some health experts are claiming now that we have too much protein in our diets. And also, meat is expensive. Some people just can't afford to order a steak when they go to a restaurant."

I nodded, trying to soak that all in. I was surprised that he had such a quick answer. I hadn't understood one reason why a person wouldn't eat meat and he had just listed about five different ones. They all sounded like bullshit to me, except the fact that ordering a steak is expensive.

Sawyer seemed to mistake my silence for frustration. "I know that I never helped with the horses or the ranching like Kylie did and I've

never really been a part of it. So, I know that I have no right to say this…
But it pisses me off too, Grandpa. I hate that someone would hang up
a poster like that and attack you guys."

I jerked my head towards Sawyer and scrunched my eyebrows
together. "I never want to hear you say something like that again," I
said, my voice low. "Don't ever tell me that you don't have the right
to say something. You've got every damn right in the world. You don't
have to train horses or raise cows. I've never expected that from you
if it wasn't something you wanted to do. All I could ever ask is that
you're passionate about whatever path you go down. But whether you
want it to be or not, this lifestyle is in your bones. It's in your blood.
Hell, it's even in your name. Sawyer **Phillip** Hyde. That middle name
was given to you because Philip embodied everything it meant to be a
hard-working, good man. And that's what agriculture is. That's the root
of it. We work hard and we try to be good people. So, don't ever tell me
that you don't have the right to do the same."

Sawyer stared back at me with wide eyes. I took another puff from
my cigar. I wasn't usually in the habit of giving speeches. "Do you
understand?" I asked him, unsure of what to say next.

"I understand," he nodded.

I finished my cigar and scrunched it against the door of the truck
before dropping it into the grass. I started the truck back up. "Let's go
find the rest of the heifers," I said and we continued to move slowly
through the field.

"You don't like Tenille, do you?" Sawyer asked quietly after a minute.

I glanced over at him. "No one ever told me who to marry. That's a
decision a man's gotta make on his own."

Sawyer laughed, "Hold up, no one ever said anything about marriage."
He visibly loosened up with the laughter. He was reverting back to his
light-hearted nature and the heaviness of the previous conversation
was lifting.

"Well, no one ever told me who to be with for marriage or… any of
the rest," I said.

He laughed again, shaking his hand and muttered, "Grandpa…" in a
reprimand that didn't hold much conviction. I drove us out of the field
and Sawyer hopped out again to shut the gate.

When we returned to the house, it seemed we had switched roles. I felt lighter and more care free after the fresh air, the cigar, and the reassurance that a man always feels in his heart after seeing his livestock healthy and happy.

And Sawyer had a few things to think about and work through his mind. As we walked into the house, he slowed up and said, "Tenille… I don't think she's made of the same stuff that I'm made of… You know, all that stuff that you talked about."

I put a hand on his shoulder and guided him toward the front door. "Well, then, I think you've solved your own problem."

CHAPTER THIRTY-FIVE

slowly

The next few days passed drama free. Maggie and I never said it, but we both seemed to be looking over our shoulder at every turn, waiting for something bad to come our way. It broke my heart to see my wife living her day-to-day life with an edge of fear. But just as Jake had predicted, nothing happened. I was about to release the whole incident from my mind until my cell phone rang. It was a Calgary number that I didn't have saved in my contacts.

"Hello, am I speaking to Charlie Hyde?" a woman's voice asked when I answered.

"Yes, you are."

"Oh, hi, Charlie. This is Kate Linderman with CTV NEWS. We met at the Stampede this year for that brief interview?"

"Oh," I said, surprised. "Of course, I remember. How did you get my number?"

"Because I'm very good at my job," she laughed, brushing me off and I was reminded of why I had initially liked her. "I'm calling because I would love to speak with you on camera again. We received a lot of great feedback from the last interview you did… And we also received some criticism. It's generating a bigger conversation and I would like to keep that conversation progressing, if you were at all interested?"

I was silent a moment, thinking. I had a lot to say. It had been building up inside me over the course of the last few days. But I still wasn't sure how to say it.

Kate sensed my hesitation in the silence. She continued, "I would like to do an interview with you on location at your home. Possibly even around the animals that you own?" She paused. "Charlie, I'd like to help you tell your story."

With that, she convinced me. "Alright," I said. "Let's make it happen."

She immediately set off trying to finalize details. I gave her directions to my house and we planned a day and time. Just before she was about to hang up, she said. "One more thing. I probably shouldn't even say this because I don't want to scare you off… But I like you and I want to be open and honest. If we do this interview, it might draw in more criticism. You may have more attention focused on you from people who won't exactly see your viewpoint."

I liked her all the more for her attempt to warn me. I thought of Maggie's face when she came home with the poster. I thought of the man who handcuffed himself to the wagon track. I thought of Hubba Bubba. I knew what I had to do. "I'm in too deep to back down now," I said and hung up.

That evening, I went over to Jake and Michelle's house to tell them about the interview. Jake immediately balked. "Call that lady and tell her you've changed your mind," he said. When I dismissed him, he began to plead. "Dad, there's just no convincing those people. They're not ever going to think chuckwagon racing is humane. One little interview and lifestyle piece on you isn't going to change anything. It will probably only make them fight back harder."

I listened to Jake because I valued his opinion. But I knew what my heart was telling me to do. To my surprise, Michelle spoke up in my defense. "I think it's a great idea. You might not change everyone's minds. But it's better than doing nothing and saying nothing. We can't be afraid to tell our side."

Jake shot back, "I'm not afraid! I just don't see how this will play out in our favor. The world's changing. People have gone crazy," he threw his hands up, frustrated. Then he walked out of the house. "I need to get some air," he said as he quietly shut the door behind him.

Michelle looked at me. "He'll come around."

I nodded. If Jake's reaction was this dramatic, I didn't know what everyone else would think. The pressure of this interview was already beginning to build.

"You know, I can help you prepare for the interview," Michelle said. "I might not have graduated but I was a journalism major for two years," she shrugged.

"That might actually be helpful." I said, appreciating her offer and her support.

When the next day rolled around, I went back to Jake and Michelle's to start the interview preparation like we had planned. Jake was working in the city and Kylie was outside riding a horse. The house was quiet and empty except for Michelle and I. It struck me that as long as Jake and Michelle had been married, her and I had actually spent very little time one-on-one. She led me into an office and started shuffling through a pile of papers, all filled with her handwritten notes.

"I've been preparing notes and ideas and questions that I think Kate Linderman will probably ask. I also watched some of her old interviews online last night to get a better sense of what she's like. She doesn't beat around the bush, that's for sure. So, we need to be ready for some heavy hitting questions. It won't just be a fluff piece." Michelle talked quickly as she thumbed through all her pages. It was nice to see her like this. She had a purpose. "Ah hah," she pulled out the paper she had been looking for and gestured for me to sit down. I found myself feeling a little nervous as she sat directly across from me. An interview preparation was far from my comfort zone.

"Before we practice answering any questions, we need to talk about what your main goal is. What do you want people to take away from this interview? What's your reasoning for speaking out?"

I scrunched my eyebrows together, suddenly remembering how good the last cigar was that I had and wishing I could smoke another right now. "I'm speaking out because she asked me to do another interview."

Michelle eyed me up. "That's not good enough," she said.

Her entire demeanor was surprising me. She held a steady gaze and waited for me to continue. I sighed and began again. "I'm speaking out because one time, one of my horses died during a chuckwagon race and if those people understood what that felt like and what that did to me, they wouldn't question my intentions so much. And also, sometimes animals die. That's a truth of the agricultural world that every single person has to come to terms with. If you're in the industry, you already understand it. But maybe we should start actually talking about it instead of sugarcoating everything so damn much."

She nodded, satisfied. "Better. We're getting somewhere now. But we're going to have to get a clear message ready." She fired up again, talking a mile a minute. I listened and tried to soak it all in but she continually kept pressing me for more and more. She wanted further clarifications. She wanted me to understand my own message. At one point, I threw my hands up in the air and said, "I don't have a message! I'm just me." And she retorted, "I know you're you. That's why I know you have a message. You've always got a lesson or an underlying meaning or some speck of wisdom in nearly everything you say. I've seen you be that way with your grandkids throughout their entire lives. I'm helping you so that you can be that very same way on camera."

I resigned. I knew that she was right. We returned to her scribbling notes on the paper and she asked me a hundred more questions.

By the time I left the house and went to step in my pickup to drive back home, I was completely drained. It was more exhausting to prepare for that interview than it was to do a full day of physical labor.

But I also knew exactly what I wanted to say.

My mind was filled with everything I'd discussed with Michelle when I got home. I went into an old storage room and started pulling out boxes. I was looking for a remnant of my past with all of my old chuckwagon racing memorabilia. Finally, I pulled out an old shoebox and saw what I was searching for. A tightly braided black mane, wrapped around a key chain. It was Hubba Bubba's hair that Rich had braided for me on that long drive home. I softly stroked the hair and let myself fall into a daydream of the past. I remembered how that was one of the lowest points of my entire life. I had fought like hell to work my way out of that hole I was in but it all started with Maggie. It started with us dancing in the living room to a Willie Nelson song with lyrics that deeply resonated. So, I tucked the horse hair keychain into my pocket and I ventured back into the living room. I looked around for Maggie before I found her sitting on a chair by the sunlight, reading a book. I gently took the book from her hands and laid it down on the coffee table beside her. I held out my hand and she took it as I pulled her up to me. I led her into the center of the living room; the exact same spot we'd danced together all those years before. I pulled out my phone and fumbled on it, cussing as I tried to find what I was looking for.

"God damn phone is ruining the moment," I muttered to myself and Maggie laughed out loud.

"What moment?" she asked, glancing back at her book, clearly wanting to get back to it.

Finally, I found what I was looking for. I hit the play button and turned the volume up on the side.

"Can I have a dance?" I asked, a sly grin on my face.

Maggie leaned in close to me. We swayed back and forth with her head on my shoulder. "This isn't Willie Nelson," she commented.

"No, it sure isn't. Thomas Rhett. You can thank your granddaughter for that."

"Mmmm," she sighed. "I like him."

She laid her head back on my shoulder and we moved slowly together. She never questioned what had sparked the dance and I never explained. We just enjoyed the moment and let Thomas Rhett serenade us, as he crooned *Sweetheart* over and over.

'Cause you're all that I adore

You're the one my heart beats for

And I can't believe you gave your sweet heart to me

light

Things were quiet. I had a regular morning and I ate lunch with Maggie and I had just moved to my easy boy chair in the living room to have a nap. My phone was still in my front shirt pocket and it started buzzing against my chest. I almost let it ring but I pulled it out and saw Rich's name pop up on the screen. I hit the answer button, thinking I would tell him that I'd call him back shortly.

Instead, Rich's voice barely came through the phone. In a raspy, heavy whisper, I heard him choke out, "Charlie. Call an ambulance."

I was out of my chair in a second. I hadn't even hung up the phone with him by the time I got in my truck and turned it around to head down the driveway, spinning my tires and shooting up rocks in the process. I was hauling ass down the dirt road as my shaky hands tried to dial 911. After a few failed attempts and a struggle to keep my eyes on the road ahead, I finally talked to a dispatcher and gave them Rich's home address.

I got to his house before the ambulance did. I rushed through the front door, leaving it open behind me and found Rich laying on the floor in his living room. He was conscious but seemed to be having a hard time breathing. I saw his right hand hanging at a funny angle and I guessed he had a broken wrist.

"Oh, Christ. Rich. You're okay," I said as I struggled down on to the floor beside him. A huge weight lifted off my shoulders when I could hear the ambulance sirens approaching. There's no feeling so hopeless as watching someone you love suffering when you don't know what to do to help them. I could hear the paramedics approaching the door and I hollered out to them to come into the living room. They assessed Rich and put an oxygen mask over his face. The panic left Rich's eyes when he was no longer struggling to breath. The medics asked me to step back and give them some space but I didn't want to leave Rich all alone. I kept pushing close to him and muttering a few words of reassurance. "God damn, you scared me. They'll get you looked after now, though." Rich never said anything back but he gave a slight nod. Eventually, they transferred him onto a stretcher and said they were taking him to the hospital. I quickly grabbed a few things from Rich's house: his wallet on the kitchen table, shaving kit from the bathroom, an extra set of underwear and socks, and then on a hopeful whim the crib board and deck of cards. I left the house, locking the door behind me and then hopped in my truck, unloading the piles of things. I quickly caught up to the ambulance and trailed them to the hospital.

I called Maggie, explaining where I went and what had happened. I'd barely gotten the story out of my mouth before she said, "I'm coming right now," and hung up.

When I got to the hospital and went in the main entrance, I tried to find out what room Rich was in but nobody would tell me. "They're running tests right now," was the same answer I got over and over. I said I understood they were running tests and I still needed to be in the room with him because I was the only family he had. Everyone gave me sympathetic looks but nobody budged.

When Maggie showed up and waited with me, time passed easier. We didn't say much to each other but just sitting side by side in that waiting room gave me a better outlook. We always had drawn strength from each other. It was one of the things that made our marriage so great.

It felt like hours before a nurse finally led us to a room. We stepped inside and found Rich laying on the small hospital bed. I was a little startled by how old and weak he appeared, curled up in that bed with a hospital gown on. My friend was getting old faster than I was and there wasn't a thing I could do about it. His eyes were closed but he opened them when he heard us come in. Some of the spark returned to his face when he saw us.

I pulled up a chair beside his bed and unloaded all his things on to a table. Rich eyed the crib board and deck of cards and said, "You are something else. A man has a heart attack and you bring a crib board to his hospital bed because you know it's the only shot in hell you've got at beating me. Well, I tell you what, even on my weakest day, I'll still hand it to you."

I laughed out loud. The deep roar when I threw my head back felt too abrasive for a hospital but I couldn't help it. Rich was one of the few people in the world who could make me laugh like that. Leave it to him to still be able to do it at this moment.

"So, it was a heart attack?" I asked when I'd stopped laughing.

Maggie propped herself on the bed at Rich's feet and gently patted his leg a few times. He smiled down at her. "Yup. The ol' ticker gave me a scare." He was trying his best to be upbeat and positive but I could see that he was already fading. He looked tired and I knew he probably needed to sleep.

A nurse walked in, her shoes squeaking on the floor as she swiveled to a stop in front of Rich. "Ah ha, my favorite patient of the day," she smiled down at him. "The wily one."

"And my favorite nurse," he winked at her. "The spunky one."

I smiled at the two of them as they continued to talk about Rich's condition. The nurse explained that he would be staying in the hospital for a few days so they could monitor him. Maggie asked plenty of questions. The broken wrist was from when he tumbled over during the chest pains. She said the cast would stay on for 6 weeks minimum before they did another x-ray.

The nurse had been joking with Rich in a lively manner the whole time. But she turned somber as she said, "I want to bring something up. Returning to a house to live by yourself is doable but not ideal. There are plenty of wonderful senior citizen lodges in the area. They can cook for you and keep an eye on you. I can bring some pamphlets by if you're interested. If you're not, that's okay, too. I just wanted to put the idea out there for you." And with that she was out of the room again, her shoes squeaking down the hallway, leaving the three of us in silence with a heavy contemplation. A senior citizen's lodge was for people who had given up and needed a place to live out their dying days. I assessed Rich from the corner of my eye. I could see the frailty of his body underneath the thin hospital blanket. Maybe it was time.

Maggie left the hospital when it was dark out. She bent over and hugged Rich tightly before she went. I stayed in my chair. Rich was drifting in and out of sleep but I didn't want to leave. Occasionally my own head nodded down onto my chest. At one point, I jerked awake to find Rich looking at me. He had a small smile on his face, perhaps he was amused.

I rubbed my eyes as he said, "Go home, Charlie." I immediately began to protest but he interrupted me. "Go home to your wife. Do it for me. Because I can't go home to mine."

I didn't object to that. I nodded solemnly and cleared my throat. "I'll be back in the morning," was all I said as I walked out the door.

The parking lot was empty as I walked to my truck. It was all I could do to stay awake for the drive home. I turned up the radio as loud as I could stand to keep my senses alert. But it didn't matter what song was playing. The only thing my mind could think about was Rich. My best friend was dying. He had made it through this scare but there would be another and he would be weaker. He was old and worn out. His wife was gone and he had no kids or grandkids to live for. My family had always treated Rich like a member of our own but it never quite was the real thing.

I didn't want Rich to die. I wanted him to be alive as long as I was. I wanted to talk to him on the phone every day and drive into his house to play crib whenever I felt like it. I didn't want to lose the one person that I could say anything around; the one person who always allowed me to just be myself with no pressure or judgment. But the world doesn't work that way and I'd already learnt that lesson. People die. Sometimes it's after they've lived a long life and sometimes it's too soon. The only thing I know for certain is that we have no control over when God chooses to call someone up to heaven.

When Philip died, I made myself numb. I ran away from the pain of losing my little brother. Every time I got close to facing what had happened, I'd push away again, never quite coming to terms with things. I was older and wiser now so, when I pulled up to my house, I turned the truck off and stayed sitting in the front seat and I thought of Rich. A man never could've asked for a better friend. I thought it was divine luck that brought us together when I was 17 years old but it was the mark of a true friendship that we had remained so close through all these years. I shed a tear or two. I waited until my eyes were dry before I stepped out of the truck and into my house. I quietly tread down the hallway to our bedroom, peeled off my blue jeans and work shirt and I crawled into bed beside Maggie. She sleepily rolled over close to me.

"You okay?" she asked.

I wrapped an arm around her and squeezed her tight for a moment. Her flannel pajamas were soft against my rough fingers. Then I perched myself up on one side and leaned over and kissed her gently on the cheek. "I am now," I said before we both drifted off to sleep.

Rich died that night. They had Maggie's cell phone number and they called her in the morning, just as I was getting ready to drive back in to the hospital. I could tell what had happened by the look on her face. She brought a hand up to her mouth and tears pooled in her eyes. "But you said he was stable," she repeated over and over until I walked over and took the cell phone from her. She gratefully sank down into a chair and buried her head in her hands. I talked to the nurse quietly, not really caring about the details because the only thing that mattered was that Rich was gone now. I thanked the nurse before I hung up.

I walked over to Maggie and stood over top of her. "I think it's what he wanted." She looked up at me, questioning. "He's back with Georgia now."

With that, Maggie nodded and put her head back in her hands, crying harder. I patted her back a few times and stood beside her.

I never cried again for Rich. Something had happened when I drove home from the hospital. A blanket of peace seemed to be spread upon me. I think God was preparing me for what was to come because I felt strong enough to handle it. Rich had lived a damn good life. Somehow, that was all that mattered. I was going to miss him; there was no doubt about that. He was the best friend I ever had. But it wasn't about me anymore. I wasn't going to cry for myself because I'd miss my friend. Instead, I would be happy for Rich. Happy he was reunited with the love of his life and happy he had lived so fully while he was here. A man like Rich wasn't meant to wither away in an old folk's home. I had seen the light go out of his eyes when the nurse mentioned she could bring pamphlets for a retirement center.

Rich had always been the life of the party. Part of that meant knowing when to leave the party.

CHAPTER THIRTY-SEVEN

goodbye

I had postponed my interview with Kate Linderman. I called her and said simply, "I have to bury my best friend."

But that wasn't exactly true. Georgia had been cremated and Rich kept the ashes in a box in his house. He had a will made up saying that he wanted to be cremated as well. I was supposed to spread their ashes together.

I knew exactly how to do it.

When I rescheduled with Kate Linderman, she arrived in her car trailing a big, white van with CTV NEWS splashed across the side. When she popped out of the car, I was surprised to see she was wearing blue jeans. She had a crisp, pastel button-down shirt on, as well. I was happy to see that. I hated when city folks wore impractical clothes on a ranch.

She pulled up to the house and I was the first one outside to greet her. Maggie, Jake, Michelle, Kylie, and Sawyer all trailed out behind me. We shook hands and she said she was sorry to hear about my friend.

"Actually," I said, "I'm glad you brought that up. My family and I are about to go spread the ashes. Rich and Georgia Melaney. It's what they wanted. You can take your camera crew and video it, if you want."

Kate Linderman just looked at me, a little taken back. I'm sure she'd already had the entire interview planned out in her mind and this wasn't part of it. I added, "You said you wanted to do a lifestyle piece on me for this interview. Well… this is my life."

I could tell by the look on her face that I had convinced her. She bustled over to the van and her camera crew, likely to explain to them what was about to happen.

Four horses were tied up and saddled to a wooden fence rail. I was going to ride Roanie. Kylie, Jake, and Maggie were all going to get on a horse, too. Michelle and Sawyer were going to take the old farm pickup. Rich and Georgia's ashes were already in the truck.

My family all stood around, eyeing up the camera crew. They seemed uncertain about the whole ordeal. But I wasn't compromising on this. "Let's head out," I said.

After I got on Roanie, I watched Maggie step into the stirrup and swing a leg over the horse Kylie had saddled for her. I couldn't remember the last time I had seen Maggie on a horse. She never really said that she was going to retire from riding but she just drifted away from it. When I had told her my plan for the day, she had said she wanted to be on a horse. She actually insisted on it. I was happy to see her sitting tall in the saddle.

"You got up there pretty easy for an old gal," I smiled at her, teasing.

She tilted her chin in the air just a little and tried to hide a smile. "Who the hell are you calling old," she said as she kicked her horse into a trot and posted up in the saddle as if she had never missed a day of riding in her life.

Kylie happily trotted up beside her grandma as Jake and I walked behind them. Sawyer and Michelle followed us in the truck, barely creeping forward.

We all knew where we were heading. There was a real pretty hill about a mile away. It was the tallest hill on our land. When Georgia had still been alive, her and Rich had come out to our place for lunch. Jake and Michelle and the kids were out, too. Georgia was already sick. She showed up looking pale and exhausted. It had been a perfect August day, not too hot and not too cold. Maggie had assessed her friend carefully and suggested we all go outside and have lunch as a picnic. Maggie had patted Georgia's hand lightly as she said, "The Vitamin D will do us all some good." Then Maggie loaded all the food and a pile of blankets into the back of the truck and we all headed to the hill. It had been one of the best afternoons we'd all spent together. The pretty view and the perfect company had lifted Georgia's spirits. Rich had often talked about how special that lunch had been.

When we finally got to the hill, everyone knew what the plan was. Michelle and Sawyer brought the ashes out of the truck. They had been split four ways. Michelle silently handed them to me, Kylie, Jake, and Maggie. No one was saying much but the silence didn't feel heavy. It felt like a family coming together to do one last act of love for two people that had been an integral part of our lives. Jake had more sleepovers with Rich and Georgia when he was a young boy than we could ever count. They always had loved him like they would've loved their own son. When Kylie and Sawyer were born, Rich and Georgia had celebrated with us as if they were celebrating grandchildren of their own. It was amazing to me that this deep, life-long connection had all started with a job at the Stockyards.

The four of us lined our horses up at the bottom of the hill. We were all spread out. The bag of ashes felt heavy in my hand. I held it low to the ground. Without looking at the others, I kicked Roanie and we started going up the hill. I loped him up to the top and then spurred him in the belly again on the way down. Roanie gained momentum as we went. He seemed excited to finally be going faster than a walk. The whole way up and down the hill, I felt the ashes sprinkling out of the bag. When I got to the bottom of the hill, I dumped the remainder out as I let Roanie run for a few more paces.

I could hear the other three slowing their horses up. Roanie settled back into a walk. He dropped his head low again, having already mustered up all the excitement he could handle for a day.

I smiled to myself. The smile broke into a grin which broke into laughter. A feeling of euphoria washed over me. I could see the cameras set up a short distance from where we were riding. I knew they were documenting the whole thing on video. Rich and Georgia would have a moment of glory captured in my interview for the world to see. It was a touch sensationalistic, a little over the top, and perfectly charming at the same time: it was Rich to a tee. I had honored my friend in the best way I knew how. I'd learnt that honoring the people we've loved and lost is the best way to get through our grief.

I rode over to the cameras, where Kate Linderman was silently standing and observing. She had that watchful, neutral look on her face that journalists somehow master. She opened her mouth to speak as I approached but I cut her off, telling her I would meet her back at the yard to start the interview. I needed a few more moments of silence to gather my thoughts.

While Roanie walked along, lowering his head to the ground every now and then to try and steal a bite of grass, I contemplated all that Michelle had helped me realize with her preparation for my interview.

I thought about Kylie, my grandmother, and the love for our horses that was powerful enough to carry on through generations. Horse training is a discipline that can be learned through hard work and dedication. But sometimes a horse gives you so much that there's no logical explanation for it. It can't be earned through hard work alone. It's something bigger and there's no way to describe it other than love. DS gave me that love and Kylie's yellow barrel horse gives her the same thing. It's what makes chuckwagon racing and barrel racing so great; it's what the man who handcuffed himself to the race track will never understand.

I thought about Maggie and Philip and how together they used to have the happiest cow herd in North America. There was something so simple yet so special about the way they worked their cows. Maggie's life dream was to have a cow herd and it brought her a purpose. She felt like she played an important role in a big world when she contributed to families putting food on the table. She understood that good meat wasn't a coincidence. It was the result of good feed and a stress-free environment. And as much as Philip hustled, he knew how to bring a grounded energy to the task of working livestock. He was the embodiment of hard work; the best representation of men in agriculture. Never complained about the physical labor, instead he fully embraced it and his enthusiasm was contagious.

I thought about ol' Gene and his connection with his dogs. Those dogs were his family but Gene expected a lot out of them. They were trained to work hard and listen and be well-mannered. They were the best dogs

I've ever seen. Gene didn't leave any family behind when he died but he left a lasting impact on me. He was a quiet man who preferred to let his work speak for itself. It was becoming a lost trait to move quietly through life. Now everyone has a platform and everyone wants to make themselves heard. Gene never demanded anyone's attention. He lived how he wanted and he allowed others to do the same.

I thought about Arthur Langdon. There are good people and bad people in every single walk of life. Arthur Langdon wasn't very good to his horses. He wasn't very good to his wife, either. But he still had good parts inside of him that became more obvious to me after his death.

And smiling, happy, hard-working Frank. I had put Frank on a pedestal before I learnt that he wasn't all good, either. He'd lied and cheated and stolen. Somehow, I managed to still see the good in him. I made a choice that I'd rather see the good in him than the bad. Never did know if that was the right or the wrong thing to do.

I thought about money. I thought about how abundantly it came to Jake and what a knack he had for the business side of things. But I thought about how it didn't always make his life easier. People made comments to him everywhere he went. People always wanted something from him. And with all the money in the world, he still can't buy away his troubles. He still deals with protestors and business stress and hours away from his family. Making money is what makes the world go 'round and it's what every single one of us is after. But I know that even if I never made a dime off my horses, some of the happiest moments of my life would still be the moments I spent riding and training and working them. People say that chuckwagon racing and rodeo are exploiting animals for financial gain. I guess it takes a man in my circumstances to prove how unjustified that reasoning is.

Lastly, I thought about DS and Hubba Bubba. DS was the greatest horse I ever owned and he got to live out his retirement in my pasture. He worked harder and ran harder than any horse I'd ever seen. And ol' Hubba Bubba. I lost a good horse just because he was competing and he was a part of my team. Don't know if that makes me right or wrong, either. But I do know that it's a crying shame to hold ourselves back just because we can't always protect and control everything that happens. Philip taught me that.

When I met up with Kate Linderman, I told her all of these things I'd been thinking about. It took me a long time to get it out. I spoke my truth in the best way I could by telling her about my life and some of the most formative years. I tried to do justice to the people I met along the way. Folks said afterwards that it was the best interview they'd ever heard with someone advocating for the agricultural and western communities. Folks said I was a spokesman now. They said I was finally changing the narrative and changing the way the world sees us. Folks said when people see the kindness of it all, it might just change the world.

I don't know about all that. I just know that I told my story.

And it all started with a *goodbye*. When I was 17 years old…

"...when people see the kindness of it all, it might just change the world."

~ Gina Flewelling

Manufactured by Amazon.ca
Bolton, ON